SERIOUSLY CHALLENGED

2

CULEBRA CHRONICLES

HALF-PAST 2 PUBLICATIONS

This book is a work of fiction. Names, characters, places, and incidents are the product of the author's imagination or are used fictitiously. Any resemblance to actual events, locales, or persons, living or dead, is coincidental.

Copyright © 2024 by Chrissy Chicory

Cover Design: Caroline Marques
Illustrations: Canva.com
Editing: Enchanted Ink Publishing
Book Design and Typesetting: Enchanted Ink Publishing

ISBN: 978-1-963402-08-7 (E-book)
ISBN: 978-1-963402-05-6 (Paperback)

Library of Congress Control Number: 2024901313

Thank you for your support of the author's rights.

WWW.CHRISSYCHICORY.COM

Dedicated to my three daughters, whose
smiles and laughter are the magic in my life

SERIOUSLY CHALLENGED

2

CULEBRA CHRONICLES

CHRISSY CHICORY

CHAPTER 1

BABS

The full weight of Babs's decision to join the summer court weighed heavily on her shoulders. She glanced up into the darkness of the stormy afternoon. Heavy clouds brewed, periodically releasing onslaughts of raindrops that landed with a pitter-patter on the sprawling woods below. As the thunder echoed around the ragged cliff, the recent months of training with Verity played through her mind. It had become increasingly grueling. After nearly a year of preparation, there were only a few days left before the challenges. If she failed to pass them, the work of the past year would amount to nothing.

A thunderous sound shuddered through the cave as Verity huffed, increasingly frustrated with Babs's lack of concentration. Babs's furrowed brow and weather-worn face turned toward her mentor, who mindlessly stoked the dying fire in the cave's center back to life. Wild orange flames danced and licked around Verity's powerful build, throwing her into a dark silhouette against the wall. She was spattered with greyish mud from the cold rain that poured down relentlessly outside. "Phasing is not an optional skill! You must act instinctively. The ability to travel by simply seeing where you want to go in your mind's eye is a basic skill of the fae. There may be a day in which your life, or lives of others, will depend on it," Verity said, her voice reverberating off the cramped walls of their lofty shelter overlooking the forested valley.

Babs stared at the opposite side of the pulsing flames, where a hulking figure of black fur lay unmoving. Gwylm was sheltered from the rain and thunder in his tranquil slumber, his large chest rising and falling with powerful breaths. Not even the most daunting storm could perturb this great wolf from his repose. Their bond was so strong that even from afar, Babs knew where he was and could feel the calmness radiating from him.

"Babs, again," Verity's voice encouraged. "There will be time for rest later."

In response to her command, Babs let loose a large swoosh of air from her lungs through clenched teeth. She stiffened her body and unfocused her vision, sensing Verity's eyes burning a hole into her head. Her mind became blank as her arms and legs became numb. She lost all sense of herself, straining to hear and feel every noise that surrounded her.

Verity lengthened her arms straight out in front of her, loose white sleeves billowing as she struck two vibration bars together that were attached to her crimson gloves. A deep invisible wave knocked Babs back. Nausea rippled through her stomach, goosebumps rose on her deeply tanned skin, her eyes closed involuntarily. When she fluttered them back open, Verity was nowhere to be found.

"Behind you. Harness this ability so that you can be at the back of your enemy at will." Her voice was barely audible from outside the cave.

Babs let her dark eyes follow the line of her teacher's gaze. Verity's hands were planted on her narrow hips, and her feet were spread apart, light illuminating her fearsome stare. She rolled thick strands of damp hair behind her ears, exposing her soft golden skin to the rain. Wet tendrils beaded up along her brows, dripping into the shadows that fell over the edges of her sharp cheekbones. Fat little raindrops splattered onto the back of her neck, soaking through her handspun woven uniform until the heat rising from her body was mixed with the earthy floral scents emanating from the nearby trees.

Babs gobbled air into her lungs, willing the searing burning sensation to ebb. Verity nodded toward Babs's gloves.

"Energy, frequency, vibration—these are what our worlds are made up of. You are used to working with earth energy, ground in its familiarity. Feel the soil beneath your feet. Connect to the physical plane. See in your mind where you want to go, and layer onto that, the vibrational travel. Trust in the process. See the waves and merge with them. Let the intuition of your fae side lead."

Babs hated feeling like she wasn't in control of her body, even for the smallest moments. Her sister Cricket was way more comfortable with this airy stuff. But she was learning to walk between the worlds, through matter itself. She was beginning to see through the illusion of separateness.

The mud pulled at her feet, connecting her to the earth and everything it enveloped. She could feel the rock, the roots of trees, and brush as though they were extensions of her body. An abundance of tiny creatures moved in concert with the subtle changes in atmosphere, as if they were also caught up with this sense of connectivity. She raised her awareness to a higher plane, feeling an almost spiritual connection with the air that hovered just above this microscopic world.

In a trance, she tapped the bars with her fingertips, sending her wish into the air. Aches and energy surged through her body as if electricity were running between each cell. When she opened her eyes, a smell akin to burning leaves filled the air. An invisible force had propelled her out to the misty edge of the cliff's lofty summit. Through the steely clouds, the sun emerged for its final moments. A brilliant kaleidoscope of salmon and burnt orange flooded the heavens, casting a haunting luminosity on the wet earth below. A strange lightness replaced her fear. As the last bit of energy dissipated, mystical warmth spread throughout her being even as she dry heaved for the umpteenth time.

Verity closed the distance between them and said, "Yes, well done. Come back in and sit."

Babs let out a deep breath, walked back to Gwylm's side, and crumpled to a heap beside him, burying her face in his warm fur. "That felt better—not great, but something was different." A frown graced her face. "It's just so hard."

"*It's coming easier to you. I felt it this time.*" Gwylm's deep voice filled Babs's mind. Gwylm scooted closer and rested his head in her lap, letting out a deep, contented sigh. She slowly ran her fingers through his thick fur coat as he drifted back into sleep. Babs drank cautiously from her water bottle, struggling between queasiness and dehydration. Her body ached from exhaustion—not from physical work or pain, but from fear of failure.

Verity sighed. "No doubt growing and encouraging life is more natural to you. Farming and nurturing animals — that is how you have spent your talents thus far. Using your hands, yes, they are filled with power. But don't limit your belief — and therefore your ability — to the more subtle side of magic. You need to learn how to quiet your mind," Verity said calmly, her sharp eyes locked on Babs's.

She looked up at her teacher, exhaustion creeping through her muscles. "You would think after a year of training — " Babs fiddled with her red serpentine belt nervously as she spoke.

Verity let out a low, throaty laugh. "A warrior isn't made in a year, Babs. It takes a lifetime. We're all climbing a ladder, never stopping to look down or back. If we stop climbing, we're no use to anyone, least of all ourselves."

The sky flashed with a bolt of lightning, followed by another. Babs drooped forward toward Verity's gaze and blurted out what was on her mind. "I feel so insignificant compared to all the others in the court."

Verity leaned against the rocky wall of the cave, letting her gaze wander. "Comparing yourself to others, are you?" She stared out at the rain. "You aren't indifferent or complacent — I find both of those traits unforgivable. Instead, you have great ambition. That is foundational to success. But I sense in you a deep insecurity, the root cause yet to be revealed. What could have possibly caused such insecurity in one so capable, and who had grown in a home filled with love?"

Babs's throat constricted, and her stomach clenched. A sickening warmth swam in her belly, slowly making its way up to her chest. Gwylm sat up, feeling the change in her. Her hands found their way toward his thick fur as if seeking comfort from a source that had grown so familiar. In her mind's eye, she could still see Nadine's harsh face; it had been a year since Gwylm helped her get rid of her oppressive force, yet the trauma seemed to linger in Babs's fragile frame even still. Not having words to explain her intensity of emotions, Babs simply shrugged and posed a deflecting question. "Why am I still getting sick?" she blurted out between unstable breaths, feeling as though some part of her should be used to this phasing by now.

"It's not a matter of getting used to it. What you are doing is changing *your* frequency to match the vibration, allowing it to carry you from where you are to where you wish to be. You are changing yourself to be able to move *through* the vibration. That is how you are traveling. Right now, you can do it well enough to get to the place you want to go—consistently—but you are not matching it perfectly. It's like hitting C sharp on a keyboard when you meant to hit C minor. Close, but it hurts the ears, or in this case—your stomach."

Babs took another sip of her water. The past year, she had sacrificed all of her time. She had switched the path that she was on. It would all be for nothing if she couldn't pass the challenges and truly become a member of the summer court. "Am I good enough to pass the challenges?"

Verity smiled. "We still have time. I have only lost three students to the challenges, in all my years. You show no signs that you will be the fourth. You are as strong and as capable as your aunt Habina. She found her unique place among us with the healers. I have no doubt you will find your place as well."

Babs stared into the depths of the cave. This time last year, she had been unaware of the summer court, lacking knowledge of this ancient realm. Heck, she and her whole family had thought her aunt Habina dead. Reflections of her past swirled around her like a maelstrom. She shuddered as she remembered how shocked her family had been when she'd chosen to embrace her fae side over the human world. Gran, along with Mama, had certainly done their best to keep the court concealed. But destiny proved stronger than their will alone.

Even in her new home with the summer court, Babs still made time to visit her mother aboveground, but the dark dwellings below always enveloped her in their mysterious comfort whenever she returned. Within the court she felt safe, cocooned in its timeless aura, and renewed by the power of the ley lines.

"Were you afraid before you faced the challenges?" Babs asked, curiosity getting the best of her.

Verity gave her a sidelong glance. "You are asking about ancient history there."

"You are not that old! You can't be that much older than me."

"You think you can tell how old a fae is, youngling? Have you not spoken with your Gran about me?"

Babs was at a loss.

Verity looked at her slyly. "To answer your question, it was more about the dishonor I would bring on my family if I failed. Quite simply, it wasn't an option."

"What do you mean?"

Verity smiled faintly. "Sabella, the queen, is my older sister."

"She's your *sister*? That explains why she leans on you so. Do you share other siblings?"

Verity's eyes glazed over; her features relaxed. "I have but one sister, the queen. She is most beloved. We are of Inanna's line."

"I see." Babs thought of her two sisters. She was grateful to have them both.

Verity averted her gaze. "The records of all the fae lineages are kept in the library. When the challenges are over, you'll gain access to that space so you can read up on your own family history. It's more important than you think."

"Well, let's hope I don't disappoint," Babs replied with a nervous laugh.

Verity gazed into the distance and sighed. "I didn't fail the challenges, and you won't either. I am a servant of the summer court—it's the path given me—and you are choosing the same for yourself."

Verity patted Babs's knee and smiled warmly. "How did we get on the topic of me? Look, you're doing just fine with your training."

"Thank you for your patience," Babs said, her gratitude evident.

"Tomorrow we're going to work on phasing the three of us from here in the woods, to the Queen's Hall, and back again. You've been successful doing that on your own; adding Gwylm and me shouldn't be much more difficult."

"Just widening my awareness?"

Verity nodded. "That's one way to look at it. Get a good night's sleep and meditate before bed. Visualize it in your mind's eye and practice while you dream. With enough focus, you'll be able to do this with ease."

Babs smirked. "If a daughter of Inanna's line says I can do it . . ."

Verity gave her an amused look. "Do your homework. We start first thing tomorrow morning."

"Yes, Your Royalness."

Babs returned home, bathed, and tried to rest in bed, but sleep eluded her. She felt both nervous and excited about what lay ahead. She'd come a long way since she'd first arrived at the summer court, but she knew there was still much to learn.

As she lay down in bed, she closed her eyes and focused on her breathing, trying to clear her mind. She visualized herself and Gwylm phasing in and out of the woods and the Queen's Hall. She could feel the power within her growing stronger, and she knew she was ready for tomorrow's training.

A feeling of dread trickled into Babs's thoughts, and she felt a familiar, yet threatening presence surround her. She opened her eyes to see Gwylm staring out the window from the foot of the bed. His eyes were glowing in the dim light, and she could see the wildness in them.

She held out her hand as Gwylm cautiously stepped over to the window, his tail straight in alert. *"Come look,"* he spoke to her mind. She tiptoed to his side, placing her hand on his back, his fur standing on end, and his eyes trained on something.

Babs followed Gwylm's gaze. The moon had risen, full and round, spilling the pale blue light of evening across the night. Just at the boundary between dark and light stood a figure swathed in a billowing cloak, its hands raised high to the moon.

As it lowered its arms and turned toward them, beams of silver grey illuminated its shape. Goosebumps rose on Babs's arms as unease settled over her. With a blink, the figure was gone.

CHAPTER 2
CRICKET

Cricket sat uncomfortably in the plush back seat of the limo alongside Caroline, the soon-to-be bride, and her three cousins. They all clutched tall champagne flutes, overflowing with bubbly liquid that threatened to spill onto their elegant dresses. Their laughter was like tinkling glass bells. Caroline's cousins sat in provocative poses, taking selfies with the bride-to-be. Their soft-tone satin slip dresses proved a neutral background to the Cartier and Van Cleef displays that dazzled their wrists and dainty necks. The family resemblance was easy to see. They all shared hazel eyes that showed high intelligence through the shadow of their long, exaggerated lashes. It would have been their most striking feature if not for their full, luscious lips glowing with lip glosses of varying tints. Their sleek, manicured fingers and slender arms shone from a coating of glittering gold dust, and they carried handbags made of metallic-embossed leather. Their long, lean Pilates bodies showed off strong arms and legs flowing out of their silken dresses.

"What a great night this is going to be, and right here, in

this limo, I am going to make our first toast of the evening!" Cricket gushed, her face beaming with delight. It was a welcome change to have a peaceful and ordinary evening, no chaos, no supernatural occurrences. "To the elegant soon-to-be bride! May her marriage bring her all the joy and happiness one could wish, and her wedding be a storybook fairytale."

"A toast to me," Caroline cheered, her eyes twinkling with excitement. She radiated like a beacon of beauty in her cream slip dress and Chanel clutch. Her thin lips were painted a delicate shade of pink, and her Jimmy Choo pearl heels added just the right amount of elegance to her look. "Let's get this party started! Driver, head to Martini's!"

"What's on the schedule for the evening?" Pricilla asked, her full pouty lips demanding attention.

"Cricket, fill the girls in," Caroline ordered, propping her feet up on the seat across from her.

Cricket had just met the three women, Caroline's cousins from Chicago. But it was like she already knew them. So many of Caroline's winter break stories revolved around that city and its magical winter wonderland. She could almost see herself in the scene, draped in furs, walking through a gentle snow to the Lyric Opera House. It sounded so exotic and enchanting to Cricket. She herself had yet to see snow. Caroline swore it was not as ideal as Cricket made it out to be.

"Tini Martini Bar for drinks, then a private ghost tour led by Bash. He's my boyfriend and Caroline's former co-worker," Cricket said with a smile.

"Yes, we all went to school together," Caroline added. "For some crazy reason, Bash left working with me and started his own ghost tour company."

"Nan will want to hear all about the ghosties when she and Mossey get here," Pricilla said, spilling her champagne as she gestured wildly.

"Nan and Mossey?" Cricket inquired, glancing at her phone when it chirped. It was her aunt Habina; she'd have to get back to her tomorrow.

Kimberly laughed. "Our grandparents on our mother's side, Nan and Mossey Nettles." She looked to Caroline. "Are they driving up in the Mossey Mobile?"

"Mossey Mobile?" Cricket had no idea what they were talking about.

Caroline rolled her eyes. "Mossey Mobile 3.0, I believe. They keep getting larger models." She smiled. "Our grandparents are on the eccentric side."

"They retired to Key West ages ago. Now they only travel by the Mossey Mobile," added Pricilla with a wide grin on her face. "*Oh, Mr. Nettles, do watch where you're going,*" she imitated in a high-pitched voice.

Seeing Cricket's confusion, Audrey clarified, "It's a giant RV. Nan likes to stop off places. She's entirely sworn off air travel."

"And Old Mossey, or *Mr. Nettles*, as Nan calls him, has heartily obliged." Pricilla quoted, "The secret to a happy marriage is—"

All the girls chimed in, "Forget the word *no*." They burst into laughter over the family joke.

"So, we're doing a ghost tour tonight?" asked Pricilla.

"Yes! A ghost tour seemed like the perfect idea for our bachelorette party," Caroline beamed. "I know this isn't Chicago—"

"Don't be a silly goose," Kimberly interjected. "Your town is charming. It's a really nice change of pace. And

OMG we can't wait to visit you when you move to New Orleans."

"I love visiting that town, but to live there?" mused Audrey.

"I've only been there three times, but the parts I've seen look very exciting," said Caroline. "Michael loves his new job with the law firm. And to be honest, I'm ready for something new. The historical society doesn't have upward mobility. It's just the one job, nine to five. Look at Bash. He's a poster child for what can happen if you go for your dreams. I know it will be an adjustment."

"Not that big of an adjustment, really. It's just St. Augustine with puke," teased Cricket.

"Cricket, I'm not going to live in the French Quarter, just play there." Caroline laughed.

"New Orleans? You'll love it!" Kimberly gushed. "It's definitely a city like no other—so full of life and culture, and of course the music! Michael is lucky to have found a job with an amazing firm that's located in such a cool spot."

Cricket could see the excitement in Caroline's eyes. She'd been stuck in the same position for years at the historical society, with little hope for stretching her abilities. But finally, here was an opportunity to start anew. She was ready for an adventure.

"Show us the ring again!" Audrey demanded.

The cousins gaped in awe as Caroline held the antique engagement ring up to their faces, basking in its delicate craftsmanship. Its pavé diamonds and princess-cut center stone glimmered in the light like a miniature galaxy of stars.

"This ring is one of a kind; no store could ever replicate it!" Caroline said proudly, delighting in the knowledge that her fiancé had gone through great lengths to find something truly unique for her. "It was handmade right here in St. Augustine, and the antiques dealer told Michael that he felt it was especially lucky; I love how history can still influence our lives today!"

Cricket's eyes sparkled, imagining Bash giving her a piece of jewelry with an old-world charm that could never be found in a modern store. A ring from the 1920's perhaps?

"It looks like Michael really has you figured out," Pricilla said, gazing at Caroline. "It's so romantic, like the perfect fairytale."

Kimberly chimed in, "I admire the effort that's gone into the wedding preparations. "Didn't you get the groom's great-grandmother's dress reworked?"

A soft smile crossed Caroline's lips. "The seamstress was incredible. She did such a beautiful job giving it new life. The lace was nearly a hundred years old, so she had to be very careful."

As the limo came to a stop Cricket asked, "Are we ready to take this town by storm?"

Audrey laughed. "What a great backdrop for selfies!"

Cricket dug through her bag and found the final touch for Caroline—a white rhinestone tiara! Audrey added a Bride-to-Be sash to complete the look.

"Let's do this!" shouted Caroline as she flicked open the door. Silk and satin cascaded out of the limo, avoiding the rain puddles, as Pricilla and Kimberly took photos of their glamorous bride-to-be. They threaded through the crowd at the entrance, receiving appraising gazes while they waited in line to talk to the hostess.

Eventually, they were welcomed into Martini's. Jazz music hummed in the air as they excitedly stepped inside.

The clouds parted as the moon rose above them, illuminating their night of fun.

Cricket finished sending a text to Babs, confirming that they would meet at their mother's house for breakfast in the morning.

Caroline gestured for them to come inside, and they were led to their table with a beautiful view of the water filled with sailboats. "Answer me this: Who is going to have the best night ever? Yes, that would be us! Bottoms up, my dears."

As the night progressed and the drinks kept coming, Cricket noticed that Caroline was starting to relax and let loose. She playfully tapped her martini glass and her cousins joined in with laughter.

"Oh no! Cricket, you got some of your drink on that gorgeous dress of yours! Don't worry, it'll come right out."

Caroline wobbled in her four-inch heels across the dark maroon carpet to Cricket and started dabbing away at the wet spot on Cricket's dress with a napkin. "That cucumber cocktail was clever of you — no chance of a stain! By the way, thank you for stepping in as maid of honor when my sister had to back out. I know she would have been here if she could."

Cricket smiled and patted her satin, maid-of-honor sash. "Of course. It's easy enough since you've made such detailed lists and diagrams for all of us to follow — you did most of the work for me!" Cricket looked towards the bridal party, who were now focused on the boats gliding across the water. She chirped enthusiastically, fumbling with her wallet as she stood up and motioned for the ladies to follow her to the bar to pay the tab. "Are you all ready to go?" she asked with a smile.

When they reached the bar, Caroline set down her YSL clutch on the marble top of the bar and called out, "Girls, if you need to use the restroom, now's the time to go! We're gonna get the pee scared out of us!"

Giggles and laughter filled the air as the trio of cousins sauntered through the restaurant, heading towards the ladies room. Their playful antics accidentally led to a bamboo chair being knocked over, but they quickly set it back upright while still laughing uncontrollably.

"Do you think they are having fun?" Caroline asked Cricket in a low voice while looking down at her newly manicured nails and admiring her sparkling engagement ring that adorned her finger.

"Obviously." Cricket laughed. "But what I really care about is that you have fun. Are you?"

Caroline looked down at her pale pink cocktail dress and bride-to-be sash. "It is exactly what I wanted for my bachelorette party—classy, giggly, and totally tipsy drunk fun! What girl wouldn't have the time of her life all dolled up like this on a weeknight out on the town?"

Cricket locked eyes with the bartender, who gave her a slight nod that signaled he understood she was ready to pay her tab.

"Are you nervous at all?" she asked, truly curious about how Caroline was feeling. Cricket still felt a flutter in her stomach whenever she saw Bash smile, even after a year of dating. But marriage? They were still so young! She was still trying to figure out who she was; and she guessed that he was too. Maybe it'd be enough for now to simply venture through life together, side by side. She marveled that Caroline was at the place in life where she was ready to sign up for—*till death do us part.*

"No," Caroline replied, "I've spent so much time making sure everything is just perfect. Mom had her opinions, and his mom had hers. It sounds terrible to say this, but I'm just ready to get it over with and start our honeymoon already." She sighed. "I'm ready to get married. I hope the next few days go quickly. I know that I want to be with him forever. The wait is torturous!" She looked off into the distance. "My future's waiting for me in New Orleans. I can feel it."

Cricket slid her credit card onto the plastic tray and couldn't believe it when she saw that she owed nothing.

"What?" she asked, looking around trying to figure out who had paid for her tab.

The bartender blew his bangs out of his eyes and smiled. "Your tab's paid in full. You young ladies have several admirers that have been fighting over covering your rounds."

Cricket laughed. "That's hilarious."

The bartender handed her a crumpled stack of napkins and receipts adorned with phone numbers from several different guys. She smiled and stuffed the ball into her bag after handing the bartender a fifty-dollar tip. "I'll make sure Caroline's cousins get their fan mail," she said, bemused.

"They would appreciate it, I'm sure," he responded before going off to help another customer.

Cricket's thoughts wandered as she considered Caroline's precisely laid-out plan for the upcoming week. Was there a similar list for her life? College finished by this age. Career established by that age. Married to the perfect man by this age. Adventures completed by this time. Babies added at that time—it seemed so linear, maybe it could be that easy. But it also seemed terrifying. Caroline was always so sure about things. She didn't second guess like Cricket.

"You're right, New Orleans is where your destiny lies. But let's focus on the here and now and make sure we appreciate every bit of this special night!"

Caroline interjected, "I'll do my best to savor it, but I must admit that Audrey's wedding last year was something else . . ."

Cricket put her hand firmly on Caroline's shoulder in a reassuring gesture. With a warm smile, she said, "Caroline, your weekend is about you and Michael, nobody else. Let me take care of everything so you have the perfect wedding. Deal?"

"Deal," Caroline said with a tired smile. Her eyes glistened, and she held Cricket's hands in hers. "I'm really lucky to have you here with me. Thank you." Caroline grabbed the martini from the bartender with a wink. "Oh, you know me too well," she said, taking five big gulps before setting it down with a clink. Cricket eyed Caroline's empty glass and was handed her own cucumber martini.

"Okay, one more before we hit the road!" Cricket laughed as she drank the martini swiftly.

"The girls are back from the ladies room. Shall we head to the next destination?" Caroline crooned, offering her arm to Cricket as they both teetered.

"I believe we shall," Cricket agreed, steadying them both as they swayed together. "Ladies, let's go out the back way! That gets us closer to the meeting spot."

The flock of tipsy girls stumbled onto the bumpy cobblestones, each trying to capture the perfect selfie angle. "Does everyone have their lucky charm?" Caroline slurred. She reached into her purse and grabbed a Bratz Chloe doll.

Kimberly pulled out SpongeBob, while Pricilla had Polly Pockets, Audrey a Pokémon card, and Cricket produced a vintage Raggedy Ann doll from her tote.

"Whoa, yours is ancient!" Pricilla hiccupped while adjusting her bridesmaid sash.

"It was my aunt's." Cricket swayed on her feet.

Kimberly leaned in. "I think I remember my mom having one with freckles. Yours only has blush."

Caroline chimed in before they could delve further into it, "Okay, ladies, hold on to your amulets — or whatever you brought — because now we're off to explore the spookiest parts of the city!"

CHAPTER 3
BASH

W ho's my good girl?" Bash cooed as he smoothed down the silky black mane of his favorite horse, Banshee. Her coat shimmered as the car headlights danced across her body. Not that he didn't love Shadow, but Banshee had such a mischievous streak that pulled at his heart. She didn't care much for humans and didn't mind if they knew it. She was smart enough to watch out for wayward pedestrians ignoring the traffic lights, and powerful enough to feel at ease sharing the streets with impatient Uber drivers. Both horses were solid black, their coats gleaming with health, and their large round bellies betrayed all the treats they were given. The tall feather headdresses stood proud atop their heads.

The carriage itself had been in rough shape when Bash acquired it. But he'd lovingly restored all the black leather seating, polished and refitted the antique gold lanterns, and hand-painted the parts that needed touch-ups with gold leaf. A few decorative scenes of mythical creatures dressed up the side panels, as well as an arched roof over the bench seats along the driver's compartment. When he had finished his work, it looked brand-new. No one would have guessed its bones were more than a hundred years old. It never ceased to amaze him all the skills one could acquire with a library card and YouTube videos.

Bash donned his usual costume of top hat and tails, enjoying the elegant vibe of it all. Cricket had taken it upon herself to help him revamp his work wardrobe, and he enjoyed it much more than the dress slacks and button-ups he used to wear at his nine-to-five job. Ever since he and Cricket had become a couple, Bash felt like he could be himself around her, no longer feeling the need to hide his psychic abilities to fit in. Before last year, academia had been the perfect place for him to disappear in—filing and organizing in the stacks, studying and preserving other people's lives. But when he took the time to examine what he was good at and what his purpose might be if he decided to embrace his abilities instead of hiding them, day by day he began to feel braver. He'd courageously asked himself: If I could do anything, what would it be? To his astonishment, a bit of drama and flair demanded release. He decided to trust his instinct, quit his job, and start his own business conducting ghost tours. He was determined to write his own story worth preserving.

After a grueling two years of intense physical therapy following his car accident, Bash's father was able to walk once more. The incredible progress he made surpassed Bash's wildest expectations.

Despite the seemingly endless road of rehabilitation that lay ahead of his father, he was adamant that he no longer needed Bash to "coddle" him and provide constant care. Now that his dad was in good health, Bash confidently moved out and rented a small log cabin on his buddy Ryan's family ranch. There was plenty of room for his beloved horses, Banshee and Shadow. The cabin was conveniently situated not too far from Old Town—close enough to be accessible by bike or horseback but far away enough to avoid the light pollution and chaotic city living.

Bash knew he had found his new home as soon as Ryan showed him the rustic cabin tucked away on the wood line at the edge of the ranch. He could hardly believe that he would have the opportunity to spend his days caring for horses and tending to the animals on the ranch. Although it took some time to adjust to waking up with the sunrise each morning, Bash quickly fell in love with country life. He was deeply grateful for all of the fresh milk, eggs, cheese, and honey that came right from their own hard work. Every day presented a new challenge as Bash learned how to help care for such an expansive property—mucking stalls and helping Ryan's father, who could use a little assistance, as he was getting up there in age. The physical labor had taken its toll in the most refreshing way; his shoulders no longer ached from long hours spent sitting at a desk. Bash couldn't help but feel proud of himself and the hard work he was putting into building his own business with Ryan's help.

"Bash!" a voice shouted, bringing him out of his daydream.

He looked around and spotted them: Cricket, Caroline, and her cousins. They were in fits of laughter as they nearly stumbled down the street. Bash couldn't take his eyes off Cricket. Her hair was tied up in a twist, with carefree curls framing her face. A deep longing welled up inside him to undo the clip in her hair and run his hand through its length. His fingertips ached to trace their way down the length of her neck. His heart raced as desire flooded his body. They hadn't been able to spend even a few moments alone lately, and he knew something had to change. Perhaps after the wedding was done, he could convince her to slip away for a short holiday in the Keys, or maybe a bike excursion in the Georgia mountains.

Cricket rushed ahead of the group, grabbed his lapels, and pulled him closer. "Hi there, handsome," she murmured in a low voice before planting a firm kiss on his lips. He instantly recognized the refreshing taste of the cucumber martini from her lips. She had clearly already sipped on a few of them. He suddenly had an urge to cancel their plans for the night and take her home. There was a clearing by a stream not far from his cabin where they could relax under the stars and enjoy each other's company.

"Do I taste cucumber martini?" he asked with a grin.

"On my fourth," she replied, slightly slurring her words.

"My lucky night," he teased, as Cricket kissed him again. He closed his eyes and savored the moment.

She had been his closest friend during college, but last year, he found out she was part fae and had supernatural powers. He shared his own secret with her—his ability to communicate with the spirit world, and their friendship blossomed into something even greater. They had faced a few bumps along the way, like Ambrosias, the winter prince who had *claimed* her in front of the fae courts. But Bash knew they'd get through this obstacle together; he'd promised her that much. And it was all worth it. Their bond strengthened and energized him. He felt invincible with her by his side. She lovingly ran her hands up and down his back.

"It's been a really fun night so far," she said, her words snapping him out of his daze. "Do you think you can put the cherry on top?" Her words snapped him out of his daze.

"Whipped cream and sprinkles to boot!" he said with a playful grin. He stepped away from her, putting some distance between them to clear his head and get back to business. But it was hard to focus when Cricket looked so irresistible. "What a pleasant surprise! You made it right on time!" He tipped his tall hat with a wink and bowed toward Caroline and her cousins as they drew near to pet the horses. "Caroline, are you ready for the tour to end all tours?" He tightened his grip around Cricket's hand. His gaze darted around the area in search of any unseen visitors. Thankfully, none of Caroline's cousins had tagalongs. Sometimes people had an unknown presence lingering with them, as if some intangible force had attached itself to their being.

It was common knowledge among the locals that St. Augustine's ghosts were territorial. The situation could turn nasty if they were forced to share their space with an unknown soul. These guided tours could be prone to agitating specters, and that was not his intention.

"A friendly wager between us, Bash?" Caroline asked with a mischievous glint in her eyes. She shifted her weight from one foot to the other and crossed her arms.

"Uh-oh, anyone is a fool who wagers against the summa cum laude, Caroline. What do you have in mind?" He couldn't help but smile at her happiness. "You never did forgive me for leaving the historical society, did you? Work must be unbearably boring without me."

Caroline rolled her eyes. "It has been boring, but I will forgive you—I'm proud of the success you've had with your business. You sure have an interesting way of bringing history alive for all the vacationers." She cast an appraising glance around the carriage.

"After breaking out of that cage, there's no way I could go back to a nine-to-five job," Bash responded. "If you ever want to branch out—"

"No, no," Caroline cut him off. "I'll leave the 'ghosties' and outdoorsy stuff to you and others like you. But when I settle down in New Orleans, trust me—I'll be looking for a regular job in some specialized archive! That's where I really belong, indoors and in the quiet."

"We can't wait to visit!" chimed Audrey.

"When do you head out?" asked Bash.

"Michael's job has had him out there for three months already, staying at an extended-stay hotel. So, now that he has the lay of the land, after the honeymoon, I will go with him to pick out our apartment and coordinate the double move. I'll take some time to settle in and then find a job."

"Double move?" Cricket asked.

Caroline glanced upward and rolled her eyes in frustration. "I have to go through both of our apartments and sort out what we're taking with us and what we're getting rid of," she explained.

"That sounds like a lot of work," said Audrey.

"It's a full-time job," Caroline agreed.

"Well then," Bash said, rubbing his hands together eagerly. "A goodbye tour? What kind of wager have you got in mind?"

Caroline let out a light chuckle, and her eyes glimmered with glee. "If I actually see a real ghost on this tour — something that I can either find proof of, or know the history of — then I'll tip you one thousand dollars," she said, her voice slightly slurred from the drinks she had earlier.

The cousins all laughed at the playful wager, while Bash smiled to himself, knowing he'd be a thousand dollars richer by the end of the night. He was relieved that nobody was actually expecting to find any ghosts tonight. It was much easier to give a history tour when people were just here for the stories. When someone really believed in ghosts, but wasn't sensitive enough to pick up on them, they would inevitably go away disappointed. Tonight would be full of old tales about this town, and he welcomed it with open arms.

"The ghosts are fickle, so no guarantees. Plus, the stories told, well, it's a lot like the game telephone, if you know what I mean. But let's do our best to find them." Bash opened the door to the carriage and folded out the small footstool. "Ladies, climb on in. Each of you has a kit at your disposal. A GoPro hat goes on your head to record the entire evening from your perspective, and an EMF reader so you can know where to look. I will tell you all the stories, tell you where to point the gear, and walk you through everything so that you can have an enjoyable evening. All your footage will be edited and put up on my website, and you can link any of your social media to it seamlessly. Any questions? No? Okay, let's get settled in and get to it." He pointed to the horses, "Banshee and Shadow like carrots. I have a bag of them if you want to help treat them throughout the night.

Bash settled in on the driver's side of the carriage and grabbed the reins, as Cricket scooted across the black leather seat and snuggled in next to him. He leaned over to whisper in her ear, "Love you, babe."

She was the first girl he had said it to, and now that it had come out, he wanted to say it always. He loved her, and her family. Family for him consisted of just him and his dad. Cricket came with a big, wild, and crazy family. He really liked her sisters, and he couldn't get enough of her mom's cooking.

"You too." She kissed his cheek and laid her head on his shoulder.

Now to work. Show time.

"Tonight, we embark on a journey through the hauntingly beautiful streets of St. Augustine," he began, his voice becoming deep with suspense. "It's known as the oldest continuously occupied city in the United States of America, it's no wonder that many have reported supernatural occurrences here! As we traverse this miraculous area, let's remember to remain respectful and courteous to its inhabitants—both living and those in spirit form. Who knows what kind of exciting encounters await us tonight!" He clicked his tongue, and Banshee and Shadow merged slowly into traffic. "We have several bottles of chilled champagne in the ice bucket, so be sure to grab some if you're feeling thirsty," said Bash.

"It's time to see some spooks," Pricilla said as she popped open the first bottle and passed filled glasses around.

"We'll circle the roundabout and take a moment to appreciate the Bridge of Lions," Bash continued. "Did you know that these two magnificent lions have been guarding the city since 1927? They were modeled after two historical Medici lions found in Italy. Legends say that if the city is ever in danger, the spirits of the lions come alive and protect its borders. Now let's see what your EMF readers have to say. Go ahead and wave them over the statues and check for any unusual activity!" Audrey and Kimberly excitedly waved their devices while Pricilla filmed them.

"Do you know their names, Bash?" Caroline asked.

"Fiel and Firme, Faithful and Firm. Do you want to tell us the other two on the Anastasia side of the bridge?" Bash asked, knowing she was dying to share her knowledge.

"Pax and Peli! Peace and Happiness," she beamed as she clinked glasses with Kimberly.

"You are absolutely correct," Bash said. "I wish you and Michael pax and peli throughout your wedding and into your marriage."

The carriage erupted in giggles.

"That is a great toast to go with champagne," said Kimberly.

"There's some water bottles in the cooler as well," Bash informed them, seeing that most of the champagne was being spilled, not drank.

"I'll switch to water," Cricket said.

"Oh no you won't, not yet," said Caroline, passing her a half-filled flute.

"Pax and Peli." Kimberly lifted her glass.

"Pax and Peli," all the women shouted in unison as they sipped their drinks.

"Now, waters all around," said Bash, giving a wink to Cricket. Cleaning puke out of the carriage at the end of the night did not sound appealing. At least the upholstery was leather, easy to clean. The traffic around them slowed, the faint whisper of the wind carrying the sound of laughter and music from the British pub.

"Point your EMF readers that way, and you may be able to pick up some supernatural energy," Bash instructed.

"Ohhh, my reader's showing red!" Kimberly squealed, clutching her SpongeBob toy tightly.

"Mine too, mine too!" Audrey echoed, gripping her Pokémon card close.

"What's with the toys?" Bash whispered in confusion.

Cricket gave him a mischievous grin as she pulled out her Raggedy Ann doll. "Talismans," she explained. "It was Caroline's idea. She's actually afraid of ghosts."

Bash was taken aback. "That's unexpected; she could easily scare them off with her librarian glare."

"You're horrible," Cricket chided.

"Why did she want to do a ghost tour then?"

Cricket gestured toward the back seat of their carriage towards the three cousins.

Bash ran his fingers through his hair, "Caroline wants an exciting evening for her cousins, but not too frightening.

Well so far, the night has been G-rated. We can keep it that way but keep it interesting, I think."

Cricket smiled and leaned her head on Bash's shoulder.

"Should we check out the Kings Head British pub?" asked Kimberly.

Bash tapped his fingers on the horse's reins, "Oh, I think we can skip it, don't you think, Caroline?" The pub was known to house aggressive spirits that liked to reach out and touch, especially in the upstairs apartment. No need to risk anyone getting shoved or their hair pulled. That wasn't for this group. If Caroline ended up with scratch marks all over her before the wedding, she would never forgive him. "I have a better stop for us," Bash announced over his shoulder. "Focus on the right side of the carriage; you will find the old city gates coming up soon. Take lots of pictures with your cell phones. Many orbs and full body ghosts are often sighted in this area guarding our city streets. Someone might even see the spirit of a little girl in white who enjoys dancing and singing—she also loves crossing the street to get candy at the candy shop nearby. Maybe she will be attracted to your toys?"

"There isn't anything showing up," whined Pricilla.

"Nothing on the footage," Kimberly pouted.

Bash brought the carriage to a halt at a red light. Floating right by them was the spirit of the little girl in white, grinning up at him. Bash gave her a mischievous wink; while he knew he shouldn't show favoritism, she was definitely one of his favorites. She jumped and skipped around with joy, and Bash wished that everyone could be as carefree as her.

"Pricilla, hold your Polly Pocket outside the carriage—that's it! Now let's get everyone to take photos and videos of Pricilla's hand."

Caroline quivered with excitement. "Oh my gosh! The EMF detectors are going crazy!"

Cricket gave Caroline's hand a comforting squeeze. "See, not spooky at all! I bet when we review the EMF readings and video footage later—we'll find something exciting!"

The carriage clattered along, the noise of horseshoes clopping against the pavement blending with the sounds of merry laughter from people walking nearby. The aroma of barbecue lingered in the air, tempting everyone with its deliciousness.

From past experience, Bash was sure that the cameras had picked up the little girl too—she often showed up as clusters of pale blue and pink orbs, like balls of cotton candy.

The Tolomato Cemetery stood ominously at the edge of town. The large black iron gates stood wide open, allowing entry to those willing to explore its secrets. Old tombstones worn by time leaned at odd angles, while above ground crypts lay neatly in rows claiming their rightful space. Large tree branches covered in moss hovered protectively above the graves, hiding them from the evening stars.

"Do you feel like you are being watched? Look for the spirit of a little boy about five years old playing around that large oak tree," Bash urged.

"What tree?" Caroline shivered as goosebumps rose on her arms.

Cricket pointed. "Right there in the middle of the cemetery."

Bash guided the horses into the grass and stopped in front of a massive iron gate. "Ready to ghost hunt? Let's all get out and see if we can connect with the spirits."

"You guys go ahead. I'll just stay here and keep the horses company." Caroline bit her lower lip, glancing nervously at the cemetery. "I don't feel comfortable walking around a graveyard in my heels — they always get stuck in the grass."

"Don't be scared! You have your Bratz doll for protection. Here, we can all leave our shoes in the cart," Pricilla said, laughing before slipping off her heels.

"This is gonna be so much fun!" Kimberly said, ripping her shoes off and running between tombstones ahead of everyone else. "My adrenaline is already pumping!"

Bash strolled up to the horses to give them some carrots while they waited for the rest of the ghost hunters.

"It looks like we have found our fearless leader," Cricket said, giggling. "Come on, Caroline. Hold my hand. I promise you are safe."

Caroline reluctantly kicked off her shoes, grabbed Cricket's hand and walked slowly into the cemetery.

Bash couldn't help but smile. People's reactions to graveyards always amazed him. Some were silent and still, others quivered in fear, and then there were those like Kimberly who seemed just as comfortable here as they would be at church on Sunday.

Pricilla pointed her flashlight around the cemetery and shivered. "What stories do you know of from here?" She pressed her phone to record, as the group carefully navigated between the tombstones, eyes peeled for strange shapes in the dark.

Bash's voice cracked with tension as he spoke. "First, you should know where you are standing — this is the oldest cemetery in the country."

Caroline took over. "Before the Catholics, it was a burial ground for the Guale, the Native American tribe that was here before the Spanish."

The high stone markers rose up in rows around them like silent soldiers standing guard over the dead below.

Bash nodded in agreement. "Do you want to tell them how many people are buried here?"

"There are at least a thousand according to the parish death records held at the Diocesan Archives."

"But there's not that many grave markers, a hundred at most," Audrey protested. "It's small."

"Creepy, right?" added Caroline.

"Yes," a voice filled the night air like a ghostly whisper. A shiver ran through the group, and they could feel their courage waning. All eyes followed the eerie moonlit walkway to the back of the graveyard, which was illuminated by an unnaturally white chapel. Another group of tourists were carefully gathered around it. "Many Catholic clergymen have been buried here, some with terrible secrets," their tour guide said ominously.

Bash saw a dark figure dart around the back of the chapel in a hurried flurry. He cautiously scanned all around it, but everything seemed eerily still. Even the wind seemed to pause in apprehension. Nothing appeared normal about that place for just one moment.

"Did you just—" Caroline stopped in her tracks and gasped softly.

"What did you see?" Bash inquired, having had his eyes trained on the spot in front of him while she had been looking somewhere else.

"White, I think I saw a blur of white."

Spirits were usually inoffensive, but a somber energy overcame him. His instincts went on high alert.

In unison, the group at the far end of the cemetery fumbled to switch on their flashlights and marched down the center path toward the gates.

"Can you believe that?" Bash heard from the group.

"Our next stop will be the distillery," a loud, arrogant voice echoed through the night breeze. "You think that was scary, there is way more to come tonight."

Bash rolled his eyes and clenched his jaw in annoyance. Tony always had a knack for testing Bash's patience. As if on cue, Tony turned and stared directly into Bash's eyes.

"Oh, hey there, horse boy!" Tony jeered, his beer gut moving up and down beneath his Jaguars jersey. "I got the cemetery all riled up for you. You might as well play "We Will Rock You," because the game is starting. Take the floor little man, take the floor. If you make it through the night after following me in this cemetery, feel free to meet up for brewskis at White Lion. I'll let you buy me some rounds to say thanks."

"Right." Bash tilted his head, as if he would ever voluntarily spend time with Tony. His mediumship was undeniable, but his motives were barbarous. Tony didn't care about the spirits at all; they were simply entertainment. His intellect didn't stretch farther than football stats and grilling. Not that Bash didn't follow the games himself, but there was more to life than football and hot dogs.

"Bash, I saw her again!" Caroline's voice jolted him back to the moment. He took a deep breath, pushing his irritation with Tony aside.

"Take us where you saw her." He was surprised that Caroline had seen something. She was very analytical. Usually that personality was not tuned into the frequency to see or feel the afterlife. "Caroline, how far back does your family line go here in St. Augustine? I mean, are there any relatives of yours that were here a hundred years ago?"

"No, my family's from Chicago. My parents moved here right before I was born," she replied.

"And Nan and Mossey moved down to the Keys not long after that," Pricilla added. "Our side of the family is all that is left in Chicago."

Caroline continued walking towards the front left corner of the cemetery. Bash found it interesting. That was the only area with the original stone fence barrier still intact.

The girls stared wide-eyed as Audrey and Pricilla raised their meters and swept them back and forth. The group followed, while orange dots turned on and off on their EMF readers. Caroline's bare feet lightly grazed the grass as she ran several yards ahead of them.

"I know I saw—" Caroline huffed. "There, did you all see it?" She spun around, her eyes widening as she searched the trees.

"No," Cricket said hesitantly, her gaze darting around. "Could it've been the flashlights from the other group?"

Bash didn't see anything, but he shut his eyes and focused in on the atmosphere. He slowly inhaled and exhaled as he tried to pick up on any subtle shifts in energy. He heard a female voice mumbling somewhere in the distance and felt a chill run up his spine when he realized he wasn't familiar with this energy. He turned to Caroline and noticed an ethereal fog surrounding her head. "Do you want to go? It's getting late."

Confusion swept through her expression. "Why would I want to leave?"

A knot of dread tightened in Bash's chest. Caroline hadn't wanted to step foot out of the carriage, and now she was adamant about staying. An unknown entity was clearly manipulating her, but for what purpose? What was their connection? He wouldn't usually be worried . . . but Tony had just been here.

"Aaaaggghhh!" Caroline screamed in agony as her body writhed from the intense pain.

Everyone turned to see Caroline desperately clutching at her hand. Bash's face paled when before them all, a ghostly figure rose up from the grave before them. She was dressed in a tattered wedding gown caked with dirt and mud. Her face had decayed from the passing of time, exposing bones and withering flesh. With deathly bony fingers, she grasped onto Caroline's hand as if claiming it for herself. Slowly, the two began to levitate, their feet hovering mere inches above the ground. The ghost clung to Caroline's limp body with an iron grip and began to merge within her. Caroline's eyes, now completely white and glassy, stared off into nothingness, entranced by this supernatural force.

"Oh my God! What is going on?" Kimberly shouted while recording the scene on her phone.

The air filled with a sickening smell of rot, making everyone gag and retch. It seemed like the entity was eager to take Caroline away, as she kept shaking and convulsing her slim form as they floated higher into the air.

"We gotta get her outta here! Now!" Bash yelled as he leapt forward toward Caroline.

"What do we do?" Cricket wailed, her voice laced with panic.

Bash ordered, "Back away! Everyone take cover in the cart and get out of this cemetery now!"

Pricilla clenched her fists tight, refusing to budge an inch. Audrey gasped, wide-eyed with fear. Cricket yanked her hand forward, a silent command for them to join hands and form a circle around Caroline. "I can disperse the energy, but it's up to you to handle the ghosts," Cricket whispered into Bash's ear.

Bash was no ghostbuster, despite his ability to see and sense the energy surrounding them. He had seen other specters throughout this graveyard before: a little boy here, a friar over there. But they were harmless residual hauntings, simply echoes from the past without conscious intention behind them. This was different — he could feel the weight of unseen panic and despair in the air. Pale peach light ominously pulsed around the barefoot satin-clad bridal party as they held hands tightly, willing Caroline to be released.

"Cricket?" Audrey's voice could just be heard above the groans escaping from her cousin that floated above.

Cricket's eyes were tightly shut, her skin pale. "Caroline's energy is linked to us now. We are grounding her. I can't pinpoint the connection between her and the entity."

"Okay, I'll try to reason with the spirit." Bash entered the circle and walked to the center, directly next to the ghost bride. He faced her, reaching his hands up to touch the hem of her dress. "Please let my friend go."

The entity within Caroline ignored him. She was floating roughly five feet above the grave, twirling weightlessly. Caroline was completely entranced, seemingly unaware of what was going on.

His pleas with the spirit continued, but were in vain.

Bash slammed his foot on the ground in frustration. He peered down at the time-worn gravestone. "Can you tell me your name?"

Caroline's body convulsed violently as she murmured incomprehensible words.

"Cricket," Bash said, "can you drive the cart here?"

She glanced back at the vehicle hesitantly.

"You mean for me to . . . drive over the graves?"

"The entity isn't giving her up. We need to take control of the situation now."

Cricket nodded in agreement and spoke with conviction. "I can provide us some time."

As she closed her eyes, she summoned the energy of the elements around her. With a graceful flourish, she extended her arms, and beautiful wings sprouted from her back. Bash felt a surge of awe as he watched her effortlessly lift into the air, bending time to her will. He was enveloped in a cocoon of magic as his ears popped, and Cricket zoomed toward the carriage with incredible speed, while all around him stood frozen in time.

It seemed that Cricket had indeed been reaping the benefits of her studies with her aunt Habina lately; such powerful spells used to exhaust her entirely, but now exuded from her effortlessly.

Bash reached into his pocket and pulled out a small bundle of sage, along with a lighter. He quickly sparked the flame, then carefully ignited the end of the sage. With deliberate movements, he waved the smoke around Caroline, causing it to dance and twirl around her. "Spirits of the hallowed realm, I send you on your way with blessings and peace. Our intrusion has disturbed you. We ask for your forgiveness, and bid you a safe journey to the other side. Be at peace."

There seemed to be no change in Caroline, as Cricket arrived back with the carriage. The two horses stamped impatiently, neighing and snorting with agitation.

"Settle down, girls," Bash soothed. He smoothly took the reins from Cricket and leaned in for a quick kiss. "You're a marvel."

"I know." She smirked with a devilish grin.

He nodded and helped her up onto the carriage. Cricket slapped her palms together in front of her face, then flung them apart with an adrenaline-filled yell. Everything around them jumped to life.

"What just happened?" Kimberly gasped in awe.

"Climb aboard!" Cricket shouted over the chaos.

They all scrambled into the back seat as Bash gave the horses a nudge forward.

"Forget nice," he growled, clenching his fists. He sprung into action, pulling Caroline close and dragging her inside the carriage with all his might. As though summoning an invisible power from some unknown source, sparks began to swirl around them. He clung to her tightly as mist thickened around the two of them, turning blacker than night. She shuddered violently in his arms.

Caroline's breath hitched, and she whispered a name. "Rebecca."

Caroline held her breath and opened her eyes, looking up at Bash with a face devoid of emotion before scanning the faces of her cousins that were pressed in upon her. "Did I pass out? I thought I— Never mind," she mumbled weakly as a strange energy still lingered in the air around them. She sat back, resting her head against Cricket's shoulder. "I think I drank too many martinis. I need . . . water."

"Martinis don't make you go full *Stranger Things*," said Pricilla, handing her an opened water bottle.

"Are you all right, Caroline?" Bash questioned, his voice laced with worry.

"Fine, just cold. It's been a long night. I think we should call it."

"That's a good idea. Let's get you guys back," Bash replied. "Everyone okay?" He glanced around the carriage as the cousins gawked at their phones in anticipation of what they had caught on video.

"What did you do back there?" Cricket murmured, her eyes wide with wonder.

Bash tilted his head to the side and pursed his lips. "I'm not sure. Something just came over me."

"Do you think it's finished? Or is it only the beginning?" Cricket added fearfully.

"That remains to be seen," Bash replied uneasily, a foreboding feeling gripping him tightly.

If the entity crossed over to the other side, it was the first time he had been a part of something like that. He had some long overdue studying to do on the topic of actual ghost busting. Before engaging the horses, he pulled out his phone to text Ryan.

Bash: Can you meet up tonight?

Ryan: What's up?

Bash: Time to level up my character

Ryan: Hell yeah! Where are we meeting?

Bash frowned. A sour taste filled his mouth.

Bash: White Lion

CHAPTER 4
BABS

Babs was a mess. She couldn't shake off the overwhelming anxiety that weighed heavily on her heart. She had been staring at the ceiling for what seemed like an eternity, growing more restless and impatient with each passing minute. The thought of failing the challenges consumed her mind, leaving no room for anything else.

In exasperation, she gave in to her restless energy that pulled her from bed, and before she realized it, she had wandered the old path that led to the alligator-infested pond ruled by Liande. The stillness of the night was broken by the croaking of frogs, chirping crickets, and the occasional splash of an alligator in the water. The air was dripping with moisture. The back of her neck felt sticky. She sat at the edge of the pond, cross-legged, closed her eyes, and listened to the song of the wood.

A dark wave slowly crawled through the heart of the murky pond, as if something was stirring in its depths.

Babs felt a chill as a sickly phosphorescence emerged from underneath the water. Liande's outline slowly became visible, and Babs couldn't help but be entranced by her primordial, reptilian aura. Her piercing gaze held a primal sexuality—lurking with sinister amusement.

"We have matters yet to be tended to, you and I." Liande's voice was like a soft whisper from the past. "That which lies between us is yet incomplete. You have changed much since our last encounter. Fury no longer burns in your gaze, and yet all the softness that gathered at the corners of your eyes is missing as well." Her head shook slowly from side to side, almost hypnotically. "But there's something else about you now. The feral stink of the court waifs about you." She took a deep breath and shook her head as a low cackle escaped her lips.

Babs drifted back to the memories of Liande and her fear of her. Was it only a year ago that she felt that way? As she emerged from the depths, Babs took in her night-like scales with new eyes, no longer filled with dread. She had seemed manic the last time Babs saw her. Tonight she seemed subdued, calm even.

"I don't know what came over me." Babs spoke in a measured tone, as if piecing it all together as she went along. Her words floated out like dreams, slowly coalescing into understanding.

"I summoned you to my realm, as before." A sorrowful longing tugged at the corners of Liande's lips, as a melancholic smile formed. "You are between, young Culebra." Her dark glassy eyes twinkled with an otherworldly wisdom.

"Between what?"

"You are not yet what you will be, and are not what you once were. It's the pause at the top of an inhale, that is where you find yourself." Her voice trailed off, her gaze distant and haunting.

"What do you know about it?"

Liande stretched out her fingers and caressed the surface of the water, causing ripples to form. The reflection in the pond began to shift and change before her eyes, revealing glimpses of distant lands and strangers. Babs had always been fascinated by Liande's ability to peer into the lives of others using the pool's mysterious power. Unexpectedly, an image caught her eye — a fleeting glimpse of her sister Cricket. Babs tried to reach out toward the vision, but it quickly faded away like a wisp of smoke, leaving behind only a lingering sense of concern.

"I've been through many metamorphoses in my time. This last one was the most challenging, forced upon me." Liande paused, her voice growing stronger with determination. "But it will be worth it, in the end. I will have my revenge."

"Nothing has been forced upon me. I've made my decision. It was my choice to join the summer court," Babs declared firmly.

"Ah, the futility of choice," the creature replied with a serene smile. Her grin widened, revealing razor-sharp teeth. "You may believe you are in control, but destiny is already set in motion. The web that ensnares you was spun long before you were even born. All glimmers of your mother's hope are gone — the path to live out your days in obscurity is lost to you. Your generation of the Culebra line will fulfill the prophecy."

Babs couldn't imagine her life any different than it was now. She thought of Gwylm, now a part of her, with whom she had gained wondrous strength. Then her mind drifted to Verity, who had opened her eyes to the mysteries of the fae, teaching her how to engage each element, to work with and to serve. She took solace in Aunt Habina's wisdom, watching her discover healing secrets with awe. Babs was certain that she had found her place in something much greater than herself. Her life before this seemed so small, claustrophobic even.

Liande tilted her head. "I can see your mind is set. Your thoughts are plain upon your face. Yet I fear you will look back on this night and lament that you did not heed my warning. It is the greatest flaw younglings have." The alligators swam gracefully in a mesmerizing pattern, their webbed feet creating small ripples that lapped against the shore.

"Oh?" Babs crossed her arms across her chest. "What is this greatest flaw?"

"You lack the ability to hear what is actually being said."

Babs shrugged. As if she would be schooled by this creature.

"No matter. Remember, young Culebra, you owe me a favor. The time is near. I foresee our alignment. You will come to me." Her tail swished against the water.

"I haven't forgotten." Had it not been for Liande sending her to meet the summer queen last year, her sister Cricket would have died from the Drake curse. It was an odd turn of events, but Liande's actions had a significant impact on the trajectory of her life. It was strange to think that someone else's actions could shape one's future so profoundly.

"No, I would hope you hadn't. And you have kept silent?" Liande hissed.

Babs remembered Liande's unusual demand. "If anyone from the court knows you're here, it is not from my lips that they have heard it. I don't break my promises."

"You will be held by your word. If I read the pool correctly, destiny is moving swiftly."

A shiver ran through Babs's body as she tried to decipher the meaning behind the cryptic words. Despite her uncertainty, Babs had learned not to question Liande's intuition. However, a sense of unease lingered in her gut, and she couldn't shake it off.

Just then, Liande's head snapped toward the water, her nostrils flaring as she sniffed the air. "My visitor approaches earlier than I expected. Away with you!" she hissed.

Babs strained to perceive what Liande was sensing, but she couldn't discern anything.

"Go!" Liande commanded.

Babs waited until Liande began to turn around before ducking behind a tree. She held her breath as she listened to the rapid beat of her own heart.

Suddenly, the water started to churn and bubble, and a group of figures emerged from the depths. Babs strained her eyes to see them better, and as they drew nearer, she could make out their features. They were definitely not human—their skin was pale and smooth, almost translucent, and their eyes glowed with a strange, otherworldly light. They were fae. Babs had never realized the lake was a portal.

Her eyes were drawn to one figure that towered above the others. Babs watched on as Liande bowed, looking small in the midst of the strangers.

The figure stepped forward, revealing himself in all his terrible glory. His silver eyes shone with the raw power of a glacier against a darkening night. The pale blue skin of his face was slightly translucent, like ice; his steel-blue armor clung to his body as if frozen within an ice sculpture. A crown made of metal and crudely chiseled gems glowed a cold blue in the moonlight. Faint tendrils of mist rose from him into the air.

"Greetings, Liande." His voice reverberated in the chilled air. His accompanying soldiers dressed in shimmering armor formed an unbreakable circle around her. Their swords were pointed inward, trapping her in a tiny circle with the leader. The warriors stood motionless and silent, their eyes glinting darkly like distant ancient stars.

Liande bowed her head respectfully. "Your Highness, you flatter me with your presence. What does the King of the Winter Court require of me?"

Babs froze, her body tense with fear as the man's cold, blue eyes pierced into hers. She couldn't move as he seemed to stare straight into her soul. Her heart raced in her chest. It was as if she had stopped breathing altogether under his intense gaze. She felt as if he were reading all her thoughts and memories at once. Breath ceased to enter her lungs.

The winter king released the spell and turned his attention back to Liande. "I require your assistance in locating the missing item," he said, his voice calm and collected.

Liande's arms encircled his neck. Her movements were sensuous and flirtatious, more so than usual. "What exactly is missing, my lord?"

"Don't toy with me. You know I seek the crown." His posture remained statuesque, unaffected by her touch.

Liande's posture froze for just a moment, and Babs could see the tension in her body. "You know it's veiled from me. Do you come here to torment me, Your Highness?" Liande replied, her voice steady but tense. "Is this undeserved curse not enough? Is your heart so cruel that you have no room for pity? I have been banished unjustly, forgotten by both courts." She moved around the king with a lithe, lizard-like motion that was both disturbing and attractive, her hand gliding lightly along his chest.

His eyes narrowed as he regarded her. "Do not test me, Liande. I know that the crown resides in the near lands. You spy upon all, banished or no." Anger punctuated his voice.

"The winter court's patience is at an end. Your sister, the summer queen, has proven to be useless in returning it to us, even after we took the prisoner. Summer's rule is weak. The king has been away far too long. The queen cannot keep her subjects in line or control her lands. The crowns were meant to be worn, the responsibility of rule wielded between both courts. We have been without the crown for far too long."

Liande hesitated, looking down at the water surrounding her.

Babs watched on.

"How fares the chosen?" Liande purred her words into the king's ear with a sultry tone that was intended to weaken his resolve.

The king's slender fingers quivered as he lifted them up to touch the edge of his crown. "She is not your concern."

Taking an alluring breath, Liande stared up at him with passionate eyes. "My affection for winter has not waned," she murmured.

"Nature demands balance. The winter prince must have the crown to present to his chosen one. Only then will our court be complete once again."

"The telling," Liande murmured. "Sister against sister. I wonder—" She dragged her clawed fingers across the surface of the pond, and as each droplet of water met her nail, it shimmered with the reflection of possibilities that her eyes alone could interpret. "Eight crowns rest upon eight heads; summer and winter balanced not. Violence, cunning tricks played out for power's sake, but also courage and determination that will bring justice." Liande's eyes grew dark. "I see how the prophecy may come true—a time when both courts may unite under one banner."

The king scoffed. "What are you muttering? Eight crowns? Has summer picked a new princess?"

Liande hesitated. "The pieces begin to fit together." She looked down around her, then sharply up, directly into his eyes. "I will wield my influence to return the lost crown to the realm of winter. In return, give me your vow to return me to my true figure. Restore my glamour and grant me the crown that now resides on my sister's head. I wish to be queen of summer and take my rightful place beside the summer king. As a son of Ishtar, this should prove an easy task."

The man's lips curled into a sly grin, and Babs felt a knot form in her stomach.

"Ah, so you bid your time to this end?" the king asked, his voice dripping with amusement. "It is against my nature to incite war. Summer politics is not my concern. And yet I have been patient, and it has gotten me nowhere. Sabella brings this onto herself." He turned to his guards surrounding them. "Very well. You all bear witness. I accept Liande, eldest daughter of Inanna's line, lover of the summer king, true mother of the winter prince, eldest sister to Sabella and Verity. If Liande should return winter's lost crown, I will use my full might to return the glamour that was so cruelly taken by her sister and will place upon Liande's head the queen's crown so that she may rule as an ally of the winter court."

Liande nodded, her eyes fixed on the regal king. Babs could see the desperation in her gaze, and she knew that she was willing to risk everything for this one chance to seize power.

"But be warned," the king continued, his smile turning cold. "If you fail to deliver, I will ensure that your punishment is more severe than you can imagine. The punishment will be upon your son, the winter prince."

Liande nodded once more, her expression grim. "I understand."

"Let us seal the pact in the fashion of the old ways," Liande demanded.

The winter king's grin widened as he grasped Liande fiercely by the back of the neck. The soldiers turned their backs on the two entwined figures.

Babs watched in horror as the deal was made before her very eyes. The sovereign hungrily took what was offered. Liande gave body and spirit fully to him; her gaze stayed upon his until delight consumed her completely, reveling in the act of unity.

Without a word, the king and his guards disappeared into the depths of the portal. Liande was left in the center of the lake, alone and spent.

"I know you are there; you witnessed the pact." Liande's voice was hoarse and thick.

Babs hesitantly stepped out from the safety of the shadows, wishing she were anywhere else. Her mom and gran had warned her about how complicated life could be in court, but she never thought she'd find herself in such an uncomfortable situation. She longed for her bed but instead mustered the strength, braved through her trepidation, and ventured toward Liande.

"The summer queen is your sister?" Babs asked, her voice barely above a whisper. "Verity—"

Liande's eyes were filled with determination and a hint of madness. "I foresaw this day."

"I would think war between the courts is not something to take lightly."

Liande turned to her, her eyes clouded with memory. "How like your gran you sound." Amusement filtered through her voice. "I now see why they did what they did. For I have seen the shadow of your future. I knew you were key, but this—"

Shock hit Babs as worlds collided within her mind. "You know Gran?" She hadn't really considered what Gran's life had been like before taking up residence in the human world. She had only thought of her mom falling in love with her dad and giving up the faerie realm for him. She assumed that Gran and her aunts had followed her so they could be together. Of course, it went horribly wrong, and they were separated anyway. It had never occurred to her that something else entirely could have happened before her mom and dad met.

Liande continued as she reached the edge of the lake. "War began long ago; it is a cycle without end. As to my part in it, Sabella bested me, deceiving the court into believing that Ambrosias was her child. Few know the truth."

"Like the winter king?" Babs picked at her fingernail.

"Information is power. He has gained quite a bit of power over me, knowing my love for Ambrosias."

"And the summer king, does he know his son is yours?"

Liande's features went dark. She grasped at her stomach. "Sabella's spell is powerful. The court, including the king, saw and remembered what she wanted them to see. I have been forgotten by all, erased. They have forgotten me entirely."

Babs remembered Verity's strange behavior when they spoke of sisters. "Maybe the spell isn't as ironclad as you think."

Liande sighed. "I bided my time in the shadows. I patiently moved the waves of destiny." Colors shimmered all around her on the water. "Sabella's unwillingness to suffer the presence of my child — the king's child — has handed me an alliance with winter, where my son has risen to power. A synergy will be created not seen in eons. I see his equal joining his side."

Babs nodded, her head spinning with the implications of the tale. She could understand Liande's determination all too well. She had her own kind of determination, and hers was just as personal. With a deep breath, she stepped closer, her heart pounding with fear and anticipation. "I agreed to not reveal your presence to the summer court all that time ago. But I will not commit treason to the court that I am about to serve," she declared, her voice trembling. "I am to face the challenges, and—"

Liande raised her hand to demand silence. Her eyes were opal flecked, hard as glass one moment and liquid the next. "Yes, you will face the challenges and indirectly bring about the telling. You will serve me as your queen. There is to be war, and you will help me win it." She ran her finger-tips along Babs's lips.

"I will give you a gift to mark your allegiance to me." Liande closed her eyes, and a pulsing energy emanated from her body. A moment later, Babs felt a hot breeze flow over her skin. She looked down and gasped as she saw symbols etched into her flesh, glowing with a pale blue light.

"What is it?" Babs asked, a mixture of fear and dread coursing through her veins.

"It is the mark of our court, yours and mine." Babs looked as the same markings appeared on Liande's arm, a perfect reflection. "It is visible to our eyes alone and will give you a knowing, making it easier for you to navigate the intricate politics of the court."

Liande leaned in closer, her lips meeting Babs's and teasing them open with her tongue. With a strong burst of energy, she exhaled a warm breath into Babs's mouth. Babs found herself lost in the intensity of Liande's embrace, feeling the strange energy dance along the surface of her skin, and a near opposite energy swirled within her. She felt different, empowered in a way she couldn't explain. A surge of life magic coursed through her veins. She could feel the pulse of breath as if it were her own, as if every inhale and exhale were a palpable connection between them. The mingling of their essences created a symphony of energy that danced and swirled around them, filling the air with a vibrant luminescence.

Her senses heightened. Babs could perceive the world in a new way. Colors seemed more vivid, each hue saturated with a brilliance that was previously unseen. She had already seen auras, but this was different, more. The sounds around her became nuanced; the song of birds transformed into a symphony of intricate melodies, the rustle of leaves an intricate rhythm. Even the scent of flowers carried on the wind held deeper layers of fragrances that whispered tales of enchantment.

With every moment that passed, Babs felt a newfound strength within herself. Liande had breathed into her an ancient wellspring of power. She could sense the ebb and flow of magic around her, pulsating in harmony with her very being. It was as if she had become one with the mystical energies that permeated the fabric of existence itself.

Liande smirked, a hint of mischief in her eyes. "Welcome to the game, little one. Remember, nothing is as it seems. But this will give you insight and truth. You will see underneath the glamour. With just a single touch of your hand and focused intention, you'll be able to tap into anyone's hidden thoughts. I will share in your vision, and you in mine."

Babs's eyes glazed over. Her mind went dull. All her muscles relaxed. She couldn't resist the spell's effects. Her body sank deep into a submissive state.

Liande caught her in her arms. "Sleep well tonight, young Culebra. When you wake up, everything will feel right, and you will follow your fate as I intend." She traced the curve of Babs's cheek with a finger. "You are to be my most valuable asset in this war. Sister against sister. Back to your warm bed, little sleepwalker. You will need your rest, for tomorrow, all will change."

Even as her feet stumbled her toward home, Babs's mind drifted in and out of sleep, sinking into a cold darkness without any resistance.

CHAPTER 5
CRICKET

Pricilla and Audrey had sloppily thrown themselves onto the pull-out couch, not caring about their bedtime attire. Their shoes were scattered around the room, while the throw pillows and covers awkwardly wrapped partially around their snoozing bodies. Kimberly was in the bathroom raising her voice with an off-key song as she presumably ran through her nighttime routine. Cricket, meanwhile, had just tucked Caroline into her own bed, turning off the main lights before carelessly wandering to switch off the lights in Caroline's closet.

The closet was astonishingly precise, like a curator had put it together. All Caroline's clothes were represented in this precious oasis, from dress pants and skirts to her button-down shirts and cardigans that she could mix and match for work. Then there were the dresses, all solid colors that Cricket knew hit Caroline just above the knee. Soft scarves were artfully folded into a cube of vivid color. A petite jewelry box with a glass lid revealed glittering gold and pearls. Her heels, ballet flats, and loafers stood in perfect formation, their pristine condition an indication of Caroline's commitment to caring for them. Along one wall, her purses and bags were artfully displayed—from lightest to darkest. Navy was the deepest hue to be found—black would clash against her porcelain skin tone. It was rare that someone living in Florida would have skin untouched by sun, but Caroline—a rare woman indeed—showed no signs of tanning. And then there were the yoga pants and tees, along with her lonely pair of tennis shoes—the only clue to her workout routine. Every garment was hung or folded with utter meticulousness.

Cricket stepped into the living room and was greeted by the gentle breeze from the ceiling fan. She smiled as it tousled her bangs. The steady hum of the refrigerator drifted in from the kitchen. Funny how each place had such a unique feel to it. Caroline's apartment felt fresh and pristine, like she had just moved in yesterday. Cricket admired the neutral color palette, noting all of the careful planning that went into it. It almost seemed too perfect to exist outside of Pinterest boards. As she surveyed her friend's soon-to-be former home, Cricket couldn't help but wonder if Caroline would miss it when she moved in with Michael.

She wondered what Caroline's New Orleans condo would look like. What would her new life bring? The thought of moving away had never occurred to Cricket. She had never considered that kind of freedom before, and it caused a strange stirring of excitement in her belly. But no matter how much she craved it, Cricket knew that leaving her family was not an option. The possibility of creating a new life entirely of your own making was definitely an interesting idea.

"You could have that with me," Ambrosias's sensual voice beckoned in her ear.

A warm breath caressed her skin, and a thrilling tingle ran down her spine. She spun around and came face-to-face with his tall form and powerfully built frame. His gaze burned with intensity and amusement. His long white locks danced playfully along his shoulders as his lips curved into a mischievous grin.

Cricket glanced over at Caroline's cousins, lying there fast asleep. She looked deep into Ambrosias's gaze, seeing a spark of something ancient and wild.

He whispered, "Do not worry, I have woven a veil of glamour around us. No one can see or hear us now. You desire a world all our own? Then look, for this is our secret kingdom." With that, he spread his arms wide, and his fingertips glowed blue. When her eyes adjusted, they were standing in a peaceful meadow blanketed in starlit snow. A campfire blazed under the night sky, a pile of furs and blankets beckoning them forward.

Cricket stood awestruck, taking in the beauty of their surroundings. She had never seen anything like it before. The snowflakes felt like soft kisses on her face as they fell from the sky. The air was cold but crisp, and the stars above them were so bright they seemed to light the whole meadow. She turned to Ambrosias, who stood watching her with an amused expression.

"This is beautiful," she breathed as snowflakes kissed her face.

"It's our secret place," he replied.

Cricket stepped forward, mesmerized by the serene beauty of the meadow. She knelt in the snow beside the campfire and held out her hands to feel the warmth emanating from the flames. Ambrosias sat beside her upon the pile of furs, his eyes locked onto hers.

"Ambrosias—" Cricket felt the champagne swirling through her body and wished she hadn't had that last martini. "I've never seen snow."

He grazed his fingertips along her neckline, sending shivers down her spine. Her messy ponytail was pulled away from her face, revealing wild eyes that looked up into his with a hint of embarrassment. She wore just an oversized shirt, but for Ambrosias it didn't hide the curves of her body.

"My sweet one, there are so many places I wish to share with you, to see them through your eyes for the first time. I find the idea captivating."

He swept her into his arms, laying her down onto the pile of thick fur rugs. His eyes sparkled in the firelight as he slowly unraveled one to wrap around her body. He stood there and drank in the sight of her.

Cricket's body trembled with anticipation under his gaze, and she couldn't help but feel a sense of danger and excitement. She had always been drawn to the unknown, and Ambrosias was the perfect embodiment of everything she had ever craved. He leaned down, his face mere inches from hers, and his lips hovered over hers as he whispered, "Let me show you the true beauty of snow."

With a flick of his wrist, the snow around them began to glow in a soft blue light, dancing with wisps of magic. Cricket gasped, entranced by the stunning display of power.

A year ago, Ambrosias had laid his claim on her in front of the summer and winter fae courts. Aunt Habina was certain there was a sinister intent behind it. Yet Cricket couldn't deny that the alluring man she was slowly coming to know seemed so different from the cunning trickster that everyone kept warning her about. Had she been foolish to let down her guard around him? Or was she foolish for listening to others?

"Why did you bring us here?" Cricket shyly looked away, her cheeks now flushed.

Ambrosias tenderly swept a wayward strand of hair from her eye and rested his hand lightly on her shoulder. His dark eyes glinted in the flickering light.

"I could feel your melancholia; I thought I would come lift your spirits," he said in a soothing tone as he curled an arm around her shoulder. "My little enchantress, you have no idea what kind of magic we can create together."

Their connection was indeed increasing. She, too, could sense his emotions, faint though they may have been from afar. At first, she'd confused them for her own, but then clarity came, and she realized it was him that she sensed. A warmth slowly spread through her as she acclimated to his spell.

"I know you're restless, darling. That's why I'm here." Ambrosias's voice was smooth as silk, laced with a seductive power that made Cricket's skin tingle. "You deserve so much more than this mundane existence. Imagine all the wonders we can discover together. Take your place as Princess of Winter by my side—where you belong."

Cricket scoffed. "I don't want anything to do with the courts. They already have Habina, and soon they will have Babs. You were born into it, Ambrosias. I was not, and I plan on staying far away."

Ambrosias pulled her close, softly brushing his lips across her ear.

"I need to talk to you about your sister joining the summer court."

"Babs? What about her?"

"Winter court's relationship with your family might be complicated, but I need you to know that it has no effect on us, no matter what happens tomorrow."

"Our family has nothing to do with the winter court."

Confusion crossed Ambrosias's face. "Why would you think that?"

Worry gripped at Cricket's stomach. "My sister is safe, right?"

"Are you asking me to interfere with summer? Are you asking for a direct favor?" Amusement twinkled in Ambrosias eyes.

"No, I'm just asking—this whole *challenge* thing, she's going to be all right—right?"

"Verity trains your sister." His shoulders stiffened. "She will be successful. I don't speak of the challenges, I speak of after—when she is a member of the summer court. Things will come to light that will be, well, challenging," Ambrosias whispered.

"I don't understand." Cricket sighed.

"Once we're together, Cricket—nothing will be the same. We'll have power beyond your wildest dreams." He gestured grandly to the night sky, where stars twinkled like scattered diamonds.

"Can you please be less ambiguous?" Cricket pleaded with her eyes.

He chuckled softly and leaned in close, his breath hot on her skin as he whispered into her ear, "Remember this: when you're overwhelmed by everything in the mortal realm and it all feels too heavy, I'll be here waiting, ready for you."

Cricket felt an indescribable longing within her, and she forced herself away from him. He was so captivating, with that quietly looming presence that radiated strength, yet beneath it all she could sense the danger that lay hidden in its depths. That was what drew her most to him, for underneath it all, he was a mystery. She enjoyed her life as it was, running the store with Gran, and she was content with her relationship with Bash. Although she had to admit, they hadn't had much time together since he started his ghost tour business, and most of her time had been given to Caroline over the last few months. Things would slow down soon. She owed it to both of them to give their relationship a chance.

She looked up into Ambrosias's mysterious gaze, feeling as if his words were entering directly into her mind. His voice filled the intimate space with a gentle power. "We have time. Your rightful place is by my side."

Cricket tried to shake off the feeling that Ambrosias's words had left her with. She had never felt so conflicted about anything in her life. She had always been reserved and careful with her emotions, but when she was near him, he turned her thoughts upside down and inside out in a matter of minutes. She knew deep down that he was dangerous, but there was something about him that made her want to throw caution to the wind and dive headfirst into the unknown.

As they lay in the frosty winter land, Ambrosias leaned in closer to Cricket and placed a hand on her cheek. She felt the warmth of his skin seeping through her own. "We will be together soon, my chosen."

A mystic wave of energy washed over Cricket like a comforting spell. Her eyes fluttered open in amazement to find herself back in Caroline's living room, her ears met by the familiar soft snores of the cousins' slumbering. It took her a moment to adjust to her surroundings.

She was puzzled. Ambrosias had never mentioned either of her sisters before, and Cricket felt an eagerness to discover what he knew. She would have to ask her aunt Habina if she had any information the next time she saw her.

"Hey, go ahead and use the bathroom," Kimberly said as she stepped out of the steamy shower, a towel wrapped around her head. She had swapped out her sleek dress and heels for cotton pajamas. Thick black glasses graced her face, and fuzzy slippers kept her toes warm. Cricket would have barely recognized her without her makeup and clothing style.

"I'm good, thanks," Cricket replied with a smile.

"Okay." Kimberly shrugged. "I was going to make some chamomile tea. You want to join me? I need some help sleeping after the night we had. It's crazy how Audrey and Pricilla can crash so easily." She smiled as she peered at her cousins.

"Yeah, that sounds good," Cricket said with a warm smile. Sleep wasn't coming anytime soon. Her mind was racing, and her stomach was still tumbling. She followed Kimberly into the kitchen; the light was dimmed just enough for them to see their way around.

Kimberly pulled out two matching porcelain mugs with an ivy pattern swirled around them from a cabinet above the counter. *These must be Caroline's Mom's old set*, Cricket thought.

Kimberly put a tea bag in each mug, then asked, "Do you take honey? We have local stuff."

"No thanks, just the tea," Cricket responded.

"I like my honey with a bit of tea," Kimberly said as she filled the silver kettle on the range. "It won't be long now; this burner is just for boiling."

"Fancy," Cricket said. She hadn't had a chance to talk with Kimberly much this evening. She was looking forward to getting to know her.

Kimberly folded her arms across her chest. "So, weird night tonight," she began.

Cricket nodded in agreement. "It was definitely a, ah, unique ghost tour," she replied. She'd gone on so many adventures with Bash that nothing seemed to faze her anymore—until tonight, when Caroline floated off the ground.

Kimberly laughed nervously. "You can say that again." She opened the pantry and grabbed a package of cookies. "I don't spook easy," she continued, tossing a cookie into her mouth. "But when Caroline lifted off the ground . . . I'm not gonna lie, I was terrified." She offered some to Cricket, but she declined politely. Tea was all she could handle; it wasn't nearly enough to calm the nerves that had been frazzled throughout the night.

Cricket wished that she could have talked things through with Bash before they all separated for the night. She had promised to keep an eye on Caroline, and so far, that hadn't been too difficult; all she'd done was sleep since they arrived home. She had sent him a text saying as much, but he had only sent back a quick reply that he and Ryan were going to go check out the cemetery together tonight.

"I didn't get any footage of Caroline levitating. I dropped my phone on the ground in the middle of the chaos . . . along with my SpongeBob!" Kimberly mused.

"No worries." Cricket chuckled. "Bash is still near there. I can text him and see if he can grab it for you."

"You don't want to go back? Aren't you curious what happened after we left?"

"Not really." Cricket shrugged. "I'm fine not ever returning to that particular graveyard. Besides, Caroline has a very tight schedule for the wedding, and I want it to go perfectly. I think it's best we just chalk it up to a weird night and move forward."

"Really? You're not giving it a second thought? I can't wait to watch the GoPro footage. Hopefully we got some good stuff!"

"I'm sure Caroline wouldn't want anything embarrassing out on the internet."

The tea kettle's whistle filled the air, and Kimberly quickly pulled it from the burner.

"Yeah, of course. Here." She poured the water into the cups. Cricket grabbed her mug. "Let's sit at the table."

They both tugged at the invitingly comfortable cream velvet armchairs from the ornately carved French country table, which was adorned with delicate hand-painted details.

"Bringing the carriage into the cemetery. Crazy! That can't be legal." Audrey folded her legs up underneath her, settling in comfortably.

Cricket hadn't given it that much thought. "Well, it seemed the right thing to do at the time."

"I should say so. It worked. We got her out of there."

Silence settled between them as they sipped their tea.

Cricket grinned. "This is good. My stomach needed it."

Kimberly smiled, her eyes drooping in the late hour. "Chamomile tea helps every time," she said softly. She took a sip of her tea and gave Cricket a curious look. "Do you have any good ghost stories? I've been addicted to all those ghost-busting TV shows lately."

Cricket thought for a moment, trying to come up with a good story that wouldn't be too frightening or traumatic for the moment. But ghosts weren't really her thing. If she had asked about cursed objects, or fairies, well then, that she could speak to. She smiled as she thought of Bash's ghost tours, and was happy that he hadn't forced her to watch all the reality TV around it. Instead, they had watched cheesy romantic ghost films.

"As far as ghosts, I think tonight tops anything I've seen so far," Cricket replied quietly. "As for those shows, I know Bash is really into them, and his best friend Ryan can talk about them forever."

Kimberly gazed off into the distance. She spoke softly. "I've seen full-bodied ghosts in the Chicago theater. My sisters know about it too."

Cricket gave Kimberly a gentle smile. "That must have been an interesting experience. How did you feel when you saw them?"

"Stunned more than anything else," she replied, cupping her hands around her cup of tea for warmth. "It felt like there was a connection to the place. Like I was connected to it. Maybe it's just that I grew up hearing my family stories."

"Maybe," Cricket agreed.

"I love that life is so mysterious and unpredictable. To me, it's all about living with an open mind—if I'm wrong, so be it—at least I'd have lived a life full of curiosity and adventure!"

Cricket sighed, rubbing her eyes as she thought of the Drake's Diary incident. "Yeah, curiosity and adventure are wonderful, but I have learned a lesson that I wish I would have learned theoretically instead of personally."

"What's that?"

"Some things are dangerous and have consequences. Some mysteries should remain mysteries."

"I get it," her new friend replied quietly, taking a sip from her mug. "But at the same time, I think what's even scarier than keeping your curiosity open is living a life with no risk—a tiny, safe, consequence-free life. Not for me."

No wonder Caroline loved visiting her cousins. Kimberly was so interesting to talk to. Cricket didn't have any, just sisters, and they were close. She knew what was on their mind before the words came out.

"I like the way you think," Cricket said.

There was just something about Kimberly, something about the wee sacred hours of the morning at a slumber party that makes one open up in a way you otherwise never would to a person you don't really know. She radiated goodness, nearly angelic.

"I believe." Cricket looked into Kimberly's eyes. "I believe there are things out there that are stronger and smarter. Older and different. Some are a wonder to behold, others dangerous. I believe we need to be discerning in what we open ourselves up to, what we allow to touch our lives. What we invite in should be greatly weighed. And if a darkness or evil is found. I think it's our responsibility to deal with it, so that those that come after us will inherit a little bit more of a brighter world."

"Heavy." Kimberly smiled. "Do you think all darkness is evil?"

"No, darkness is a part of the cycle. The sun sets every night, giving rest. Winter, the long rest. It's not darkness itself that is evil. It's the nature of darkness to cloak. Unfortunately, evil things like to hide in the dark and prey on those that are resting." Cricket folded her legs up beneath her in the chair. Her mind wandered to Ambrosias.

"So, it's primal that we fear the dark."

"Of course. It's nature's way of keeping us safe."

"What do you think we encountered in the graveyard? Do you think it was just something in the dark, or something evil?" Kimberly tapped the side of her teacup.

"It didn't feel evil to me; but it was obviously dangerous to Caroline. Maybe chaotic or confused would be a better explanation. How did it seem to you?"

"To be honest, I really don't know. It happened so fast." She scooted her chair out.

"Do you hear something?" Cricket asked. Both women strained to hear. A gurgled mumbling was coming from Caroline's bedroom. "Let's check on her."

"Yeah, she did drink a lot." Kimberly smiled and rolled her eyes. She grabbed a big silver cooking pot that was hanging on the wall and held it up to Cricket. "Just in case. Getting puke off the carpet is a pain in the ass."

Light streamed into the bedroom from the two tall windows at the head of the bed. The smell of lavender puffed from Caroline's diffuser. Cricket had one just like it set on a timer in her own bedroom.

Caroline lay still in the middle of the bed, head resting on a plethora of pillows of all shapes and sizes. Layers of cotton blankets covered her small frame. The story of the princess and the pea floated through Cricket's mind. Caroline looked like a faerie princess, peacefully sleeping, waiting for a prince to kiss her ruby lips. Then her neck twisted violently to the left, then right. The action was so swift, Cricket wondered if she had seen it correctly. A low moan escaped Caroline's lips.

Kimberly quickly went to the side of the bed. "Hey, Caroline. You feelin' okay? I brought a puke bucket." She placed her hand on Caroline's shoulder. "Are you asleep?"

Caroline's eyes fluttered open. She pulled her hands out from under the covers and examined her engagement ring. In the low light it glimmered, sending soft blue light all around them. Beneath her nails, the skin of her fingers was a deep purple. Thin lines of dried blood lay in the grooves of her cuticles.

"I'm getting married," she said, in a soft, hoarse voice.

"T-minus four days, but who's counting?" teased Cricket.

Caroline's shoulders drooped as she went into a coughing fit. Her cheeks flushed an alarming red, and her lips were tinged with blue-black where they had been pressed too firmly together. Her fingers shook as she held a long finger up into the air, pointing at some unseen force.

Kimberly thrust a glass of water into Caroline's shaking hands, desperately hoping that it would soothe her throat and help her get back to sleep. Water spilled out onto the nightshirt, staining it with droplets that glistened in the moonlight as Caroline coughed and wheezed, struggling to find some relief.

"I wish that horrid scratching noise would stop. It's getting on my nerves," Caroline said while turning over. "Stop the scratching!"

Cricket exchanged a nervous glance with Kimberly. "Do you hear scratching?" Cricket asked.

Kimberly leaned closer to Caroline and brushed a strand of hair away from her forehead. "Yes, I do hear scratching," she whispered. There was something about the way Caroline's voice had sounded that was not quite right. "Caroline, are you feeling okay?"

Caroline's eyes flicked open again, and this time they were not her own. The pupils were dilated, and they shone with a strange, otherworldly light. "Rebecca." The voice that came out of her mouth was not Caroline's. This had to be the spirit from the graveyard.

Kimberly's heart skipped a beat as she heard the unfamiliar voice. She hesitated for a moment before placing a firm hand on Caroline's wrist. Caroline, or whoever was inhabiting Caroline's body, looked directly at Kimberly with a piercing stare. The air was starting to feel suffocating, thick with dread and tension.

"Who's Rebecca?" Cricket asked, her voice shaking slightly.

Kimberly's grip on Caroline's wrist tightened. "Caroline, is that you?" she asked.

But there was no response.

The quiet room was suddenly filled with the relentless sound of scratching, which seemed to be coming from all directions at once, growing louder and more urgent by the second. Without warning, Caroline's body began to convulse, her limbs thrashing wildly as if she were having a seizure. Her eyes rolled back into her head, and she let out a blood-curdling growl.

Kimberly looked at Cricket.

"I need out! Let me out!" Rebecca's voice boomed through Caroline's throat. "I'm not dead. Let me out!" Caroline began to flail about.

Cricket's mind raced as she tried to think of what to do. She had never dealt with spirits, let alone possession. But there was one thing she knew, they had to figure out what Rebecca wanted and why she was possessing Caroline. "Rebecca, if you can hear me, tell me what you want," Cricket said, trying to keep her voice even.

The thrashing slowed down, and Caroline's body seemed to relax slightly. But when she opened her eyes again, they were still not her own. "I want my life back," Rebecca hissed. "I want another chance. I was too young."

Cricket stepped forward, her fists clenched tightly. "We want to help you," she pleaded. "Tell us how to help you."

Caroline's head snapped back, and her eyes glowed a

bright red. Her body lifted off the bed, hovering a few inches above the mattress. Rebecca was more powerful than they could have imagined. "They buried me alive!"

Her terror-filled voice boomed throughout the room, echoing off the walls and sending chills down Cricket's spine. Kimberly stepped toward the bed, trying to soothe Caroline's thrashing body, but she was thrown back by an unseen force.

"We need to put her to rest," Kimberly said breathlessly, struggling to stand up.

Cricket nodded, her eyes transfixed on Caroline's floating form. "Okay, but how do we do that?"

"I want to live!" Rebecca's voice continued. "I desire to live!"

Cricket took a step forward, her palms held out in front of her. "Rebecca, we want to help you." Her fingers instinctively clutched the crucifix that Bash had given her for protection last year. The necklace had become a constant companion, never leaving her neck. She took it off with care and held it in her palm, feeling its weight and comfort.

Kimberly chimed in, "But you need to let Caroline go. She's not strong enough to handle this."

"I want my husband. I deserve to live my life," Rebecca sobbed.

"Hush, calm down. We will help you," Cricket soothed.

Rebecca's eyes locked onto Cricket's, and for a moment, there was a flicker of recognition. "You . . . you can help me?" she asked, her voice slightly less hostile.

Cricket nodded, keeping her voice calm and steady. "Yes, we will help you. But we need you to release Caroline."

Rebecca hesitated, her eyes darting back and forth between Cricket and Kimberly. Finally, her body began to tremble, and the red glow faded from her eyes. Caroline's body floated back down onto the bed, her breathing slow and steady.

Cricket and Kimberly exchanged a relieved glance, grateful that they had managed to calm the situation down.

Cricket's voice lilted through the air, singing a lullaby of ancient magic. Her hands glowed with a soft ethereal light as she slowly moved them over Caroline's body, and her words wove an enchantment that filled the room. The moonbeams grew brighter in response to the spell. They swirled around Caroline's body, wrapping her in serenity before finally lulling her into a deep slumber. With care, she placed the necklace around Caroline's neck, believing that it would keep her safe from any danger.

Kimberly's eyelids grew heavy as the enchantment seeped into her being. Cricket may have been at a loss on how to deal with a spectral presence, but she knew enough about alchemy to manipulate the energies surrounding them. A soothing wave of slumber washed through the house, lulling even the restless spirit into contented repose. As Cricket pondered the next move, she reveled in the tranquility that had descended upon them—suspended in a dream state. Then, startled, she realized that it felt more like Ambrosias's magic than her own, and it felt good.

CHAPTER 6

BASH

The inviting aroma of stout beer and salty crinkle fries filled the cozy pub. Bash slid onto a tall bar-stool, its metal legs screeching over the terra-cotta tiles.

His gaze was fixed on the trio of televisions hanging above the bar surrounded by cheering twenty-somethings. The atmosphere in the room was electric as they rooted for their beloved player, watching him deftly maneuver past his opponents and make a daring dash toward the goal line. A cacophony of cheers erupted when he successfully leaped over the line, igniting a frenzy of celebrations. In this pub tonight, sports reigned supreme.

"Dude, when you said level up, I didn't know you meant the game!" Ryan teased as he walked up.

"Two Guinnesses, two orders of fries, onion rings, corn nuggets, and mac and cheese balls," Bash ordered. He was feeling like devouring some junk food.

The bartender nodded and began working on their order of beers.

"The game is a plus. That we are meeting Tony is the minus. He will be here any time," Bash informed him.

"We aren't meeting up with *him*, here of all places."

The White Lion was known to have a few unruly spirits lurking about. While the food was enjoyable and the music top-notch, Bash made sure to steer clear of Tony. He wasn't necessarily a bad guy, but he had a knack for getting on Bash's nerves.

For casual drinks, he preferred Meehan's as their usual spot. Bash couldn't resist their addictively delicious chips and the relaxed camaraderie that always surrounded him when he hung out with Ryan there. Maybe it was a sense of nostalgia, as this was the bar his father had introduced him to when he was younger.

Bash adjusted his foot resting on the stool leg. "Had an issue tonight in the graveyard. It involved Caroline, and I'm afraid we need to pick Tony's brain on this one."

"Did we have to meet him on *his* turf? And are you sure he does have a brain?"

"Brain or not, he knows ghosts."

"Reluctantly, I agree." Ryan coolly leaned forward, resting his elbows on the bar, dressed in his well-pressed tee that accentuated his toned physique and held his signature aviators by the neck when not wearing them. His pristine Levis and trusty G-Shock gave him an appearance of discipline and order. Ryan had never completely dropped his military bearing. Every morning he rose before dawn, jogged five miles, and then proceeded to the daily ranch duties without skipping a beat.

Even when Cricket spent the night, Bash would rise early, meeting Ryan as the sun peeked over the horizon to go for the run and get the morning chores done. While Bash was working, Cricket would remain in bed, dreaming away. When he returned from his morning routine, the aroma of freshly brewed coffee always awaited him. Cricket would be curled up on the couch, wearing his T-shirt and peaceful-ly looking out the window while sipping her coffee.

"Buddy, where'd you go on me?" Ryan asked. "You got a goofy grin on your face."

"Ah, nowhere, sorry, a little daydreaming." He brought his mind back to the task at hand. "I've already sent all the GoPro files from the evening to our server. I don't want any of it to go on the website. Caroline is a friend, and I know she wouldn't approve of it going out. But I am hoping we can get some kind of information from the audio or video that will help us figure out what happened."

"When do you want it?" Ryan popped an onion ring in his mouth just as it was set in front of him.

"If we head right back to the ranch after this, do you think we can sift through it all by tomorrow around lunch-time? I'm meeting Cricket."

Ryan looked around the room. "We need to make this meeting with Tony fast then."

As they stared patiently, the frothy bubbles gradually settled atop the ice-cold beers. They lifted them up in sync and eagerly took the first gulp. The rich and smooth flavor of a Guinness on tap was unparalleled, and this place did not disappoint. It was like heaven in every sip.

The game went to commercial break, and the music blared Run DMC with Steven Tyler's high-pitched voice from Aerosmith wailing "Walk This Way."

Tony swaggered into the room with an air of confidence, his gait reminiscent of a duck, feet pointed outward. With-out missing a beat, he lifted his chin toward the bartender, and before he had even reached the bar, his Bud Light was already on a thin paper napkin waiting for him.

"Hey there," Tony called out while fingering his gold chains about his neck. "Doug—they have my tab tonight."

He nodded in Bash's direction, as he headed across the floor. "Excuse me," he addressed the blond sitting on the stool next to Ryan. "Can you scoot down a seat? This one is mine. My buddies here will get your next drink. Hey, Doug—get the lady a fresh drink. We can't have a beautiful dame like her staying thirsty now, am I right?" He looked her up and down, letting his gaze linger on her chest. "As long as you don't root for the Giants. You wouldn't want to be rooting for the enemy now, would ya?" He laughed at his own joke. She picked up her purse and moved down a spot, tucking her hair behind her ear. "That's a good doll."

"Highlight of the evening?" Bash casually inquired.

"Ah, the hot dame. Did you get a load of the broad in my group? No? Too dark to get a good look? Anyway, the redhead was a jumper, ya know—real skittish. And she seemed to always land right here." Tony spread his arms and legs out wide and laughed, his belly jiggling up and down. "Love me the squealers. They make this job. Am I right?"

Bash washed down his onion ring with a swig of his beer, hiding his features. "Was she jumpy in the cemetery?"

"Nah, the only ones roamin' about there were the friar and one of the cardinals. They're both harmless. The group didn't seem to pick up on them. Too subtle. Real light energy, ya know. But they didn't hide from old Tony." He raised his empty glass to the bartender. The room erupted in cheers. Tony stopped to check out the screens. "Ah man, I missed the play!"

"You didn't see a woman in white in the cemetery?" Ryan pushed.

"Nah, like I says. Just the friar and one of the cardinals."

"Have you *ever* seen a woman in white in the cemetery? Or heard of a ghost named Rebecca?" Bash questioned.

Tony took his new beer from the barman and downed half of it. "Look, the only woman in white I know of is over on the wall across from OC's, the restaurant by the water. I's never seen one in the cemetery. What gives?"

Bash looked at Ryan. Ryan rolled his eyes and nodded in the affirmative.

"Just had a run-in with a woman in white in the cemetery tonight. I'd never encountered her before. Was hoping you might know something."

Tony's jaw went slack, and a vacant look crossed his face. Several moments passed. "Well, as you know, I only sees them. I don't hears them." He pointed at his eyes and ears for clarification. "But I know our residents pretty well. If I was to guess. Either our lady in white from OC's got lost tonight, and I's don't think that's likely, she never leaves her post on the sea wall. Or the construction of the new cemetery wall woke someone up."

Tony had a good point. The spirit realm did not take kindly to changes in the physical world. A few years ago, a car crashed into the front wall of the cemetery, forcing the city to rebuild it entirely. This sudden construction could have disturbed those who were at peace before. The chaos of identifying individuals buried in each plot was compounded by the fact that multiple bodies were placed in most graves. He would have to go through the records and see if there were any clues to a grave for a woman named Rebecca.

Bash put down cash to cover the bar bill. "Thanks, Tony, that was helpful."

"Have a good one, Tony." Ryan stood up.

"You callin' it early?"

"Yeah, we need to head out. Horses need to be taken care of."

"You boys enjoy. I'm off the clock." Tony chuckled and turned his attention back to the big screens.

They drove the horses slowly to the edge of the cemetery. The night was late enough that every tourist was already settled in their hotel room. As they stopped outside the stone walls of the graveyard, every fiber of the air seemed to become still and silent. A feeling of dread and isolation descended upon them as they beheld the evening gates, now shut fast and tightly to ward off all unwanted visitors.

Bash pointed to a tombstone nestled close to the original stone barrier. They both climbed out of the carriage before making their way solemnly to the edge of the cemetery wall.

"Yeah, this is the side that the car drove right through about a year ago," Ryan said in a quiet voice. "It damaged the original stone barrier so bad the whole thing needed to be replaced." His finger brushed lightly against the surface of the fence. "But this grave is nestled closely to the remaining original stone fence. See, look."

"You know, on previous tours, tourists have felt the breath of ghosts on their necks. Or felt fingers brush at their hair. People regularly saw black shadow people or caught glimpses of full-body ghosts, usually in turn-of-the-century clothing. If any of those things occurred on the tour, we always got a perfect star rating. That was what people were looking for, proof, fun." Bash kicked at the grass.

"Right, but not too much fun, not too much proof. Just a harmless story to tell people when they get back to the office after vacation. A light touch from the beyond. Just a little giggle. A reassurance."

"Ryan, a ghost has never picked a person up and just hung out in the air with them, not on our tours. It was just me and the girls." He ran his hand across the back of his neck.

"Um—Cricket's not just any girl."

Ryan was right. Bash had watched her powers multiply over the past year. She could do things he could only dream of—manipulate time, travel between realms, wield powerful magic, fly. But this was different. This was not her area of expertise. It was his, and he was feeling like a novice. He didn't have the answers they needed. It's not that he took it lightly, he had just blocked off the parts of the supernatural that made him feel uncomfortable. Until now, he had felt safe and secure on the other side of that drawn boundary. This spirit completely ignored that boundary and did as she pleased. What if something happened to Cricket? He would never forgive himself. "Yeah, she didn't show any fear or hesitation. She never does."

"Dude, I don't know how you keep up with her," Ryan teased.

She did have a lot on her plate. She'd been making up for lost time with her aunt Habina, picking up with her magical studies where they had left off. Plus, there was Ambrosias, who was insistent that she was his chosen one. Were they meant to be together? Was her destiny determined? In the end, were he and Cricket supposed to just be friends? "There's never a dull moment, I can tell you that. She brought the carriage into the cemetery to help get Caroline out."

"Shut up—she didn't. You guys had the carriage *in* the cemetery? Are you looking to have our business license revoked? Hell, the city could sue us." Ryan pointed at the new gate and fencing.

Bash jumped the stone fence, clearing it easily. A puff of dirt erupted from the ground behind where he had stood. Ryan followed him quickly, hopping over the low wall in one leap.

Bash strode over to the tombstone and knelt, leaning forward to study it. Ryan came up behind him, holding a bright spotlight from his phone under the name Rebecca on the stone. The word had faded away by time, only parts of the word still discernible: most of the first name and some bits from the last name and an unreadable date.

"Okay, so the ghost told you her name, then took Caroline for a twirl up in the air?"

"No, she took her for a twirl while merging into Caroline, then told us her name, right here." He pointed up. "Ryan, I need a minute."

"Sure thing, we can chill in the graveyard. Y'know, get some quality spooky vibe time. Do you promise me we'll get chased by a guy with a chainsaw later? Get that full horror experience!"

"Hey, that's second-date material right there."

Ryan took a puff of his vape and held it out to Bash, who waved it away with a smile. "Gotta keep this temple of mine pure and clean, brother."

"Yeah sure, like those onion rings you gobbled down were exactly healthy . . ."

Bash felt a chill run down his spine as he opened up to the spirit realm. A gentle breeze caressed his face, brushing away any last remnants of hesitation. He reached out with reverence to the ghostly figure in white, searching for some sign of acknowledgment. The shadows seemed to move around him, dancing in synchronized patterns, beckoning him further into their domain. Soft glowing orbs of energy danced in the night like fireflies. They mingled and spun, drawing closer to Bash, feeding off his energy. The silence deepened.

"Are you picking up anything? Do you see her?"

Bash gracefully settled into the earth, Ryan slowly arranging his posture to match Bash's. This wasn't the first time they had settled in at a graveyard in the time between night and day. Bash's eyelids fluttered closed as he reached out with all his being. He could feel himself melting into the ground, merging with the living energy of the planet. The chaotic noises of his mind dulled to a whisper, like he had crossed into a different realm. The faint sounds of the night swirled around him until it all finally faded away. For a moment, Bash could feel something else, something deeper beyond this world, waiting for him.

"Rebecca, are you here?" He sent his thoughts out. *"Rebecca, are you willing to speak to me?"*

The stillness of the air filled with anticipation. Bash's call vibrated through the stars, a plea to be answered from beyond. His energy pulsed throughout the astral plane, seeking answers from the spirit world.

"Any luck?" Ryan asked. His clothes were damp, and the night air clung thick about his skin.

Bash opened his eyes slowly, the disappointment evident in his expression. "No, nothing yet. But there's something else here."

Ryan's eyebrows furrowed in confusion. "Something else? What do you mean?" he asked, shifting his weight and readjusting his crossed legs.

Bash took a deep breath and closed his eyes again. He could sense the energy—a dark, primal energy—swirling around him. It was like a wet, oozing sensation running down his spine. He tried to push it away, but it clung to him like evening dew.

"I'm not sure. It's like a thickness hovering around us. I can feel its gaze sizing me up, waiting for something."

Ryan's relaxed posture stiffened at Bash's words. His eyes darted around the cemetery, searching for anything out of the ordinary. All he saw were the gravestones surrounding them, the occasional gust of wind that sent dried palm fronds scurrying along the ground illuminated by weak beams of light from the nearby streetlamps.

"Do you think it's dangerous?" Ryan's voice was low, barely above a whisper.

Bash opened his eyes slowly, scanning their surroundings for any sign of danger. The heaviness continued to loom, like a hungry predator stalking its prey. It was an unwelcomed presence.

He looked up at the moon, its light casting an eerie glow on the gravestones.

"I'm not sure, but I don't want to invite contact. Let's get out of here," Bash said, standing up and brushing the grass off his jeans. "Rebecca isn't here. I just hope she went back to rest and isn't with Caroline."

Ryan nodded in agreement and stood up as well. As they made their way toward the cemetery's gate, the oppressive energy seemed to follow them. Bash could feel it wrapping around his body, causing his thoughts to race and his heart to pound.

His eyes were drawn to a figure that emerged from the shadows. It was tall and slender, concealed by a dark cloak with a wide hood that hid all features entirely. Bash sensed feminine energy that felt extremely familiar, as if it had always been with him in some way or another.

The figure took a step toward them, her eyes fixed on Bash.

"Destiny has declared, the time for our paths to cross

is now, Bash Wellington," she claimed, her voice low and authoritative.

Bash was startled to hear his name. He focused all of his attention on connecting to this entity. "Are you a spirit that has passed?" he asked, squinting his eyes to try to make out her features. For a moment, he thought he saw the gleam of one yellow eye.

Ryan scanned the cemetery, seeing and hearing nothing but Bash's voice. He took a few steps back and pushed Record on his phone, focusing on Bash, noticing a rigidness run through him.

"I am one who watches; you have been in my vision for some time now. I know what brings you back to this place." She walked in a slow circle around Bash.

He noticed something dragging behind her yet couldn't make out what it was. His breath became heavy and labored.

"When last you were here, you were careless, unfocused." She circled round to face him. "You cared more about impressing those around you than being respectful of where you were and who lies beneath" — she paused and looked up — "or around."

Bash opened his mouth to speak but couldn't will the words to form. It was as if his jaw was cemented shut. His hand rose to his face.

"When traversing the realms, one ought to be careful." She tsked. "Have you spent time studying them? Watching?" She raised a green-clawed hand to his face and traced the outline of his cheek. "I thought not. You clumsily walk in and out, summoning unknown beings."

Bash calmed his mind and forced his speech. "No."

"No?" She threw back her head as a manic cackle escaped her lips. Her hood slipped off, revealing a humanlike head covered in green scales. She closed the distance between them, daring him to look away.

Weak in the knees, he proclaimed, "No. I am very respectful. You may know my name, but you don't know me."

"Defiance. I see why she is drawn to you. You are both alike in that." Her laugh simmered to a chuckle. "Were you respectful when you stumbled into a war between the courts? Or are you speaking of your great respect when you awakened a sleeping bride just steps from here?" She walked in a slow sultry circle around him. "I will show you the meaning of respect, little mortal."

She pointed at his chest, and he immediately fell to his knees. All he could hear was the blood throbbing in his ears. A torrent of water surged from her cloak, soaking the grass beneath them and quickly spreading to him. He suddenly felt his knees sink into the mire of the earth until he was fully submerged in its murky depths. He sucked in a desperate breath as searing-cold brackish lake water rushed over him, filling his lungs and burning his throat. His arms thrashed violently while he fought against the unyielding current that had swallowed him up and dragged him away from the graveyard into the depths of a lake. He could hear Ryan's voice in the distance, calling out his name. Bash tried to shout back, but the water had taken hold of him, muffling his cries for help.

Bash gasped for air as he bobbed to the surface of the lake, his clothes soaked through and weighing him down. He coughed and sputtered, his lungs still burning from the brackish water. In the distance, alligators bellowed and splashed around him. Panic seized him, but he managed to keep his wits about him as he tried to swim to the shore.

It was then that he saw her. The creature from the cemetery was standing on the banks of the lake, watching him with a cold, calculating gaze. Bash felt chilled to the bone as he realized that she brought him here, to this alligator-infested pond, not to simply teach him a lesson on respect, but to terrorize him to get his full attention.

As he swam closer to the shore, Bash could hear the woman's voice in his head, hypnotic and alluring, dangerous.

Bash knew he had to make it to the shore before the alligators caught up to him. His arms and legs felt heavy, weighed down by the soaked clothes that clung to his body. He felt as if he were moving in slow motion, but he refused to allow himself to give up.

He blinked, and he was back in the graveyard, no evidence of water at all. He snapped his head around to look at Ryan, who seemed frozen with his phone pointed out in front of him.

Catching his breath, he moaned, "Who are you?" as he looked up at the cloaked figure.

She tilted her head to one side. "I am the one that holds the remedy to your predicament." The figure reached into the folds of her black cloak and produced a small vial filled with a shimmering liquid. "This is a potion that will send the spirit of the bride to the realm in which she belongs," she explained, handing it to Bash.

Bash took the vial from the creature's hand and examined it carefully. The shimmering liquid inside seemed to glow with an otherworldly energy, and he couldn't help but feel a little bit skeptical.

"What exactly is in this?" he asked, raising an eyebrow.

The creature gave him a cryptic smile. "Ingredients not found in this world," she said. "The bride has merged with the living vessel."

"Our friend, Caroline," Bash answered. "How do we free her?"

Drawing closer, the woman pointed toward a lonely corner of the cemetery. "Your friend must drink this potion at the site where the bride's body was laid to rest on the upcoming full moon," she instructed, her voice low and ominous.

A wave of remorse washed over Bash. He wished he'd been more attentive, and if he had acted earlier, Caroline would still be safe. He was determined to make things right and put an end to her suffering.

Bash panicked. The full moon was two days away, the night before the wedding. He couldn't let Caroline run around with a spirit inside her. "Do I have to wait two days to give her the potion? Can I give it to Caroline earlier?"

"The potion draws its strength from the moon. If you wish to free your friend and send the spirit on, it must be on the full moon."

Bash nodded, slipping the vial into his pocket. For a moment, he thought he saw a flash of something in her eyes. Was it amusement? Or perhaps gratification? "I will do as you say. Why have you come to me? Why help a stranger?" His intuition was piqued.

"You are no stranger to me. I see all."

"The potion, it won't harm Caroline. It's safe, right?"

The figure nodded, her features softening slightly. "Nothing is without cost or risk." Her voice dropped low. "Your friend is full of youth and has a vivacious spirit. She dreams freely. No harm will befall her from the potion."

Relief flooded over Bash. Why this supernatural creature was taking an interest in him and their situation was beyond him, but he was grateful the universe was working toward good and including him in that goodness.

"You are a small distraction I aim to put on a different path. Oh, don't look so concerned. Liande always treats her subjects fair — and you" — she leaned in close to his ear, her breath causing goosebumps to rise on his neck — "will do your job well, I foresee."

Apprehension gripped his stomach.

Liande walked away to the shadow, her voice trailing on the wind. "The potion will bring about that which you desire. Free your friend from the wayward spirit, mortal."

Bash took a deep breath and watched as Liande's cloak swished behind her, disappearing into the darkness of the cemetery. The vague sense of apprehension he had felt since entering the cemetery intensified. He wondered what kind of world he had stumbled into and what kind of powers he was dealing with. He couldn't help but replay the encounter in his head. Liande's hypnotic voice and alluring presence seemed to still linger in the air around him.

The image of Caroline's face flashed before his eyes, and he knew he would do whatever it took to save her from the clutches of the bride's spirit. But he couldn't shake off the feeling of unease that Liande's words had placed within him. A chill ran down his spine at the entity's words. He didn't know what to make of her cryptic responses, or how she knew him, but he knew that now was not the time to push for answers. He turned to look at Ryan, his eyes blinking rapidly, as if he were waking up from a dream.

"Let's get out of here, buddy," Bash said.

"What? I thought you wanted to—"

"I'll explain on the way home, as much as I can." Bash sighed. "My head is spinning. Hopefully you caught some footage that will give us some answers."

CHAPTER 7
BABS

Babs felt a sense of unease settle in her stomach as she nestled deep into her favorite wooden chair at her mom's kitchen table. As her mom busied around the stove, she tried to remember what happened the night before, but her mind was jumbled with disjointed images. She saw Liande's face, and memories slowly seemed to be coming back to her. What had she gotten herself into? Nonspecific dread sat in the pit of her stomach as she put the pieces together. She may be forced to pick a side, but she was not picking today. All she was going to think about was getting through the challenges and finding her rightful place in the summer court.

She leaned her elbows on the table and rested her chin in her hand, feeling the warmth of Gwylm's fur brush against her leg as he lounged at her feet. She absentmindedly rubbed her arm as she took a deep breath to clear her mind of any lingering troubles. She was determined to enjoy this morning. She loved being in Mama's kitchen; if a home had a heart, the heart of their family beat loudest here.

The tranquil hum of activity—Mama baking her signature cakes, the soft drip of coffee as it brewed, and a hint of cinnamon from the sweet treats she created with her own unique flair—all created an atmosphere of cozy warmth that was unmatched anywhere else.

"Are you all right, sleepy head? Mama said with a soft smile as she ladled a scoop of western scrambled eggs over a piece of cornbread on Babs's plate. "You're awfully quiet. Here, take a second helping." The gentle aroma of the homegrown peppers mixed with the buttery cornbread created a comforting invitation that Babs couldn't resist. "You're working so hard apprenticing—" Mama's quiet voice trailed off as her hand wiped away some flour from her forehead before running her hands briskly against her apron. Her wavy hair was neatly tied back at the nape of her neck, revealing her deep brown eyes weighted by a sorrow she struggled to keep to herself.

Wasting away was not an option with Mama around. Her sturdy frame and round figure were a testament to her love of cooking, and her warm embrace could melt away any worries. The aroma of blossoms from her garden traveled with her as she moved about.

"Thanks for being so understanding Mama. The training will be over soon. Things will get back to normal," Babs said.

As she spoke, her mind wondered as to the truth of her remark. There was no going back. She had chosen a life within the summer court, one bigger than the life her mother had chosen for herself.

The atmosphere between them was thick with unspoken words. As much as she wanted to bridge the gap between them, she had no idea how to communicate in a way that wouldn't shatter all the fragile polite gestures they had woven together to maintain their delicate relationship.

Mama took a seat at the table. She tucked a strand of Babs's freshly washed hair behind her ear. The dampness darkened its already dark natural brown to a near-black shade. Only a tiny bit of dark blue could be seen at the tips. It tickled Babs's shoulders, sending a cold shiver down her spine. "When the trials are over, we need to have a talk. I have some things to tell you."

A large bite of cornmeal lodged in Babs's throat. "Hmmm." She gulped her warm coffee. When she looked up, she saw her mom's knowing stare—serious and penetrating. Babs was startled, taken aback by the intense expression on her face, something she had never seen before.

Mama continued, rolling her shoulders back. "Now that you will be a part of the court, there are histories, family histories, you need to know about. Prophecies. I need to be the one to tell you." One small tear streaked down her cheek. "There were things we did, choices we made—"

"Mama." Babs moved to hold her mom's hand.

"It's not easy to talk about this, but it's important for you to know," she said solemnly.

A sense of trepidation arose in Babs's heart. She was suddenly nervous about what her mother wanted so desperately to tell her and yet was obviously afraid or maybe ashamed of telling. What could it be that would cause such an emotion?

"Family, that is the center of life. Love." Her eyes rested on her wedding ring. "It's time you knew about our past." She wiped her tears away. "I just want you girls to be happy and safe. I want your lives to be filled with love and warmth. We built that here, till your father was—" Her voice cracked.

Babs's mind drifted to Father, whom she knew only from the photos around the house. He had disappeared on the day she was born. News articles she'd found at the library said there had been a massive hunt for him, but eventually the police declared the case cold. There were no clues about what happened and nothing to suggest foul play either. The file was tucked away in an old filing cabinet at the police station where other unsolved disappearances were kept. Babs couldn't help but feel that it was strange, so many people lost without a trace—especially in this area. It seemed almost surreal.

Mama had never revealed to her and her sisters the true story. They assumed that she was a hopeless romantic, leaving candles in the windowsills each night, wishing for her husband's return. In a way, she remained frozen in time, standing there determinedly, unwilling to let go of the man she loved more than life itself. But now that Babs knew the court was right here, she wondered—

"Mama, I want to hear what you have to say, honestly, but right now I need a clear head. Can we talk after the challenges?"

"Of course, I'm sorry." Mama gave a disappointed smile. "I just wish all of you would stay in the mortal world! I know with Zadie, it can't be helped. But you and Cricket!" She wiped her hands on a dish towel and looked out the window. "With Caroline getting married, perhaps that will inspire your sister. Do you suppose? At least that way—" She grimaced and glanced at her watch. "She's running late; the eggs are probably cold now. Is she still attending the wedding with Bash?"

Mama had made so many wedding cakes over the years; her fingers were itching to make one for a Culebra wedding.

"As far as I know, they're going to the wedding together. I like him; they seem good for each other, at least for now," Babs replied honestly. She noticed that Bash was sharp enough to fit in with the family and open-minded enough for honest conversation. It would be fun having him around more often, if her sister Cricket willed it so. Plus, a seer with abilities such as his could come in handy in certain situations.

"Maybe I will talk to him at the wedding reception—"

The back door opened and in walked Cricket. Large sunglasses covered most of her face, and a ball cap graced her head. "Mama, it smells—"

"I know, divine. I'll make you a plate."

"No thanks, I'm just going to grab some coffee."

Cricket trudged toward the cabinet, and after rummaging through it, she grabbed a thick mug before carefully pouring a generous serving of coffee with vanilla creamer for herself. After she was done, she took her seat next to Babs at the table.

"You okay, sis? Late night?" murmured Babs in her ear as a big smile crossed her face.

Cricket let out a small groan and laid her head on her folded arms. Gwylm moved to lie on her feet.

Mama seemed not to notice Cricket's condition as she prepared a large plate of eggs and cornbread and sat it down before her. "Caroline's cake must be at the church before the service; Cricket, you need to help Babs. It will fit in the back of her truck. She will drive, but you need to sit in the back with the cake, yes?"

"Mmmhmm—" Cricket agreed through sipping her coffee.

"We've got it, Mama, no worries." Babs stood up and took her and her sister's dishes to the sink.

"Make sure you both eat big pieces of the cake."

Babs leveled her a glare. "Whatcha put in it?"

A grin crossed Mama's face. "Basic love potion ingredients and a dash of destiny. It won't change the person's core desires, but their ears will open to hear whispered secrets of fate on the wind that will open roads to joy and adventure."

"Is that what Caroline ordered?" Cricket mumbled.

Mama shrugged. "A good baker knows what ingredients are needed." She winked. "Caroline's a good girl. She deserves a good life."

"Well, we know better than to argue with you," said Babs, making a mental note to skip the cake. Mama moved briskly around the kitchen, wiping at invisible messes on the counters. "Girls, Zadie, isn't picking up my calls. Should I be worried?"

Cricket rested her hands on her head and lay down on the table. Babs found it amusing to watch. She could only guess what kind of shenanigans occurred during the party the night before.

Babs answered, "She's out on a dive, Mama. New shipwreck Tom found. She probably doesn't have good reception or is working to exhaustion. When she gets close to land, I bet your phone will light up with a ton of texts from her. She promised to try to be back in time for the wedding."

Cricket cut in, "She's fine, Mama, I promise."

"I'm sure you're right." Mama let out a breath. "She's my wild child. I never know—"

Babs laughed. "I'm going for a walk; I have the wiggles. I must prep for my last training day with Verity. I won't be long. Cricket, can you walk me out?"

"She just got here!" Mama protested. "We haven't had a chance to talk—"

"Mama, I have so much to do for the wedding. I'm meeting Caroline for last-minute errands this morning. When I left her apartment, she was still asleep, but I must get back to the bridal party." She walked to her mom and kissed her on the cheek. "Thanks for coffee. Sorry I can't stay. It's just a weird morning. I'll make it up to you."

"Yes, you will, by eating a big piece of the wedding cake," Mama said. The orange of the early morning sun illuminated Mama's face as she turned to stare out the window. Tiny gold lights bobbed around her head, flickering in and out of view. All the humor left her face in one moment. She looked tranced. The temperature of the room dropped.

"Mama?" Cricket asked.

Mama glanced out the window, her voice laced with dread. "The tides of destiny ebb and flow, bearing down with a relentless force. The pathways shall cross, merge, and change. Blood will be spilled, and war waged between all. Be wary of the usurper who will divide the Culebra line." She stared out at the horizon, her brow furrowed with worry.

Babs watched her mother slip deeper into the trance. There was something ominous about the way her voice changed, and the words she spoke seemed to be more than just a simple prediction. It was clear she'd tapped into something beyond the realm of their world. "Mama, who is the usurper?" Thinking back to her conversation with Liande, she stepped back away, making sure not to disturb her while she was in the trance.

"Sister will doom sister. All will end in heartbreak. The telling will be fulfilled."

Cricket closed the distance between her and her mother, shaking her arm lightly. "Mama."

Babs poured a fresh cup of coffee and set it on the table. "Bring her here," she ordered Cricket as she pulled out a chair from the table.

The girls assisted their Mom with getting comfortable.

"Take a sip, Mama. Are you feeling alright?"

She shook her head and smiled. "My mind wandered there for a minute. That was strange." She took a sip of the coffee, her hands shaking slightly.

"I'm going to walk Babs out. I'll be right back in. I can stay for a while, okay?" Cricket asked, worry tinging her words.

"That would be nice," Mama replied. "Not necessary, but nice."

Quietly, Cricket turned on her heels and followed Babs and Gwylm out the door. Once they were outside, Babs turned to her with a worried expression etched onto her face.

"Have you ever seen her do that before?" Babs asked, nodding toward the kitchen where the trancelike Mama still sat. "I've only seen Gran do that."

"Gran is terrifying when she does it. But to answer your question, no, I've never seen Mama like that." Cricket paused. "I thought she lost the seeing, you know, when she married Dad." Cricket sighed. "What do you think brought this on?"

Babs shook her head. "The ways of magic are unpredictable. Anything could have set her off. She seemed very emotional before you got here."

Cricket nodded.

Babs's mind was already racing with possibilities. Was this a warning of an upcoming war between all fae? Who was the usurper in their midst? Could it be Liande for wanting to overthrow her sister, or was Sabella the original usurper? While she had a lot of questions, one thing she was sure of, nothing would divide her family. Nothing would come between her and her sisters.

Babs and Cricket peered through the screen door, to find their mama quietly nursing her coffee at the table. Gwylm started to rise. "Gwylm, please stay here; I'll come for you before heading off to meet Verity. Help Cricket watch over Mama and let me know if anything strange occurs. I'll feel you even as I'm gone." He accepted this request with a nod. *"She's fine. I can feel her."* Babs heard Gwylm's voice in her head. He headed back into the house, retreating under the table.

The past weeks had been incredibly hectic, but Babs wanted him to have some well-deserved rest. Even more so, she felt better now knowing that he was looking after her mother.

"On a lighter note" — Babs smiled — "I grabbed these from the pantry." Babs handed a bundle to Cricket. "Ginger and honey snaps. They should settle your stomach. I made them myself."

"Thanks." Cricket popped one in her mouth. "I was so wrapped up in the wedding, I forgot your challenges were coming up."

"Well, I'm not really supposed to talk about it. It's not a total secret. They know you know about it. But I'm not supposed to put it on blast."

"Right." Cricket shifted her weight from one foot to another. "So, don't put it on my social feed?"

Babs offered up a half-hearted smile, trying to mask the sadness beneath it. This was the toughest part of growing up: separating from her sisters, who she used to do everything with. This year, though, they all had different objectives: Cricket was exploring new places with Bash, and

Zadie was traveling the Atlantic, hunting historic finds with Tom. While this separateness seemed normal for their age, Babs still felt a little sad. "It's cool they let you visit Aunt Habina to work with you on your abilities. They don't let just anyone visit the Queen's Hall."

"We mainly spend time in the healing rooms. I've learned so much! Plus, spending time amongst the ley lines has really amped me up. I lost so much time not properly training since she left, but picking up where we left off has been so wonderful."

"I'm glad you have her. I feel so grateful having Verity — not that I don't appreciate all the time I've had with Mama. It's just—"

"I know, Mama gave up the power to bond with Dad. I'm sure the training is completely different," Babs mused. "Things going smoothly with the wedding party?"

"Kind of a rough night, but hopefully things will be normal today." She pushed her palm against her head. "I'm going to get Mama squared away, then I return to maid of honor duties."

Babs's face lit up with a smile. "Send me pics."

"Absolutely. I will see you for the great cake delivery, and you can tell me how awesome you are doing with your secret challenges," Cricket teased.

"You got it." Babs watched Cricket walk back into the house till the wooden screen door slammed shut with a quick snap, closing her sister in the house with their mother. She turned her attention to the forest.

The sound of frogs flitted through the trees, trilling and hissing into the air. She stared hard into the tree line, which was thickening, obscuring the view beyond. She drank her fill of the morning, as she moved slowly through the golden haze toward the light emanating from deep in the forest. Dragonflies zoomed back and forth, their long bodies moving with precision around obstacles, their large eyes twirling independently in time to their wings. Even as she stepped over a fallen log and onto a tiny moss-covered flat rock, soil spilled out between her toes. Her neck released its tension with a few vigorous twists to loosen it and then softened to prepare for meditation. Her attention rested on knots formed along her spine like little islands rising out of the ocean — places her body had been hoarding stress. They begged for attention. She visualized each one becoming soft.

Let go, release. Let go, release.

All of the tension of the last few days flowed out of her like a melting glacier into the ground. She raised her hands above her head, stretching fully, one side, then the other, sensually moving like a soothing river warmed by the sun. She stretched her arms out to her sides and twirled slowly, like she had as a child, taking deep breaths in through her nose, feeling the energy of the forest rejuvenating her. She lay down, closing her eyes, feeling the heat from the forest floor enter her, soothing her sore muscles. Her thoughts flittered dreamlike.

In many ways, life was so much simpler a year ago. She was so sure of herself, arrogantly believing she had it all figured out. But now, she realized how wrong she'd been. She had been wrong about Nadine. Embarrassment brought a flush to her cheeks. How stupid was she to have believed that she was her sister, when everyone around her told her otherwise? At the start, life without Nadine was difficult and strange, but as she trained with Verity, her self-reliance grew, bringing forth a newfound trust in her own abilities. Joining the court was something she yearned for with all her heart. Now, her actions felt significant for the first time.

She ran the drills of the day through her mind. Envisioning Varity standing tall and serene next to her, Gwylm appeared in her mind. He leaned into her as she pressed her hands together, imagining the frequency of the chime, hearing it, feeling it carry them to the Queen's Hall.

The Queen's Hall, the Queen's Hall.

As she felt the luminescent energy swirl around her, her physical form began to meld and shape-shift, coalescing into a beam of light that twinkled like stars in the night. In an instant, she opened her eyes and found herself standing on the edge of the underground lake inside the Queen's Hall. She watched as peculiar ripples moved across its surface, creating ever-changing brilliant patterns. The lake's smooth surface shimmered with magical patterns that seemed to be alive, beckoning her to venture farther into the mysterious depths below. This vision seemed so real.

Torchlight danced on the surface of the colossal bronze statue of the queen sitting on her throne, eyes focused on the center of the lake, sword in hand at rest in front of the waterfall. Echoes of the water crashing reverberated all around the monstrous cave.

On her first visit to this space, she had run as fast as she could to get behind the waterfall to return the cursed treasure and help her sister Cricket break the pirate Drake's curse. That event, unsealing the tunnel, brought Aunt Habina back to them and changed the trajectory of Babs's life from simple farm hand to one of the summer court.

Her gaze was glued to the lake, usually so still and unfazed. The sudden movement didn't seem natural. That was when she saw what was causing it: snakes. As something grabbed her from behind, she felt herself being pulled into the lukewarm water. She kicked and thrashed, desperate for air. Little air bubbles cascaded away from her mouth as she sank deeper below the surface. All her strength gone, she let go of the fight and closed her eyes, trying to stay calm. Every inch of her skin felt the pinch of the snakes that circled her body in a tight embrace. She pictured the lake above her in the woods and imagined holding on to her gloves, feeling them on her hands, hearing the sound of birds chirping in the trees. Her last sensation was a forceful tug downward.

In the far-off distance, a loud rumble of thunder echoed. She fought to breathe, her chest and lungs aching from the lake water she had choked on moments before. A fog of confusion settled over her—she must have blacked out while meditating. With much effort, she managed to lift herself up off the ground and determinedly made her way home as peculiar thoughts swarmed her mind.

The pain in her head felt like white-hot needles piercing her brain. Her vision was diminishing, almost as if she were looking through a long tunnel that was slowly getting narrower and darker. Hissing filled her mind, interrupted by the roaring sound of fire rising from inside her. Images flitted through her mind too quickly for her to make sense of them; all she could make out were flashes of her father, the winter court, and something about Cricket.

CHAPTER 8
CRICKET

Cricket was so thankful for her moped; this morning, luck was shining down on her, as she hit every green light. When she arrived at the Blue Hen Cafe, a dozen cars were inching around the block, searching for parking spaces. She pulled to the front of the building and found Caroline and her three cousins standing together, waiting outside the entrance. Kimberly had texted her that all was well so far that morning, no encounters with Rebecca, and it seemed Caroline was unaware of anything being amiss. Cricket hurried to join the group. All four women were wearing espadrilles, short sundresses that hugged tightly at their chests, oversized sunglasses, and sun hats. From a distance, Cricket thought they might have been quadruplets or a squad of cheerleaders — yet Caroline stood out like a diamond with her snow-white complexion.

Cricket felt slightly underdressed. She'd tied her hair up in a high ponytail, pulled on a ballcap, aviator shades, and a comfortable dusty-rose-colored V-neck T-shirt. Her khaki miniskirt hit right above her knees, while scuffed white tennis shoes gave her silent movement as she walked. She had added a swipe of lip gloss and some eyeliner to hide the effects of her late night—the only cosmetics she needed. With no time to shower and change before meeting them, she hoped she could squeeze that in sometime today.

"You wait in a line for eggs?" Kimberly asked, clearly baffled that someone would wait for something that wasn't a posh club with table service.

"No, not the eggs, it's the chicken, biscuits, and gravy. I promise you won't regret it! Right, Cricket?" Caroline asked for confirmation.

"Agreed," Cricket said with a smile. "But I think I'm just going with coffee today." It was still way too early for her to consider putting food in her stomach. Last night's vigil by Caroline's side was making it hard for her to stay awake. At least the ginger candy from Babs had calmed her stomach somewhat.

"I'm having a mimosa," Pricilla said, gesturing toward one of the tables in view.

"Caroline, party of five," the small girl behind the podium called out above the crowd.

The group of women followed the waitress to their table. Wooden chairs slid smoothly against the linoleum floor. The cream-colored walls were adorned with art of countryside life—chickens, roosters, and the like. You couldn't look anywhere without seeing a painting of some type of wildlife. The low roar of morning chatter filled the atmosphere, while the smell of coffee was almost overpowering. The perky brunette server handed out menus to each person and said, "I'll grab some water for you all while you check out the menu."

"Mimosas for everyone!" Caroline exclaimed, her finger rotating in a circle.

Cricket shook her head no and silently mouthed "coffee" to the woman. She was relieved to see Caroline acting so normal this morning. Her phone buzzed.

> Bash: Can you meet for lunch?

Could something today not be about food?

> Cricket: Quick lunch, crazy day.
> There's so much I want to discuss with
> you in person. It's too much to try and
> explain through text messages.

> Bash: Our sushi place—we do really
> need to talk

That they did. She needed to fill him in on more details about the frightening encounter last night. Sushi would work; she could get udon. Carbs, she wanted carbs. But later, much later. Just caffeine for now.

> Cricket: *Can't wait to see you*

> Bash: 🤍

"If someone would pay attention," Caroline said with a slight emphasis on the "someone."

"Sorry. Bash." Cricket apologized while putting her phone away. The waitress returned to the table and handed out all the water glasses.

"Your drinks will be ready shortly. I'll be right back." The waitress rushed away again.

"As I was saying," Caroline continued. "We go from here to the nail salon for mani-pedis. Next is lunch and relaxation in the salt cave, followed by ice cream and then massages. A quick wardrobe change for the evening, then we have plans to visit a winery for drinks and dinner. Any objections?"

"No way, that sounds like a great day!" replied Audrey without looking up from her menu.

"I'm having lunch with Bash and helping out at the store this afternoon, but I can make it back for dinner."

Caroline's forehead was drenched in sweat. Her eyes quickly bounced around the room as she folded the menu and started fanning herself. "It's so hot in here. They need to turn up the air conditioning or something!"

The server arrived swiftly with four mimosas and a coffee balanced on a tray delicately handled with her practiced hand. "Cream and sugar on the table. Ready to order?"

The members of the group leisurely placed their breakfast orders, one following another. Cricket couldn't help but marvel at the server's impressive memory and ability to handle all of their requests. She knew she would not do well as a waitress; keeping track of multiple things at once was not her strong suit.

"Can you hear that scratching sound?" Caroline questioned with a look of horror.

Cricket and Kimberly exchanged worried glances. The atmosphere was filled with the clattering of kitchen appliances, chairs being pushed in and out of tables, and the ringing of bells as people walked in and out of the restaurant.

"Maybe it's coming from the chairs—they do make a weird noise when they move," Pricilla suggested, adjusting her seat.

Caroline stayed still, fixated on nothing that anyone could perceive. Cricket put her hand on top of Caroline's, and noticed it was clammy to the touch.

"It's so stuffy here. It feels like the walls are closing in," Caroline said shakily, her pupils enlarged with fright.

"Have some ice water," Pricilla recommended.

Caroline delicately held a glass with both hands and sipped slowly.

"You've been biting your nails?" Audrey exclaimed, her voice rising as she peered at Caroline's fingers. Underneath her nails were swollen, red, and bleeding. "It'll take some serious work to cover up that damage."

Caroline's bottom lip started to tremble in response.

"Everything's going to be okay," Kimberly comforted, extending her arm over the table to pat Caroline's hand. "It's just pre-wedding jitters."

The waitress returned with a spread of chicken, biscuits and gravy, pancakes, French toast, oatmeal, toast, and a bowl of fruit and yogurt. Everyone grabbed their own small plate to sample the variety of breakfast goodness before them.

"Not going to eat, Cricket?" Kimberly asked.

Cricket glanced at the table. "Could you pass me the toast?"

Kimberly handed her the toast and butter.

"This spread looks amazing," Audrey remarked. "It's just what we needed to start off the day."

"Oh, dear Lord," Pricilla crooned. "These biscuits and gravy are out of this world!"

Caroline gulped her mimosa, and drops of sweat formed on her brow. Cricket had a feeling of unease in the pit of her stomach. Was Rebecca going to make an appearance again?

Cricket's eyes met Kimberly's. She could tell she was thinking the same thing.

The rest of the girls at the table were consumed by their breakfast, while the families and couples surrounding them talked amongst themselves.

"Caroline, may I have some of your fruit?" requested Cricket.

"Sure," Caroline said, handing her the bowl with her left hand. Cricket noticed her wedding ring glimmer in the light as she took it from her.

Cricket's mind raced as she looked at Caroline's ring, wondering if it had any connection to the spirit in the graveyard. She usually avoided using her ability in public, but Caroline seemed distressed, and the incident the previous evening was terrifying. "Can I . . . look at it? Your ring."

Caroline extended her hand, presenting the diamond for inspection. She touched it gently and mentally commanded it to reveal its secrets.

Dizziness engulfed Cricket as the ring transported her to the past.

Cricket's eyes widened at the overwhelming sight – the hospital was a somber and desolate place; its walls seemed to be closing in on her. Long rows of beds cradled the sick, their white sheets resembling shrouds. Silver trays held countless medical instruments, stained with dried blood that emitted a thick scent, lingering in the air like a fog that filled her lungs. The stench of death hung heavy in every corner, almost causing her to lose consciousness. All she could see was hopelessness extending as far as her gaze could reach.

"Rebecca, this patient requires assistance," said the distressed voice of a man wearing an apron streaked with red above the moans and hacking coughs.

"Yes, certainly, Doctor," came the soothing response from the far side of the room. Cricket watched the brave woman before her in awe. A brunette with her hair twisted neatly into a bun busied herself with tending the ill. Her small hands were both gentle and quick as she worked to ease their suffering.

Cricket felt a wave of dizziness, and suddenly everything was dark. The ring had more to show her. When she regained her senses, she realized she was standing in the shadows behind one of the columns at the Cathedral Basilica.

"Dearly beloved," the priest declared solemnly. His quiet melodic voice echoed through the grand cathedral. Its vastness seemed to swallow the meager gathering of friends and family present for the wedding of the nurse. The smell of incense wafted in the air as the priest began his sermon. Cricket glanced over to the groom, who stood with a strong sense of purpose, though his anxiety was palpable. He carefully placed a ring on the bride's finger, Caroline's ring, only for the bride to swoon to the floor moments later. An eerie silence fell upon the congregation, unable to mask their despair in this solemn moment.

Cricket was overwhelmed by a wave of confusion, and everything went dark again. Then she realized the ring had even more to show her. When she regained her bearings, Cricket found herself back in the sterile white room. The bride was lying in one of the hospital beds, her lips stained by crimson liquid and her skin having taken on an ashy grey hue.

"No, Rebecca, no," the groom wept.

"She was of pure heart," the priest said softly as he pulled the white sheet up to cover Rebecca's face.

The young man shook with uncontrollable sorrow, tears streaming down his face. "I don't have any money for a proper burial," he murmured shakily between sobs.

The priest gave him an understanding look and put a comforting hand on his shoulder. "Don't worry yourself, my son. I will perform the service. As for the plot, she can go in the paupers — "

"No! She deserves better than that," the mournful husband replied with a broken heart. He tenderly shifted the fabric of the sheet to expose Rebecca's still hand. He slowly took off her wedding ring, kissed it, and extended it toward the priest without lifting his gaze. "Find her a proper burial spot."

"Leave your worries to me. Let me take care of everything else while you grieve. I believe we can fit another grave in the corner of the cemetery."

Cricket felt a chill as the ring transported her to a world of pure, abject horror. The darkness was absolute and oppressive, the air thick and heavy like an all-encompassing fog that choked her lungs and pounded on her chest. She could barely make out Rebecca's desperate cries for help as fists pounded against wood — muffled by the coffin trapping her inside. Cricket heard fingernails scratching desperately at the wooden planks, until understanding dawned in a wave of horror; Rebecca was buried alive beneath the earth — and she had no chance of escape. Terror flooded through Cricket's veins, a palpable, hopeless feeling that made her heart race faster than it ever had.

Her breath hitched as she gathered her senses, the past fading back into the walls of the Blue Hen Cafe. The sounds of people murmuring and plates clanking came flooding in, grounding her to the present. She never could have imagined that the first bride to wear Caroline's ring had been buried alive. She had heard such stories before, but not one so close to home.

"Are you okay, Cricket?" Audrey inquired, her face full of worry.

Cricket took a swig of her coffee in response. "Yeah, it's just kinda loud in here. I feel a bit overwhelmed."

Kimberly chuckled. "So graveyards don't bother you much, but diners do?"

Caroline stared at Cricket intensely with eyes that reminded her of Rebecca's. Her voice was low and gentle when she spoke. "Can you even fathom it?"

CHAPTER 9
BABS

I'm telling you, I phased into the Queen's Hall, and something tried to drown me," Babs said, throwing her hands up in frustration. Gwylm gave up pacing alongside her and stretched out alongside the large tree.

Verity regarded Babs compassionately. "Explain it again, please."

"I was practicing my visualization, became very relaxed, and actually phased into the Hall."

"Was there anyone around?" Verity prompted in a soothing tone.

"No, I don't remember seeing anyone."

"Did that strike you as odd?"

Babs began to tap at her temple in an agitated manner, attempting to calm her nerves. "No, before I knew what was happening to me, I was in the lake. Snakes surrounded me and nearly drowned me, but I was able to phase back to the woods above."

"What kind of snakes?"

"I don't know—lots of big swimming slithering snakes." Babs tried to contain her rising panic. "And then in the forest,

I had all these flashes, pictures entering my mind—but it was so fast I couldn't . . ." Babs broke off, overwhelmed by emotion.

"Might it have all been a dream?" Verity murmured soothingly.

Babs felt her body shaking with rage. She raised her shirt expecting to find dark bruises on her sides instead of the flawless skin that she saw. "I don't get this!" She looked into Verity's eyes in desperation, searching for an explanation.

"Where did you phase from before coming to the Queen's Hall?"

Babs's body stiffened. Strange visions invaded her mind. Had she been to the pond where Liande dwells? Or had she been at home? Why were her memories muddled? She rubbed her arm absentmindedly. She had been at Liande's. They had talked. Why was she having a hard time remembering?

"Do you have a sister?" Babs asked.

Verity paused. "You know I do. We spoke of it before. What's going on?"

Babs struggled not to let her emotions show. She tried to keep her confusion hidden. Babs rubbed at her arm, feeling a stirring of magic, primal. She felt a wave of protection glide upon her skin. A renewed confidence seeped into her pores. She felt the eyes of Liande upon her.

She shook her head. She was just lacking sleep, she supposed. "Just in the woods, near my farm. Things didn't get weird until I was in the Hall."

"I see." Verity squinted her eyes. "Was there anything else?"

Babs thought back, sorting through her fuzzy memory. "I felt like I was on fire inside."

"Ah, that's a good hint as to what happened to you."

"What do you mean?" Her head throbbed with pain. She rubbed at her forehead.

"It sounds like you have been touched by the ancient source of life-energy. If so, your latent powers have been kindled by the serpents of old. Now that your true powers are waking up from their dormant state, your individual capabilities will amplify as you cast away your old self and evolve into this new version. How interesting that it coincides with the coming of the full moon."

"I don't understand."

Verity glanced at Gwylm. "Phase the three of us to Queen's Hall. I want to take you to the healers and have you checked out."

"Can I touch your arm? I think it'll make it easier for me to take all three of us."

Verity wrapped her arm all the way around her.

Babs closed her eyes and delved into the magic that lay within. Gwylm leaned against her leg, his warmth radiating through to her soul. Verity's arm was a welcome, soft embrace, coaxing Babs to relax into a calmer state. She summoned forth a bright pearl of light from her core, imagining it unfurling outward until it engulfed them all in its warmth. Feeling the power surge within her veins, Babs raised her gloved hands toward the sky and released a shimmering incandescence from her fingertips, weaving an invisible lattice with its unearthly glow. With one more exhale, she opened her eyes — only to find they were successfully transported to the Queen's Hall, just as she had been the night prior.

She spun around swiftly, expecting to find someone or something lurking in the shadows. But there was nobody — no snakes, nor any other signs of life. Her abdomen felt hot and comforting as if she had just ingested a cup of warm milk before going to bed. No nausea for the first time after phasing. "Verity?" she called out, her voice echoing off the cavern walls. Gwylm raced away to a group of women and leapt onto one of them, causing laughter to burst from the entire crowd. The other wolves circled him and pranced in a friendly greeting.

"No need to worry," Verity said in a comforting tone. "Gwylm has the right idea — let's go meet them."

Babs trailed behind her, and she found that the light was playing tricks on her eyes: everything had fuzzy edges and was bathed in soft hues.

"Is it just me or does the lighting look different?"

Verity glanced at her and asked, "What color do you see around me?"

Babs thought for a moment before replying, "Gold."

Her mentor just gave her an intrigued look and said, "Hmmm."

"So, Verity. Your protégé is to undertake the challenges tomorrow," the queen's voice pronounced regally.

"Yes, Your Highness." Verity bowed with confidence.

Babs watched closely as the two sisters interacted. Verity had mentioned that they were related, but Babs found it hard to believe. There was no outward display of warmth between them. The queen was bathed in a powerful amethyst aura that reached out and consumed all those around her. She watched as every color was drained away by the queen's commanding presence until only its own mystic magenta light remained. Even Varity's radiant glow could not stand against this power.

"Do you think she is prepared?"

"As prepared as any of us ever were. She will do well. I am certain of it," Verity replied confidently.

"I see." The queen stalked around Babs, her eyes a piercing green that demanded attention. The woman's fingers dug hard into Babs's chin and forced her to look up. Babs cringed and felt herself pull back, but the queen held her grip steadfast. She felt as though she were being compelled by the queen's hypnotic aura. Reality faded out of existence as heaviness took over.

A brilliant pink cherry tree shimmered in the golden sun. Opposite it was a pond, lily pads floating on its still, clear water. As she stared across the bridge, which swayed slowly above the pond, a chorus of songbirds trilled from within the trees.

Babs basked in the cherry tree's aura. She felt as if all her worries and fears were being washed away. The tree's petals swirled around her, slowly forming the shape of a woman made entirely of cherry blossoms. The figure danced and twirled in the air, her movements so fluid that it was as if she was one with the wind.

"Babs." The cherry blossom spirit spoke in a gentle voice. "You are run down. Come rest below my blossoming limbs. Bathe amongst the lily pads."

With a gentle laugh, the tree spirit dissolved into a whirlwind of petals that softly showered down on Babs.

She put her hands on the trunk of the tree and felt a warm energy run through her. A storm of emotions erupted from within, greater than anything she had ever experienced before. A connection settled deep within her spirit.

"*Gwylm!*" she called out with her mind. In a heartbeat, Gwylm appeared at her side, watching vigilantly over her in this strange realm.

The queen's voice swirled around her. "I sense something familiar about you," she murmured mysteriously. "Here is a space between spaces. Here I seek to see you clearly."

Babs felt a wave of confusion and wariness wash through her. She pushed the emotions away, then she thought she sensed Liande peering through her own eyes, looking onto the scene. Babs was here, in the cherry blossom realm, standing by the queen, and there, standing in the alligator-infested pond, looking upon the reflections on the surface of the water, seeing her own image. Her skin began to tingle. Her breath filled with the taste of brackish water. She clearly was losing her mind. As soon as the sensation appeared, it flitted away.

"Reveal your secrets," the queen demanded.

"I . . . don't have any secrets," Babs muttered, struggling to hold her composure. A low pulsing thrum beat within her mind.

The queen's eyes narrowed as she peered into the depths of Babs's eyes. She stepped away from Babs quickly with an expression of shock upon her face.

"There is something dangerous about you, girl, something truly sinister — but what?"

The queen began to weave her hands and call on the power of something ancient and dark. The air around them filled with a crimson haze that seemed to be sentient, shifting constantly between shapes and energies as if it were seeking its prey.

Suddenly, the sky above turned a dark purple, as thunder echoed through the land. A chill raced across Babs's skin, and lights flashed from within the clouds like blue lightning strikes. The lily pads floated up off of the pond's surface, slowly turning into balls of dark red fire sizzling in the rain.

Babs's heart raced against her chest until it seemed it would burst right through if she didn't find safety soon enough. Gwylm stepped protectively between Babs and the queen as they both surveyed their surroundings carefully for any way of escape. She felt a sickly chill run through her core as the queen's magical powers wrapped around her in a stifling embrace, attempting to pry all secrets from Babs's very soul—yet nothing came forth. Despite the intense magical display, she was unable to break Babs or figure out what supposed danger lurked inside her—whatever it was that the queen sought remained shrouded in darkness beneath the surface . . .

"Your Highness," Babs whimpered.

As quick as the nightmare began, the sky suddenly went clear, the wind grew calm, and the cherry blossom trees lit up with a soft pink hue. It was as if the realm mirrored the queen's mood. The lily pads floated down to their original positions skimming the surface of the pond.

The queen's eyes roamed. "You may yet earn your place among us."

Babs was still on guard. She couldn't allow herself to fully relax—realizing that she was still alone and vulnerable to the queen.

"The waters have shown me many possible timelines. They vein out deep and wide like the roots of a tree." The queen's gaze climbed up the blooming branches of the tree. "Beautiful possibilities like the petals above. And yet I feel a blind spot. Something moves against me, but I cannot see. You are somehow a part of this. Yet it is veiled to me the part you will play. Vexing!" The queen waved her arm, and the peaceful realm dissolved.

Babs shook off her trancelike state and glanced around the grand hall. All the women had their gazes fixed on the monarch. "A moment of encouragement has been bestowed upon the apprentice," the queen declared. "This is all that will be said on the matter."

Verity stiffly expressed her appreciation for the honor, though her peers exuded hints of apprehension. "We are most thankful for your kind gesture. It will be greatly treasured. Now, if we may be excused. We need to make our way to the healing rooms." She lifted her hands to her forehead in honor, and those around followed suit.

"Go forth with my blessing," the queen voiced.

The sound of Gwylm's, Babs's, and Verity's feet striking the ground reverberated through the tunnel-like passageway as they pushed farther into the Under. A year ago, this path was unfamiliar to Babs; it was only with her fae-given sight that she could find her way. Now, her steps became effortless as if the landscape itself changed to where she wanted to be. Thinking of her destination was enough for a new route to appear.

"Is the queen always so...?" Babs stammered, her voice shaking with uncertainty.

Verity's frown deepened. "Where did she take you?" She barely met Babs's gaze. "Are you all right?"

"It was a meadow with a lily pond and a cherry blossom dryad, I believe." She kept her tone even. "Then it turned —" She attempted to catch Verity's eye, but she kept looking straight ahead, seemingly weighing her words.

"I know how it turned," Verity whispered. "We need not speak of it."

They hastened around the bend and stumbled upon the door to the main healing chamber. Verity pressed her hand against the ancient stone, and the entrance opened with a soft rumble. An enchanting melody of crystal singing bowls drifted out and settled in their ears like a blissful lullaby. As

Babs stepped inside, she was swallowed up in a blue aura of serenity. The walls were adorned with pink salt that gave off an energizing scent, like a breath of cleanliness. Vials of tinctures and potions in differing shades glowed like fireflies on vastly tall shelving. She'd come here many times before in order to bolster her strength and recalibrate her energy. Each time was like a healing journey, and it left her feeling something akin to euphoria.

"Gwylm, head back to the Queen's Hall and wait for us there," Verity said.

Gwylm gave her a hard look before turning around and shuffling toward Babs.

"He can stay," Habina stated, her voice echoing in the chamber. "Niece! What brings you to the healing rooms?"

Babs lit up at the sound of her aunt's voice.

Verity stepped forward, her expression filled with apprehension. "There might be cause for concern—last night she had a vision of snakes taking her into the portal, yet she effortlessly phased today. I'd like to have a seer look over her and make sure her magic is stable as we move toward tomorrow's challenge."

As she watched Verity fret, Habina's lips curled into a slow smile. "You seem anxious," she mused, her eyes taking in Babs from head to toe. "And I understand why; this could be a tricky situation." Her forehead creased. "No wonder Gwylm is being so protective; it's essential to keep one's balance."

"Also, on our way here, the queen took Babs to a place of in-between," Verity mentioned.

Habina cast a quizzical look her way. "Why would the queen think she required a place of in-between to interact with Babs?"

"Your aura is radiating turquoise," Babs interrupted.

"You can see auras? Since when?" Habina touched Babs's wrist lightly, taking her pulse.

"It's new, just started recently," Babs answered.

"Before you ran into the queen?" She moved her fingers lightly over Babs's temples.

Babs considered that for a moment before replying, "Yeah, it was right before then."

Habina turned back to Verity. "This could take a while — should I call you when we're done?"

"That would be great." Verity smiled at Babs before taking her leave.

"Should we start with the snakes or the queen? Or skip all of that and you can fill me in on what your sisters are up to?" Habina prodded, her tone filled with excited amusement. "It's so good to have you here, kiddo. I'm glad we have time together before tomorrow. It's a big day for you!" She pulled back the sheets on the bed in the center of the room and waved her hands, dimming the lights. "Go ahead and slip under the covers." Gwylm released a deep sigh and curled up into a ball, quickly letting out soft snores. Babs undressed as her aunt busied with linens. She crawled under the warm covers of the bed, wrapping her arms around them comfortably.

The room filled with peace, as Habina hummed a soft melody. Babs had been longing to talk openly about the things she'd seen, but wasn't sure if she should burden her aunt. Could Habina really help? Would she be honest with her?

Babs watched silently from beneath the covers as Habina sat in a chair across from her bedside, slowly sifting through wildflower petals scattered gently on top of a small table between them. She spoke softly at last: "Babs—I know you're worried about the challenges, but you have got this . . . you have nothing to be worried about—I absolutely believe in you. Here's a pillow for your neck and one for your knees. Now put one hand on your heart and the other on your belly. How does that feel?"

She let out a contented sigh, and her eyes drooped with drowsiness. It felt like she was a child once again, being tucked in by her aunt. Memories of her upbringing came rushing back: holding hands with Cricket, the sweet aroma of crayons, and the sound of Zadie's voice singing throughout the house.

"Do you want to tell me about the encounter that has Verity worried?"

Babs explained the ordeal as her aunt listened carefully.

"Do you have any physical discomforts?" Habina spoke from above.

Babs felt as if she had left her body, drifting through her memories. She mumbled incoherently.

"Excellent, you seem to be completely relaxed. I'm going to start at the bottom of your body and work my way up. I will make sure that your energy is unblocked and flowing freely. Focus on your inhalations. Inhale slowly and deeply; hold at the top. Exhale slowly, maintaining the breath before exhaling again; hold at the bottom. I'll breathe alongside you. The ley line is amping up your new power. Now we need to keep you balanced. Like riding a bike."

Babs closed her eyes and allowed herself to appreciate the sound of her aunt's breath. An inner harmony was stirred up inside of her, as if the two of them were breathing in perfect unison. Gradually, she felt a sense of peace overtake her. She could see flashes of pictures too quickly for her to process, but they unblocked as soon as they entered her consciousness. She chose not to try to make sense of what she was seeing, trusting that the insights would come when she needed them most. Stars and shadows, flames and oceans — all these images filled her mind until she felt like a conduit. She didn't need to understand what it all meant; all she had to do was allow it.

"Yes, I'm ready," she said softly.

Habina laid her hands on Babs's head with a gentle touch. All of the tension seemed to rush out as the pressure dissipated down through the bottoms of her feet. The energetic cleansing was complete.

"Babs, you with me?" Habina whispered. "Can you wiggle your toes? Open your eyes?"

Babs's eyes fluttered open. She felt lighter.

"Take a minute, there's no rush," Habina said. "You are physically and energetically ready for what will come tomorrow."

From the corner of her eye, she watched as Habina reached for a glass of water. "Do you have any advice for me on how to handle the big day?"

Habina walked to the bed, sat on the edge, and leaned in closely. It was a gesture so familiar and longed for, a tear formed in the corner of Babs's eye. "All you have to do is follow your intuition. Meditation is you speaking to the universe. Your intuition is the universe speaking back. moment by moment, follow your intuition. Don't rush."

"That makes sense." Babs shifted uncomfortably. "Can I ask you something?"

"Sure."

"Your coming here was different than me. I mean, you almost died. Had one of the fae not given you their life force, you would've perished. Do you regret that the decision was forced on you? Do you regret that your only option was to become a healer?"

Habina's fingers grazed the bottom of her lips.

"I had a choice between life and death. I chose to live. Sabella, the queen herself, was the one that saved me. That gift has granted me the ability to heal and save many since that decision, including you and your friend Bash. The calling to heal others by my skills or to share my blood — I cherish and will forever be grateful for. Being tied to the ley lines as my main source of energy, well — it feels a bit like house arrest. But the ley lines web their way around the earth. There are few places that I truly cannot venture."

"I'm glad the court brought you fulfillment and a sense of purpose, but you weren't given the choice to join or not. You were forced into it."

Habina smiled wistfully. "I grew up in the court, Babs. I had my place in it, obviously not as a healer. I guarded the portal so that the seer could prophesy without threat of intrusion. I didn't want to leave this realm. Humans have never interested me. Had things been different — "

Babs sat up, trying to comprehend Habina's world-shattering words. *She grew up in the court.* It felt like she was tumbling down a steep hill, her thoughts racing back in time.

The shop run by Cricket and Gran had been there ever since the town was founded. But Gran was now aging, since joining the human realm. Her father disappeared on the day Babs was born. Her mother lost her powers when she married and bound herself to her father. The tunnel was sealed, and Maj and Habina left their lives when Babs was a young teenager. She had defeated Nadine almost a year ago. A question she had never considered before formed in her mind: When and why did our family leave the summer court?

Habina's expression softened as she responded, "My dear, you were born into an already unfolding story. Only your mother can answer that question for you."

CHAPTER 10
BASH

I hope this brew is strong enough to keep me awake," Ryan said as he leaned on the table and sipped from his small teacup.

Bash responded, "It's been a long time since we've pulled an all-nighter." He quickly recoiled from the smell of his armpit, regretting not having enough time for a shower. Maybe he should avoid leaning toward Cricket during lunch, considering his lack of personal hygiene.

"Those appetizers were worth ordering. I'm starving!" Ryan said between bites. "The footage we got from the graveyard was impressive. It could compete with anything on the internet or TV. I can't wait to see Cricket's reaction!"

Bash shook his head. "People will never believe it. They'll say that Caroline was hooked up to wires or something. And the footage showed fog hovering around her, not the spirit that we all saw. It looks like it's just an atmospheric occurrence."

"Right," Ryan said with a smirk. "Fog picks people up all the time. It's a normal *atmospheric occurrence*."

Bash glanced up toward the door as he saw Cricket make her way through the restaurant, her ruby-red lips accentuated with lipstick. She had pulled her curls back into a bun at the nape of her neck, showing off her pearl earrings. A pair of aviator sunglasses covered her eyes, and the loose ringlets framed them beautifully. Her short skirt revealed her bronzed, kissable legs. A solitary pearl adorned the chain of a dainty rose-gold necklace around her neck. Bash couldn't help but notice that she wasn't wearing the crucifix he had given her, the one she always wore without fail.

His palms grew sweaty, and his body tensed with the anticipation of seeing her — until Rebecca floating in midair with Caroline, flashed across his mind like a bucket of cold water. The image left him feeling sick to his stomach.

He was aware that Cricket had some powerful abilities, being half fae. But those gifts were no help when it came to the danger of the departed. It was his duty to protect her. He knew there was a risk in having one foot in both the realms of the living and the dead. If she — or anyone else — got hurt because of him, he didn't think he'd ever be able to forgive himself.

Bash rose from his seat and offered Cricket a spot at the table. He carefully poured her a cup of tea and waited until she was settled before he leaned forward to kiss her lightly on the lips. She lingered for a moment, and he relished the experience. "Missed you," she finally said with a shy smile, enjoying their brief moment.

Ryan whipped out his iPad. "You won't believe the footage, seriously," Ryan proclaimed. "We skimmed through it last night, but we'll have to take another look to see if anything was missed. You'll never believe what happened the second time we went to the gravesite! I can't wait to put it on the website! I downloaded some of the files. Take a look," he said. He tapped Play, and an image from the night before filled the screen: Caroline was hovering in the air, with another woman in a long white dress who held tightly onto her hands. Their eyes met and remained locked as if transfixed. There was no sound accompanying the strange scene. "I was able to zoom in and get a close-up on the fog, but it's quite grainy," Ryan said, showing off a picture file.

Bash squinted at Ryan's little display. "What do you make of this, Cricket?"

"I can make out the figure of a female in the mist, right?" Cricket squinted at the screen.

"Man, I don't think we're looking at the same thing; all I see is Caroline in a fog," Ryan replied.

"You don't spot the female form?" Cricket was clearly puzzled.

Both men shook their heads. "Just fog," said Bash. "It's curious that you perceive what we actually saw last night, and Ryan and I can't see the form."

Cricket rummaged in her bag for some lipstick and then began to apply the gloss. "Let's hold off on posting anything online till we get the situation resolved," Cricket suggested.

"Oh, privacy, right. What if we put the videos online with everyone's faces blurred out, no names mentioned?" Ryan suggested. He was clearly focused on the business side of things.

"Maybe you could speak to Caroline after the wedding," Cricket said, glancing around the room.

Ryan agreed with a nod but clearly was excited about getting his footage out there.

"So, how has she been? Anything out of character?" Bash asked.

"Yeah, how's Caroline been?" echoed Ryan, a blush of embarrassment crossing his face as if he realized he was being insensitive.

"Cricket, you were cryptic with your text. What had to wait to talk in person?" Bash asked.

Cricket took a sip of tea and wiped at the corners of her mouth. "The best way I can describe it is that we had a rather violent possession episode last night." Cricket paused. "Then at brunch, I had a breakthrough moment of clarity when I touched Caroline's ring. It's a rather gruesome story."

"Oh yeah? What was that?" asked Ryan.

"Caroline's ring—it's an antique. It belonged to the woman buried in the graveyard—Rebecca," said Cricket.

The table went silent while everyone processed this new information.

"So, you think Caroline entering the graveyard while wearing the ring woke up the previous bride—Rebecca?" Bash leaned forward.

"Yes, I do. When I touched the ring this morning, I saw the former bride donning Caroline's ring as she wed in the same cathedral Caroline is planning to get married in."

Ryan vibrated in his chair with excitement. "Wait! The same church Caroline is getting married in?"

"Yes, I suppose it's not that odd; it is a beautiful church. If I was getting married and was Catholic, I would want to get married there." Cricket looked down at her lap and back up at Bash shyly.

The waiter set down a large plate of egg rolls, chicken wings, skewered beef, fried wontons, and crab rangoons. Ryan greedily licked the yum-yum sauce off his hands while reaching for one of the wontons.

"Would you like anything else, ma'am?" the waiter asked politely.

"A small bowl of chicken udon would be great, thanks."

"I'll put that in right away." He hurried off.

Cricket filled her teacup once more and cradled it with both hands gently. Bash observed her as she quietly closed her eyes and drank it with focus.

"We thought her name was Rebecca," Ryan said while chewing on a fried wonton with his mouth open.

"Caroline spoke her name in the cemetery last night," Bash added. "Plus, you can just make the name out on the gravestone."

"The spirit told us her name last night at Caroline's apartment as well. She said she was Rebecca," Cricket confirmed.

Ryan swallowed and continued, "Our theory was that the renovation of the wall disturbed the spirit, but your intel about the ring makes more sense."

"You mentioned something about a gruesome story. What was so bad about her getting married in the cathedral?" Ryan questioned.

"Rebecca, the bride, was a nurse tending to those stricken with a sickness sweeping the city, and she passed out at her own wedding," Cricket informed them.

"That is tragic." Bash sighed and reached out to hold Cricket's hand.

"It gets worse," Cricket whispered.

"She didn't make it?" Ryan asked, bracing himself for the answer.

"No, they thought she had died of the same thing that she had been nursing so many people through. But she was accidentally buried alive."

"What?!" exclaimed Ryan.

"Are you all right?" Bash asked. "That had to have been an awful experience, to be shown such a frightening end." Ghosts possessed a strange habit of introducing themselves through their manner of death, something Bash was accustomed to, but he assumed it would be extremely distressing for someone not used to it, like Cricket.

"It was difficult, I admit, but I am doing okay now." Her expression was solemn and her complexion ashen.

"Can you believe we know about a grave in St. Augustine where the person was buried alive? We have to be the only people who know! Otherwise, they would be shouting that out on every tour," exclaimed Ryan.

Cricket fidgeted in her chair. "Last night, Rebecca made it clear that she feels cheated out of life. Kimberly and I promised her we would help her. She seems fixated on her life with her groom. Any thoughts on how we help her, Bash? Do you know how to help her pass over to reunite with her groom?"

Bash thought it over for a second before speaking up. He needed to tell her the plan but didn't want to overburden her with all the details. "Ryan mentioned that we went back to the graveyard last night," he began.

The waiter brought over a bowl of soup for Cricket and several sushi rolls that he placed methodically around the table. "Is there anything else I can get you?" the waiter asked politely.

Cricket shook her head no, but Bash replied with a nod. He was already munching on a large mouthful of egg roll. "Just one more app platter, please."

The waiter's eyebrows rose in surprise at the two young men's appetite. With a smile, the waiter nodded and hurried away to put in their order, taking several empty dishes with him.

Bash cleared his throat, determined not to burden Cricket with any unnecessary stress. He hoped to ease her mind about Caroline. "So, at the graveyard—" He pulled out of his pocket the vial of shimmering liquid and offered it to Cricket.

"What is this?" Cricket held the vial in her hands and felt at its smooth, hard edges. Ryan and Bash looked on as she opened herself up to it. "Reveal your secrets," she whispered. Silence stretched through the slow moments. Finally Cricket handed the vial back to Bash. "It's an enigma to me, a total mystery. So, fill me in! What is it?"

"We are to give the potion to Caroline at Rebecca's grave site, as the full moon peaks in the sky, tomorrow night. This will guide Rebecca's spirit out of Caroline, and pass her on to a realm of peace."

"I've never heard of giving someone a potion to rid them of a spirit!" Cricket said, clearly puzzled.

"My intuition tells me that it will work. I think it's our best bet on helping Caroline."

Ryan ran his hands through his hair, a look of concern crossing his face.

"Ryan seems worried." Cricket clearly wanted clarification. "How did you come to possess this potion?"

Bash cleared his throat and tried to organize his thoughts to best explain about the entity in the graveyard, but his throat tightened and the words refused to materialize.

Ryan jumped in, "He had a strange episode in the graveyard last night. I have it recorded." He looked to Bash for approval.

Bash nodded in agreement.

Cricket stared at the screen. Bash clearly was interacting with some unseen force. The footage was dark and grainy but not compromised.

She watched as tiny flecks of light danced melodically in front of and around Bash like fireflies. He dropped to his knees, reached out his arm, and suddenly the vial was in his hand. Cricket watched his lips move, but there was no sound. The video came to an end.

Cricket nodded and asked, "I'm trying to understand. Bash, who were you talking to?"

Bash ran his hand across his forehead. "The universe has presented us with a solution to our problem. Caroline's wedding is in two days. This can resolve the issue in time. I know this is our answer. Trust me?"

Cricket pursed her lips, then a sense of determination entered her eyes. "Yes, of course. If you are sure, we'll do it. We'll give Caroline the potion on the full moon and have faith that it will all work out for good."

Ryan placed a hand on Bash's shoulder. "Buddy, I hate to say it, but I think we need to call in reinforcements for this one."

"Are you serious?" Bash moaned.

"As much as it pains me to say it, I know he would be able to help us out."

"Who?" Cricket asked, curiosity lighting her face.

"An acquaintance of ours who is more comfortable with this side of mediumship. His name is Tony, and although annoying, he's very skilled in the art of spirit communication. He might be willing to help us if we explain the situation to him," Bash replied.

Ryan raised an eyebrow. "And pay his beer tab at the White Lion. I just think having a plan B on hand if something goes wonky with the potion is necessary. We're taking this right up to the last minute." He put a piece of nigiri into his mouth.

"If nothing else, we can see if he can help bring in the groom to ease Rebecca's transition," Bash mused.

Ryan asked, "Can you handle Caroline between now and then?"

Cricket pursed her lips. "I am leaving here to help Gran with the store for a little while. Kimberly, Caroline's cousin, was with me last night when Rebecca really acted out. She's been texting me updates. Other than a shaky moment at breakfast, things have been okay. Once I get back with the bridal party after work, I won't let Caroline out of my sight."

Bash cleared his throat before replying, "Keep an eye on changes in her voice or unusual mannerisms. Look for colored orbs, usually blue, white, or silver."

Ryan quickly added, "And look out for fog or mist objects—we have video and still images of Rebecca showing up as such!"

Cricket shook her head. "Our night was way crazier than that, boys. I've got this."

Ryan swiped a napkin over his shirt in an attempt to clean off the splotches of soy sauce.

Cricket's face lit up with enthusiasm. "All right, so we have a plan. I will take care of Caroline while we wait for the full moon. You guys are going to reach out to your friend Tony for backup tomorrow night."

Bash grabbed the check and said, "One more thing, why don't you try to keep Caroline away from the graveyard until tomorrow night, just to be on the safe side?"

Cricket slid the lip gloss into her purse and nodded. "Sure, that won't be a problem, since the bridal party will be at the winery this evening. We will be on the complete other end of town."

"It looks like Ryan and I are joining Michael and his friend tonight; the other groomsmen won't get into town until tomorrow. We're having an unofficial bachelor party."

Cricket's face lit up in amusement. "I can't wait to hear what you think of Michael after spending the evening with him. What are the plans?"

Bash shrugged. "Not sure about the entire night, but Michael's text said to meet at the distillery."

"I'm sure it will be an amazing night. I'll text you if anything happens out of the ordinary with Caroline. I should probably head back to Baubles and Whatnots; Gran has a list of things she needs done before I meet up with the bridal party," Cricket said.

Bash leaned in and kissed her softly. "Miss you already," he whispered regretfully, wishing they had more time together. He hoped things would calm down after the wedding was over.

"You know I feel the same," Cricket responded before slipping on her sunglasses. She waved goodbye to Ryan as she navigated through the restaurant tables until she disappeared from Bash's view.

"What do you think?" Ryan asked.

"I think it's going to be okay." He pulled out the potion and held it to the light. "This is going to work," Bash said quietly.

Ryan looked back at the video paused on his screen. "I can't wait to upload the events on our web page. This will put us in a whole new tier."

"Yeah." Bash kept his eyes fixed on the grainy video, his tone solemn. "I'll reach out to Tony."

"Buddy, you worry too much. Want the last crab rangoon?"

CHAPTER II

CRICKET

Gran emerged from behind the massive mahogany desk in the front of the shop, her eyes sparkling behind her spectacles. "Your mom called earlier today; we had a lovely conversation," she said softly. As Gran walked, Tikaboo, their Cavalier King Charles Spaniel, stretched her front paws and let out a big yawn. The dog followed behind her owner, happily trotting along.

With a swift motion, Cricket tucked away the feather duster that she had been using to tidy up the shelves of Baubles and Whatnots, her family's cherished antique store. She made sure to dust in between customers as they came and went throughout the day. Although she usually mopped the floors at closing time, tonight was different; she was eager to return to Caroline's side. So, she decided it would be better to put out wet floor signs and tackle the mopping immediately.

Her main responsibility was to cleanse the store's objects of any negative energy before they were passed on to their new owners. Each object in this store held a special place in her heart; she wanted to ensure they were well preserved while waiting for their next owners. Only a handful of items in her experience had proven too challenging to cleanse and were instead stored safely in the subterranean section of the store. These items were closely guarded by a crystal skull and the family's stone canine guardians.

Most of the customers that graced their store had been bitten by the collecting bug. Cricket enjoyed collecting too, but carefully: she preferred having a small, curated collection of jewelry that she truly loved instead of many that she merely liked. One of her favorites was an old Cartier tank watch; it was slim and lightweight compared to more modern models. She discovered it years ago at an auction and couldn't imagine ever needing another one.

It was trickier for her to control the amount of clothing and shoes she brought home. Estate sales often had vintage pieces tucked away in forgotten boxes in attics. She couldn't help herself from keeping items she was unlikely to come across again.

Gran's voice jolted Cricket out of her thoughts. "I mentioned that I spoke to your mom earlier."

"Yeah, I saw her and Babs at breakfast this morning."

"That's what she told me. She mentioned that you were wearing sunglasses, didn't eat anything, and left quickly." Gran walked over to Cricket and placed a hand on her shoulder. "Did you have too much fun last night celebrating the wedding?"

"Well, maybe a little more than I should have," Cricket replied, pulling away in embarrassment.

"Ambrosias's influence is showing on you."

Cricket snatched the mop and started swishing it around the room, letting the scent of pine fill the air. "How did you hear about Ambrosias?"

"I've heard stories. Even if I'm not part of the court, I still have my contacts. I see his magic surrounding you; it's quite unusual, considering he is of the summer line, yet serves winter." Gran inhaled deeply as if to catch a scent. "He has an unmistakable aroma." She smiled knowingly. "Care to tell me what's going on?"

Cricket was perplexed. Did Ambrosias's essence still linger even when he wasn't with her? She couldn't shake the feeling that they were somehow merging together. Sometimes a thought would enter her mind and she'd realize it wasn't her own, but rather she was picking up on his thoughts and emotions. Her aunt Habina had advised her to keep the claiming a secret from their family until they understood its true purpose. However, it felt like too much time had passed, and if her grandmother knew, it was definitely time to come clean with her mother — unless she already knew too.

"Does Mama know about Ambrosias?"

"You should ask her. My question is, why would you not mention to your family that you are involved with the Prince of the Winter Court. Or any court business? You have no idea how dangerous the court can be."

"I'm not *involved* with him. Bash is my boyfriend. I am one hundred percent in with Bash. I am extremely happy with him. Ambrosias just — visits me."

"Oh? That sounds — interesting. Much more interesting than dating a human."

Cricket shut her eyes tight. Her stomach twisted in knots. She wasn't ready to think about this on her own, let alone have a conversation with someone, even Gran. Ambrosias pulled at her from deep inside, yet the hair on the back of her neck prickled warningly—being with him was like walking along a treacherous cliff edge overlooking raging seas below. On the other hand, Bash was safe and soft, like chocolate chip cookies fresh out of the oven. He made her think of her favorite pair of jeans and sneakers. She knew that no one else would make her feel the same level of comfort as he did.

Cricket glanced up to see Gran looking at her with concern. Gran pursed her lips. "All right, I will give you some space. Just know that I'm here when you're ready to talk—but don't take too long. And do talk to your mother. She doesn't deserve to be caught off guard. The news will come better from you, I think."

Cricket placed the mop back in the bucket, avoiding eye contact. Since it seemed a moment for sharing opinions, she said, "Gran, you may not care about the court, but you need to go back to that realm eventually. Your physical body—" Cricket glanced at her elderly grandmother before quickly averting her gaze. If Gran left the mortal realm, her youth and her full powers would return.

"Don't worry about me," Gran said gruffly. "I'm thoroughly enjoying my stay here with Otis; I intend to remain until his lifetime ends. I've taken preventative measures so the aging process hasn't gotten too bad," she exclaimed, spinning around like a ballerina and throwing her arms up.

"With Babs and Habina taking their place in the summer court—"

"Our house has always been divided by court business. It makes me sick to think on," Gran declared curtly, her mouth forming a firm line. "It's been so nice being away from it all."

"What will you do, then?"

Gran gave a comforting reply. "Don't think of tomorrow, Cricket. We have enough to worry about today."

Cricket sighed. "Actually, I do have something that worries me right now. Can I ask your opinion on it?"

Gran nodded as her hoop earrings jingled in agreement. "What is it?"

"You know Bash takes tourists on ghost tours, right?"

"Yes." Gran's lips became a thin line as she narrowed her eyes in concentration.

"Well, we, Caroline and her bridal party, went on one with him, and something happened."

"Yes." Gran lowered her chin and looked over the rim of her glasses at Cricket.

"To make a long story short, Caroline's antique ring woke up a spirit in the graveyard, and it is now possessing her."

"Are you sure? Were you able to ground the energy from the ring to a ley line?"

"No, the ring woke the spirit up, but nothing is actually wrong with the ring."

"Isn't your Bash good with the spooks?" Gran teased. "Can't he just whisk it away?"

Cricket walked back and forth in an anxious manner. Tikaboo followed her movements. "This will be his first time, and he has a potion that is supposed to help. It's linked to the power of the full moon. Have you ever heard of that?"

Gran had a perplexed look on her face as she said, "Mediums don't usually work in potions. Witches and earth elementals do. Which is he working with, a witch or an elemental?"

"Um, I guess—I don't know. I'm not sure," Cricket replied.

"Interesting." An amused look crossed her face. "Either way, there are potions that when used correctly can transport a being between realms. In this case, from this plane of existence to the natural transition into the next."

Cricket's eyes glanced around the room before she said, "I get this feeling that something isn't right. Maybe I'm just worried it won't go as planned."

"Your timetable is difficult. Poor girl, planning a wedding is stressful enough. To go and get oneself possessed during the bachelorette party, embarrassing," Gran teased.

"Gran, don't poke fun! This is serious. It's a real issue!"

"I'm sorry, it's just you younglings get so riled up over the simplest of things."

"I beg to differ, Gran! Possession is not a simple thing!"

"I didn't mean to ruffle your feathers, girl! Just telling it like I see it." Gran shook her head. "I have to go upstairs for a second. I left my phone in my room this morning and don't want Otis to worry if he's been calling me and I haven't answered."

Cricket gazed as Gran as she climbed the staircase leading up to the apartments.

"She thinks you're a worrier, you know."

Cricket could smell the musk of Ambrosias before she saw him standing casually against the counter, his biceps bulging and his grin hiding a secret knowing. Tikaboo sniffed the air.

"Ambrosias, why can Gran see your enchantment around me?"

"Because you are my chosen one, my love." He advanced toward her with measured steps.

"Yeah, about that. I think it's time you explain to me what that means."

"It is the only thing in life I desire." He moved forward abruptly, and she felt his frame against hers as he lifted her chin with his index finger. "Come away with me to the winter lands; become my princess and accept my claim. Just say the word, whisper it in my ear: yes." His fingertips' touch was light on her lips before moving up toward her cheek and down her neckline. "I will give you both delightful pleasure and torment, more sweet than you ever dreamed possible."

"Ambrosias, you know I can't do that. I'd perish in temperatures below sixty degrees. I'm not kidding." She pulled away from his embrace.

"Do you doubt that I could keep you warm? I'd wrap you in furs and the heat of my love. You'd never be cold, only surrounded by the comforting warmth of my heart. Your head weighted with the crown, which you alone deserve." His arms slid down along her body.

Cricket pulled away slightly. "You know I'm not interested."

"Not interested? You deceive yourself. I can tell precisely what you are feeling. It is not disinterest. Deep down you know we are destined. You are the air magic of the Culebra line. I am the air magic of the royal line; a son of Ishtar. When we combine forces, we will be unstoppable." He intertwined his fingers with hers, and she found herself short of breath. The act felt so intimate. There was something so familiar about him.

"I implore you, listen to your heart and to your body. Will you say yes to me?" His lips brushed her ear, sending ripples of pleasure throughout her. "Let's make this happen; everyone will be satisfied, both courts." He pushed against her, enticing her closer. "What do I have to do to get you to come to me? I want you willingly, without duress."

"I can't leave my family. I'm needed here." Cricket sighed.

"Imagine where you'll be in five or ten years: your sisters will have moved on, Babs is to the summer court henceforth, and Zadie will join the Mers. Your Gran will have to take up permanent residence with the fae before her body gets too old for even the healers to help."

"Are you listening in on my conversations?"

"As for your mom — once the summer court returns what is owed, she won't be alone anymore."

"What do you mean?"

"You are slowly running out of reasons to stay in the mortal plane. You know I'm right. Let me guess. Bash? I understand your curiosity for the human world. I do. But he can never provide what you truly need, or fill that incompleteness in yourself like I can. He will only hold you back. Your only choice is joining and claiming your full fae power. Be my eternal companion. Together we will do great and mighty things."

A flicker of magic sparked within her at the sight of his intense gaze, and she could feel her defenses crumbling under its enchanting spell.

CHAPTER 12
BABS

Babs gently placed her hand on Gwylm's large head, eliciting a happy pant from the wolf as she scratched him between his eyes.

Through the branches of the trees, she could see the sun had finally peeked through the clouds. Today was the day; either she would pass and join the summer court or leave this dream behind. Despite being filled with apprehension for more than twelve months, she now felt calmness wash over her. If it wasn't meant to be, then so be it. She would either follow this path or return home and work alongside her mother. That wasn't so bad, was it?

"Cast away your fears," Verity said softly beside her. "Come, take us in, all of the court wait for us."

Babs lifted her hands, and a luminous green mist swirled around them. She was used to sensing the energy, but seeing it was something else entirely. She felt a new connection as she waved her arms in sync with the undulating vapor. In her mind's eye, she pictured the Queen's Hall and felt the distance between them shrink until they were there. The mist dissipated to reveal the chamber filled with all the fae courtiers, the warriors, healers, and even those that didn't live within the court, but nearby, that relied on the court to keep the peace. Her gaze fell on Habina, her aunt, who winked in encouragement. Babs noticed she didn't feel sick from the phasing; for the first time the travel felt normal.

Verity lifted Babs's hand high and addressed the crowd. "My pupil, Babs, comes before you today to face the challenges. You all bore witness that she correctly phased herself as well as Gwylm and me into the Hall. If ever you find yourself fighting beside her, then you can rest easy knowing she is capable of guarding your safety."

A hush descended over the crowd as Babs stood before them. The anticipation radiated from everyone, and it matched her own excitement. Verity had told her that she had to phase them into the cavern, but what would come after that? Her body pulsed with energy, as a wave of anticipation washed over her, and sweat prickled on her forehead.

Verity gracefully curtsied to the queen, who was dressed in a stunning blood red gown that emphasized her regal stature. The collar of the dress reached high above her head, drawing attention to her crown, while the low-cut bodice seemed to have been slashed with a knife, exposing a slice of her chest down to her midriff, leaving very little to the imagination. The flowing skirt brushed against the floor and accentuated her strong, shapely figure. A string of rubies dangled from a gold chain just below the neckline of the luxurious dress. Her fiery crimson hair was intricately styled into cascading curls and tendrils that framed her face and cascaded down her back. As she met Verity's gaze with a cold smile, her dark eyes sparkled with anticipation.

"You may continue, sister," the queen said in an uncharacteristically kind way.

Verity's voice rose to a fever pitch, reverberating off every crevice of the rocky terrain. "We do not battle nature; we protect her. We are not vanquishers; we are defenders. Our duty is to monitor the equilibrium of all things and ensure that balance is maintained — no matter the cost." She paused for effect and then whispered into Babs's ear, "To keep this equilibrium, it begins inside you." She tenderly placed a hand over Babs's fluttering heart.

"Let the challenge begin." The queen's voice traveled across the vast watery portal.

The court members all sat silently with legs crossed as the healers carefully arranged their singing bowls in a line. When they began stroking the rim of the first bowl with a mallet, it produced a sound that filled up the space. Babs felt the lake below them vibrate as aqua light flickered around the room.

Verity beckoned to her and led her to the base of the statue. "Come, follow me," she said.

Up behind the large bronze statue was a roughly hewn staircase, which Verity and Babs began to climb, followed by Gwylm. As they wound their way higher, Babs eventually reached the lap of the throne of the queen. Verity arranged her in a sitting position, then handed her a small bronze scale to hold with both hands. Gwylm laid his head gently on her lap.

Verity glided her fingertips over Babs's head, and a ball of emerald light seeped from her skin. It softly settled on one side of the scale like a feather. Then she moved toward Gwylm, and a shimmering amethyst light poured forth, intermingling with the green, and shimmered for just an instant before shifting downward in weight.

"Call forth the balance," Verity intoned, her voice like a distant whisper of bells.

Terror coursed through Babs's veins. "How can I do that?"

"It is a unique quest for all. You and Gwylm must discover it together. The answer lies within your bond."

Gwylm made a deep rumble in his throat and snorted vigorously.

Verity smiled gently. "Have faith in yourselves — both of you."

Verity's steps faded into nothingness. Babs and Gwylm sat in reverence, peeking down from their high vantage at the queen, who sat still as marble in a meditative trance, eyes sealed shut, her voice sounding like gentle harp strings weaving together a tapestry of magic on the edge of the portal. Inexplicably, Babs was entranced by the queen's aura, a brilliant red that covered all around her and seemed to reach out to her, as if beckoning her to explore its depths. She scanned the entirety of the cavern below, mesmerized by the sight. When she unfocused her gaze, it all melded into a beautiful mandala, where each layer shifted and blended — the swirls of vibrant energy hovering just above the healers and warriors with their wolves, paying homage to the divine — a sacred work of art painted upon the world by energy itself.

Babs could feel Gwylm's vitality meld within hers. Everything around her seemed in perfect equilibrium, almost as if it had been ordained by fate. She closed her eyes and took a deep breath, feeling the gentle undulation of energy flow around her like a mosaic. Images emerged in her mind — spring blossoming into summer, autumn surrendering to winter, all perfectly orchestrated with each other. Nature was at peace, she realized. The cycle of life remained unperturbed, elucidating an important lesson: that everything has its own place and time for existence. The answer to the unasked question entered her mind.

"Time."

A softly glowing orb of moonlight manifested from the pulsing mandala of energy, drifting to the scale, where it hovered, radiating an ethereal luminescence that weighed in at a third of Babs and Gwylm's effervescent spirit. A force as great and ever-changing as time was embodied by this gesture, reminding them that life is precious and fleeting yet ever infinite and flowing.

The healers struck the singing bowls, their deep tones creating a rippling vibration that permeated the air. The cacophony of sound melted into a complex yet unified harmony of notes and fractals, reflecting the indelible beauty of the cosmos. Babs beheld visions of galaxies, each containing their own song, movement, and rhythm that expressed its unique voice while still part of an ethereal chorus. They all flowed together in a cosmic serenade.

"Harmony."

A brilliant ball of luminescent energy, pure as the sun, radiated from the core of the mandala and illuminated the balance scales with its radiant glory. The amount of light and energy that Babs and Gwylm shone was nearly equal, proving that harmony between two opposites was possible. They were close.

The world went dark and silent. Babs could no longer sense the room around her, nor Gwylm touching her lap. She felt . . . nothing. Nothing but a deep yearning, an irrepressible longing for something she'd never known. Panic rose like a wildfire within her, with each spark of fear feeding fuel to the flame. The moment stretched on without end. But then—there it was: a sound that at first seemed like thunder but soon revealed itself as Gwylm's powerful voice, bringing her instant calm. There was hope in this small familiarity, stirring something deep inside her and bringing with it a warmth and comfort more powerful than the enveloping darkness.

She strained her mind and body to seek his presence. Where was he? The mandala. Instantly, a wave of energy pulsed from within her, radiating out to transport her to safety. She was standing in the middle of the mandala. Surrounding her was a kaleidoscope of color, light, and energy. A buzzing sensation filled the air as Babs slowly took in all the beautiful energy. Everywhere she looked there were shapes and patterns — flowers, birds, animals all intricately carved into each swirl of the mandala's ever-changing surface. Each spiral seemed to have its own story to tell, with billions upon billions stories yet untold, just beyond reach of sight or sound . . .

She realized that this was where time stood still: in perfect equilibrium between two opposing forces, both chaos and order coexisting harmoniously without weight or dominance over one another; no one perspective could decipher the whole, but each independently held their integral piece that was necessary for all, achieving balance within the worlds . . . Here she experienced true freedom from outside influence, an extraordinary feeling but also daunting, considering how easy it would be to become lost within this new realm — a labyrinthine atmosphere requiring great focus during navigation back toward reality if ever escape should be successful.

Gwylm rushed to her, rubbing his flank against her side. *"I will never leave you, nor lose you."* His voice filled her mind, and she accepted the truth of it.

"Nor I you, Gwylm." Babs's feet soaked in the warm energy from the living light that cushioned her stance, connecting her to this plane. She raised both hands, reaching and receiving energy. The ley line flowed heavily through her, filling her with power. Images flowed through her consciousness, becoming a part of her. Her whole body felt as if it were being rearranged, pulled apart atom by atom and reconstituted. Was she seeing the future? The past? Her mind filled with images of the Culebra line going back further and further. Her whole being shuddered and filled with an understanding of life and death, of love and fear, betrayal and cunning, change without end. Nothing was new. We rode this cycle over and over, forever playing our parts. Was this what enlightenment felt like? Her soul trembled with awe.

"Oneness."

She blinked her eyes. She again came to the awareness that she was seated on the statue's lap. Gwylm's head lay upon hers. A bright white ball of light came out of the center of the mandala that she saw below her, landing on the scale, perfectly balancing it. It was done. The balance had been summoned. The power of the ley lines coursed through her. The illusion of separateness was now broken. She had faced the challenge and succeeded.

CHAPTER 13
CRICKET

The jazz band released a steady swirl of notes that mingled with laughter, both gently wafting through the beautiful evening. The stringed lights that festooned the roof of the winery sparkled like stars in the night sky. San Sebastián Winery was one of Cricket's favorite spots in Old Town.

"Let's order another bottle. The rosé is to die for." Caroline laughed, waving her wineglass in the air. The shifting light made the antique wedding ring shine on her finger with a brilliant white hue. The horror of last night was completely forgotten; not a trace of it remained. Cricket could see that her friend's smile was full of energy, and the delight of being a bride-to-be was evident. "We still have more than half this cheese plate to go through!" Caroline grabbed a hunk of bread covered in blue cheese, sparing a moment to admire her new manicure, and took a large bite. Her eyes closed as she let out a moan—bliss radiating from her face. "I didn't realize how hungry I was!"

Cricket spoke above the noise. "I'm going to put a tip in the musician's jar. Any particular song you want them to play?"

"Surprise us!" Pricilla said.

Cricket looked around the table. She noticed that Caroline's cousins—Kimberly, Pricilla, and Audrey—were moving their bodies enthusiastically to the music, snapping pictures of everyone else enjoying themselves, and posting it all to social media without reprieve. The singer paused to take a drink from her water glass as the jazz music shifted to a smooth, mellow beat. Cricket drank the last drops in her wineglass before getting up from the table.

She slipped off her uncomfortable shoes so she could feel every beat through her bare feet as she made her way across the familiar dance floor.

Her mind wandered, fondly thinking of all the times she and Bash had spent together here, more evenings than she could count. They shared countless bottles of wine and light appetizers before walking the street below hand in hand and ending the evenings at either his tiny cabin on the ranch, or her bedroom here in town. At this point, half of each of their belongings were at each other's place. Even when he wasn't with her, just seeing his toothbrush by hers in her bathroom in the morning gave her a sense of comfort.

Maybe when Gran went back to the faerie realm, which should be sooner rather than later, Cricket would have the wall removed that separated her and Gran's quarters and make it one big loft for her and Bash to share.

He would, of course, still need to spend time working at the ranch and tending the horses. But maybe he could live with her and just *work* at the ranch. They hadn't discussed it, but things seemed to be naturally moving toward that end. Helping Caroline with her wedding prep had really gotten Cricket to think about what direction she wanted her life to go. Looking around the rooftop winery bar, she was content to enjoy her life right here. At this moment, she didn't have a care in the world.

She reached the tip jar and placed a crisp twenty on top of the pile of fifties and hundreds. The dazzling singer, draped in shimmering sequins and bright feathers, leaned down from the stage with a beguiling smile. Her velvety voice tickled Cricket's ear. "What can I sing for you tonight, sweetheart?"

Cricket gasped in awe at the singer's glitzy ensemble. Twinkling chandelier earrings peeked out from under her wild curls, radiating an enchanting light. Long ebony hair was adorned with rhinestone loops and spangles that accentuated her jangling necklace and simple collar of her roaring-twenties-style gown, which sparkled with sequins and gemstones.

"Can you sing 'What a Wonderful World'?"

"You got it, sweetie. We have a few requests ahead of yours, but I should get to it within the hour." The singer touched Cricket's hand, and a sudden jolt of recognition shot through her. The singer's eyes glimmered an intense green, almost glowing.

Cricket was stunned, shock radiating across her face. "Uh—you are, you're fae!"

The singer winked, turning to the band, who had been looping a melody, and flicking her wrist to tell them to keep playing. "I wondered if you would pick up on my magic if I lowered my veil just a bit." Amusement danced in her voice as she spoke the words.

"I'm Cricket—"

"I know who you are, little Culebra. Maj and I go way back. And I know your gran too." A sly grin tugged at the corners of her mouth.

Cricket's brows knit together. She'd never run into a fae that wasn't her family out in the ordinary world. She looked at the tip jar again. She could see the charmed spell hovering around it.

"You know my family?"

"Everyone knows your family and that awful business with—" The woman's voice trailed off as if an invisible hand had wrapped around her throat. Her eyes grew wider, her lips thinning to a tight white line. She frantically shook her head. Cricket could feel the tension rolling off of her like waves as she desperately tried to free herself from whatever spell had caught her tongue. Finally releasing her breath in one sharp exhale, the woman's gaze transfixed on Cricket as she stood up and grabbed her microphone. "I have to get back to my set, honey," she said, her voice barely above a whisper, "and you should get back to your friends." The singer's red lipstick was garish now against the stark pallor of her face as she stared wide-eyed at Cricket before taking her place center stage.

Cricket's world shifted as she ran the startling interaction over in her mind. The realization that her family were not the only fae living in St. Augustine was monumental. The thought had never crossed her mind, but of course, the tales all speak of fae among humans. How could their presence have been cloaked from her until now? Her mind immediately began to race with new ideas. What had changed? Was it Ambrosias? Was being around him changing her somehow? What was the *awful business* that she seemed to try to speak about? Cricket threaded her way through the dancing couples and groups, back to the table. Opening her eyes, she saw the tendrils of magic pulsating out from the jazz band. A green glow swirled around the room, calming all the people, altering their moods ever so slightly to an elevated merriment, as their daily cares soaked into the wooden floor below them. No wonder the tip jar was overflowing.

Cricket felt the tranquil spell settling over her. It was a strange sensation, like being covered in a cool mist. She looked up, trying to comprehend what had just happened; the singer appeared to be completely recovered from their mysterious interaction. It seemed an invisible force had kept her from revealing something important to Cricket. She wondered what it was that she was not allowed to hear. Who had enough power to cast such a spell? Cricket remained confused and mystified by their interaction.

"I filled your glass!" Caroline slurred as she scuffled her chair around and plunked down next to Cricket. Her voice was swimming in wine like a fish in a pond.

"Thanks, I could use another drink." Cricket's mind whirled, bafflement clouding her mind.

"Wow, this wine is amazing!" Caroline smiled. She poured another full glass of the pink liquid and took a measured sip. Her phone rang out with the first bar of "Wedding March." She grinned while looking down at it. "It's my husband-to-be!" she exclaimed. "He and his friend Bobby made it to the Ice Plant. Bash and Ryan just joined them."

"Nice, that's a good spot. Bash was excited to hang out with Michael tonight," Cricket replied. She wished they all could meet up. She wanted to tell Bash she saw another fae, here of all places.

Caroline's phone rang out again. "They are ordering old-fashioneds."

"Do they make a good old-fashioned there?" Audrey asked.

Caroline's voice rang out, "Honestly the best. Make sure you stop by their gift shop and grab a bottle of their bourbon before you head back to Chicago."

"I'm not sure I want to go back," said Kimberly.

"You're joking," replied Pricilla. "You just have vacation-itis. It happens to all of us. We imagine a different life than we are actually living, but nobody ever just picks up and starts over somewhere else."

"No, I mean it." Kimberly put her phone down. "I think I'm done with the big city. I've experienced everything that Chicago has to offer. I'm still in my twenties. I'm not in a relationship, so — why not run around a bit? Try something totally different."

"You don't mean it; it's impossible," said Pricilla. "You couldn't live anywhere that didn't provide all the finer things that the big city does. Plus, you couldn't leave Mama and Dad."

Audrey studied Kimberly's face. "You're not thinking of staying here, are you?"

"No, not here. No offense, Cricket."

"None taken." Cricket reclined and took pleasure in observing the familial exchange; it made her realize that the decisions she and her own sisters had to make were universal, not unique. Somehow that brought her comfort.

Kimberly took a sip from her wineglass and declared, "I was thinking New Orleans."

"Oh my God, are you serious? Yes, yes!" exclaimed Caroline. "You could stay in our guest bedroom, once we have one, till you find a place. OMG, that would make my transition so much easier. Please — do move to New Orleans with me. We could job hunt together and help each other set up our apartments."

Audrey and Priscilla stared slack-jawed at their sister in disbelief. Audrey slowly cleared her throat. "If you are going to make a move, do it now." She plopped a piece of cheese slathered with mustard into her mouth and chewed vigorously. "Take it from me, right now your choices are boundless. But the older you get, the more you commit to life-altering decisions like marriage, career, and home—your options become increasingly limited. There's a point where you realize you have already made your choices, and now you have to live with them."

"That's complete nonsense!" Priscilla gasped. "Audrey, you and Luke have only been married for a short while, and you have an impressive career as an interior designer. But that doesn't mean you can't change your mind and try something different."

Kimberly chimed in, "You are way too young to think all of your choices in life have been decided."

"You aren't married to Chicago. You could move anywhere you wanted, if wanderlust has taken you over," said Caroline.

Audrey slowly swirled the glass of wine in her hand, her voice becoming more resolute as she spoke. "Try telling that to Luke."

Cricket couldn't help but feel a pang in her chest as she listened to their conversation. She knew all too well the concept of feeling stuck in a predetermined path. She was sidelined to her sister Zadie's heartbreak, knowing she would, at some point, go to live in the sea as a Mer with Aunt Maj. Zadie's whole life had been tinged with sadness, never quite able to commit to anything or anyone fully, knowing she would have to move on at some point in time. At least Cricket had a true choice. She could stay in the mortal realm, or she could choose to join the court. It was entirely her decision.

Caroline nibbled on a piece of bread and grinned. "So, Kimberly, are you really considering moving to New Orleans with me?"

Kimberly nodded, a determined look in her eyes. "Yes, I think I am. Honestly, I started thinking about it a while ago, when you said you guys were moving. This trip" — she looked over at Cricket — "felt like something ignited inside of me. My core is saying, 'Now! Jump now!'"

Kimberly continued to talk, but Cricket could no longer hear. She was focused on watching Caroline's expression slowly shift into something — different. The energy in the room changed, charged with something she couldn't quite place. Suddenly, Caroline's eyes turned pitch black, and her body went rigid.

The other women at the table jumped back in shock, but Cricket knew exactly what was happening. Rebecca, the bride whose spirit had possessed Caroline, was trying to take over again. It felt just like the other night.

Cricket quickly sprang into action. She had to get Caroline out of there before Rebecca caused a scene. She stood up from the table, grabbing Caroline's arm and pulling her toward the elevators to get to the ground floor.

Kimberly, right on cue, grabbed at Caroline's other side and helped half drag Caroline out of the restaurant. Once outside, Caroline's body went limp, and Cricket struggled to keep her upright.

"What the hell is going on?" Pricilla shouted, following them out onto the gravel parking lot.

Grabbing Caroline's arm and pulling her toward the car, Cricket panted. "We need to get her back to the apartment.

Now. I'm afraid the spirit from the graveyard isn't finished with Caroline."

"She's been perfectly fine all day. What changed?" asked Kimberly.

Cricket shook her head. "I don't know what triggered the episode. But we need to get her back home as quickly as possible."

With a wave of her hand, Cricket gently led Caroline into the back seat of the car. She murmured an incantation, weaving a soothing spell around her like a warm blanket. Meanwhile, Kimberly took the wheel and drove them back to Caroline's apartment, guided by the twinkling navigation spell Cricket had cast to remove all hindrances on the road.

During the drive, Caroline's body twitched and convulsed, and Rebecca's voice emanated from her lips. "It's dark. It's dark. Let me out!" Rebecca wailed.

Cricket gritted her teeth and focused on keeping Caroline safe and the rest of the girls calm. She was determined to get Caroline back to safety. When they finally arrived at the destination, Cricket and Kimberly practically carried Caroline out of the car and into her apartment.

Once inside, Caroline's body went completely still, and Cricket breathed a sigh of relief. She sensed that Rebecca had retreated into the antique wedding ring that Caroline wore on her finger. Interesting that she hadn't sensed that before. Cricket knew that she couldn't let her guard down.

"I'll stay with her for the night," Cricket said firmly to the cousins. "You all should get some rest. We'll figure out what to do next in the morning."

Kimberly countered, "We'll take shifts. I'll stay up with you. Audrey, Pricilla, get some sleep and we'll trade off later." Kimberly turned to the kitchen. "I'll put on some coffee."

"Well, this bachelorette party took a turn for the worst," mused Pricilla. "Does the wedding need to be called off?"

"No, we have a plan." Cricket took the time to explain to them all about the potion and what needed to be done. She was surprised at how calm they all were about it. But then again, they had seemed very comfortable with the spirit world when they were on the ghost tour.

"Here's your coffee," Kimberly said. "You girls go on off to bed."

Pricilla and Audrey puttered off to the couches. "What's next?" Kimberly asked.

Cricket really appreciated how down to earth Kimberly was. She reminded her a lot of Babs. "I'll text Bash. He should know what's going on."

As Kimberly hesitantly climbed into bed with Caroline, the near full moon luminously glowed through the gauzy curtains. The sky was a deep navy, and stars twinkled above. Noises from the road outside drifted in through the window. Cricket perched in the armchair next to the bed, vigilantly monitoring every breath that Caroline took.

CHAPTER 14

BASH

The hostess looked up from the seating chart, confusion etched on her face.

"I don't have that name down for a table," she replied.

Bash took in the details of his surroundings. He noticed the ornate cage at the front desk, filled with bottles of whisky glimmering amber in the light of the lamps above. The Ice Plant used to be an actual working plant back in the day. Now it was known for much more than just the building's history: a distillery, museum, gift shop—and its restaurant. With its delectable old-fashioneds and truffle fries, people from all over flocked here for free tasting sessions. Locals were regulars. Thanks to the seasonal, fresh rotating menu, there was always a surprise for the tastebuds. This was one of Bash's favorite places to go.

He smiled amiably at the hostess. "Thanks for checking. I'm sure they're at the bar." He turned to Ryan, accosting him with a determined stare. "You take point, Ry. I'll be right behind you." As he followed his friend up the wide wooden staircase, Bash felt the black iron railings creak slightly under the weight of his Allen Edmonds shoes. Above his head glowed the brilliant orbs of an elaborate chandelier, casting a gentle white light around them.

He glanced down at his watch; they were a few minutes early. For Bash, that was just how he liked it; never late and always punctual. Caroline had told him so much about Michael, he was stoked to finally meet him. She'd texted Bash earlier that evening insisting that he make sure her soon-to-be husband had a tasteful night out for his bachelor party. Michael had only one groomsman fly in early, so Caroline asked Bash and Ryan to be the party for Michael. They had happily agreed.

The cozy upstairs floor was teeming with bodies, a veritable maze of what seemed like dozens of tables. There were couples and large groups seated, and a whole crowd hid the large bar area. Ryan led the navigation, trying not to step on packages and bags that littered the cramped walking space. With so many people trying to get around, there was an almost nonexistent gap between each table.

"Do you think you can handle the atmosphere in here?" Ryan asked as his eyes nervously scanned the crowded bar. "Is it a good night or a bad night?"

Everywhere Bash looked, spectral forms were mingling with the living. He detected a sense of shared purpose in their movements. There was no mischief in the air. Bash exhaled slowly, somehow comforted by the presence of these supernatural beings. The entities seemed to be too occupied with their own affairs to pay notice to the mortals around them. Despite its heightened atmosphere, this haunt was one of his favorite spots—there was an undeniable charm to it.

"It's a good night," he finally replied.

Ryan jostled through the bustling crowd, his body shifting to allow the passing of those that brushed up against him. He turned and spoke over his shoulder. "Do you know what Michael looks like?"

"Yeah, Caroline has shown me plenty of pictures. I think that's him on the balcony side of the bar," he replied, pointing at the far end of the bar.

A faint glint of curiosity shone in Ryan's eyes, and his eyebrows rose slightly. "You go on over. I'll grab us drinks from this side," he suggested with a nod of his head toward the bar.

Bash gave a slight shrug before replying, "Sounds good." With one last look at Ryan, he weaved his way through the mass of people, making a beeline toward Michael.

He strode with purpose around the marble countertop, spotting the distinguished figure that dominated the corner of the establishment. He wore a tailored navy silk suit, perfectly pressed and with each seam immaculate. A white button-up was tucked into the trousers at just the right angle, drawing attention to his broad chest underneath. The man had an infectious grin and intelligent, almost wolfish eyes that darted around the room, taking in every detail of his environment. Bash knew without hesitation — this must be Caroline's fiancé — Michael. As he watched the man, it became clear to him that Caroline and Michael were going to make one unstoppable power couple very soon. Bash stopped just short of him and spoke up. "Hey there," he said, extending his hand for a shake. "I'm Bash. You're Michael? Caroline's husband-to-be?"

As Michael spun around, his teeth glistened in the dull light. "Yes, two days and she will be Mrs. DeVere." His English accent startled Bash. Michael reached out and grabbed Bash's hand for a firm handshake. "I've been eager to meet you and do a little cross-examination to get all the details about Caroline's college years."

Bash chuckled. "That's right, you're a lawyer." He shifted and stuffed his hands into his pockets. "Caroline's an open book. There's probably nothing you don't already know."

Michael raised an eyebrow skeptically. "Oh, I'm not so sure about that. You went to school with her. There must be some secrets. We didn't meet until after she graduated."

"Well," Bash began, his eyes sparkling with amusement, "she was a real force to be reckoned with on trivia night. She always had the answers for the craziest questions."

Michael burst into a loud laugh, his broad grin stretching across his face. "I bet she crushed everyone! Ha!" His enthusiasm was infectious. Even Bash couldn't help but chuckle.

"Bash, meet my best mate, Bobby."

The man next to Michael turned around. He was dressed nearly identical to Michael but opting for ebony rather than navy. When their hands met, Bash felt a powerful yet controlled grip as Bobby introduced himself. "Robert, from Stuart and Stuart," he said proudly.

Michael interjected, "He's referring to the law firm he was recently promoted to junior partner at."

Bash studied the man standing before him. He certainly had boyish charm with his blazing blue eyes that seemed to draw stolen glances from all the women nearby. But underneath the dashing smile was an aura of cruelty and narcissism that made Bash want to take a step back.

"Criminal defense?" Bash asked without breaking eye contact.

"How'd you guess?" Robert replied with a condescending smirk.

Bash shifted his gaze toward Michael, noting the sterility about him, like an operating room.

"Corporate finance?"

Michael's mouth gaped open in wonder. "This guy is incredible," he said in awe. "Let me grab you a drink."

"Oh, my drink is on its way. Look here. This is my man Ryan," Bash said.

Ryan strode purposefully over to them and shook both men's hands with confidence before presenting Bash with a perfectly crafted old-fashioned.

"Cigar then? I grabbed them downstairs, from the reserved batch," offered Michael hospitably.

"Sure, why not. Let's head to the railing," replied Bash nonchalantly. "It's a bachelor party, after all." With that, they all moved toward the balcony, where an expansive view of the city glittering under the night sky awaited them. Eventually, they secured a cast-iron table in a secluded corner. The air was thick with the scent of smoke, as if someone had been smoking there recently; an old ashtray sat at the center of the table, ready to receive its next cigar. Looking out, the palm trees swayed in the slight damp breeze, their delicate leaves forming a subtle dance with the stringed lights that hung above the picnic tables nestled in the small grass clearing. In the distance, they could make out rows and rows of parked cars, all patiently waiting for their owners to retrieve them at the end of the evening.

Michael cut the ends off each cigar, passed them around, and lit them in turn. "Bash, you're not the only one that can deduct. Ryan is clearly military. Haircut and posture give it away."

"I can neither confirm nor deny," came Ryan's reply with a sly smirk curling up his lips.

"Oh, I see. We are Special Ops?"

"That's classified information." Ryan shrugged nonchalantly, his face expressionless.

The group burst out laughing.

"So, Bash, I heard you are a historian just like Caroline, is that right?" Robert asked curiously.

"In a sense. We studied together at university and then both landed jobs at the Historical Society. We started off as interns and quickly moved up to full-time positions over the years." The corners of his mouth curved into a reminiscent smile. "But now I run my own business."

Michael's eyebrows shot up. He scratched at the stubble on his chin and leaned forward as if to draw every detail from Bash's response. "Oh, business doing what?" he asked, appearing genuinely curious.

"Horse-drawn carriage ghost tours," replied Bash simply in a voice full of confidence.

At that moment, Michael and Robert lowered their cigars from their lips in unison, their faces turning blank as they realized what Bash had said. "Like *Ghost Hunters*?"

"Sure, but with more of a focus on history," explained Bash thoughtfully. He rubbed the back of his neck nervously and shifted his gaze away from the two men.

Michael and Robert exchanged a look before Michael finally responded, "That's . . . interesting."

The atmosphere cooled suddenly as an uncomfortable silence descended upon them all. All four of the guys sipped on their drinks and fidgeted with their cigars, each lost in their own thoughts. Ryan shrugged and smiled at Bash.

"Can you see any ghosts right now?" Robert asked skeptically.

Bash took a draw on his cigar, then exhaled languidly before responding. "There's a gangster-looking fellow standing just behind your left shoulder," he said, his voice low and mysterious.

Robert let out a full belly laugh like staccato gunshots ringing through the air. "Maybe he's looking for fair representation."

Bash was amused when the spirit laughed along with the joke. It was a deep chuckle that echoed through the air circling Robert. The gangster spirit's eyes were full of mirth and warmth, hinting at some kind of unspoken secret.

"Michael, I heard you've just started with a firm in New Orleans?" Ryan inquired, his voice brimming with curiosity.

"It was an offer I couldn't refuse," Michael joked. "Caroline and I both figured it was the perfect opportunity to start anew in a different city. We're excited by the prospect of living in a new place. It saved us from having to decide between St. Augustine and Chicago," Michael replied, his gaze wandering out over the crowd.

"New Orleans must be quite the city to live in," Ryan said thoughtfully.

Robert snickered. "It's so cool! You'll definitely see me crashing on your sofa every once in a while."

Michael rolled his cigar along the edge of the ash tray. "Wouldn't have it any other way."

Bash's phone buzzed in his pocket. "Hey, guys, I'll be right back." He hastily made his way back through the restaurant and down to the men's room.

"Hey, everything all right?" Bash asked, an edge of anxiety in his voice.

"No need to worry. We are all safe and back at Caroline's apartment." Cricket's voice was hushed. Bash was having a hard time hearing her.

"What happened?" Bash's worries grew with every passing minute.

"Rebecca happened, at the winery," Cricket whispered. There was exhaustion in her tone as she continued. "After Caroline fell asleep, I tried to take off the wedding ring in hopes that it would help separate her from Rebecca. But it's like the ring is welded onto her finger—I couldn't even twist it let alone get it off."

Cricket's voice rose in fear as she continued speaking. "It's like her wedding ring has merged onto her finger! I'm not sure how else to explain it . . . I've cast a calming spell. It worked on the whole house. I'm the only one awake."

"Are you okay?" Bash asked.

"Yeah, just frustrated. I don't know how to help Caroline. It's killing me to wait till tomorrow night to actually fix this. I just want this over with."

"Okay, I'm going to try my best to cut out of Michael's party early. Ryan and I will get there as quickly as we can."

"No, I've got it covered over here. How is Michael?"

"It's been a fun night. He's a nice guy. I can see that Caroline will be very happy."

"That's great to hear. Let's just rid her of Rebecca and let her get on with her happily ever after."

"Cricket?"

"Yeah?"

"Next time you throw a bachelorette party, let's skip the ghost tour."

Cricket laughed. "Agreed."

CHAPTER 15
BABS

When the adrenaline left Babs's system, her body crumpled, as limp as a used tissue. She slowly descended the stairs, one heavy footfall in front of another, the numbness of shock tingling through her limbs. She had spent a year training to serve the summer court. She was mentally ready to kick ass and take names. She was at heart a pedal-to-the-metal kind of girl. Charge in first and ask questions later. But she came out of the trail altered in a way totally unexpected.

"I've sent for your things to be gathered and taken from the initiates' quarters and moved to the regular lodging wing—" Varity came rushing toward the steps. Her eyes widened when she saw Babs's face. "Oh." She stopped and leaned on the wall for support. "I didn't think—"

"What happened to me?" Babs cried, her fangs cutting sharply against her lower lip.

"It's okay—"

"I thought the only way you changed was if someone saved you from death. Like what happened with Habina. Like, the power was put in you. I thought that was what Habina said." Babs felt her legs going weak. She sat on the step. She could hear the noise of the court waiting for her to emerge on the other side of the statue, waiting to embrace her as one of them. But she couldn't will her legs to move. "I'm a warrior. I'm to have wings."

Varity slowly moved toward her. "I should have said something, but there was no chance of that." Her gaze flew up the staircase.

Babs's eyes pleaded for answers. "Cricket got wings!"

"You saw the mandala, went into it, yes? It hasn't presented itself fully in thousands of years. Do you know what this means?"

"My mama and gran are going to hate me!" Babs grimaced, feeling angry hot tears well up in the corners of her eyes.

"What? There's no way—"

"They can't stand the court. They could barely tolerate that I decided to be a part of it. But this—this they won't forgive."

"You don't understand—"

"No, *you* don't understand. When Habina left—I won't do that to my family!"

Verity grabbed Babs's shoulders and shook her roughly. "You are not Habina. Stop acting like a child! Your path is your own, and now we know just how pivotal it is. No wonder the queen took an interest in you. Somehow she must have seen."

Verity grabbed Babs's hand and dragged her to the summer court. The crowd parted as they walked up to the queen. "Majesty, I present to you Babs, our newest member of summer." Verity spun Babs around to face the crowd. "Whom here can remember the last time we had among our numbers a true balancer, one worthy to wear the crown?"

Hushed murmurs erupted through the hall. Babs took in

all the shocked faces as they stared at her changed appearance. She wiped at the hot streaks on her face.

The queen's clear voice spoke over all. "Our annals warned of the time of the telling. Many believed the time had passed without fulfillment." She paused to glare at Habina. Habina averted her gaze. "War between the courts is upon us." She paused, her gaze passing from one face to the next. "The Prince of Winter's brash behavior of claiming his chosen, in our hall no less, turned the hourglass once more, starting the countdown with every passing grain of sand. Balance is on summer's side; winter has a reluctant chosen without a crown. Our princess has been chosen by the energies themselves."

Verity stepped out of the crowd. In her hands, she held a crown of exquisite craftsmanship, adorned with gold and silver and intricately woven patterns that seemed to be formed by the very forces of nature. It was as if the trees themselves had lent their hand in its creation.

"Bejeweled with rubies and sapphires, the crowns of summer harness the power of the sun and stars," intoned the queen. "Living, ancient artifacts that were crafted eons ago under the perfect solar eclipse, they hold wonders and secrets unknown to man or beast alike—with our crowns, summer is one with nature herself. Come to me, Babs of the Culebra line." Her face broke into a manic smile. "The crown has patiently waited for its next custodian, and it has chosen you."

Babs moved forward, although her steps were unsteady. She ascended the dais and turned to face all who had gathered in the great hall. The queen lowered the relic on top of her head; it fit perfectly, as if made for her alone. Its intricate design seemed to come alive, its golden vines pulsating with vibrant energy. Whispers swirled about her head, a cacophony of voices from the past, echoing through the crown's ancient magic. The memories and experiences of all the previous bearers rushed through her mind, overwhelming her senses. She could feel their presence, their desires, and their power intertwine with her own. They spoke of grand battles fought, of alliances forged and broken, and of the delicate balance between summer and winter that had been upheld for centuries. Tales of love and loss, of sacrifices made for the betterment of all the realms wove patterns through her mind. Each voice carried with it a unique tone and cadence, a testament to the countless souls that carried this very crown upon their heads. Amidst this barrage of sound, Babs struggled to find her own thoughts. She clung desperately to her sense of self, fighting against the overwhelming tide threatening to consume her identity.

Yet amidst the chaos, a voice arose within her — a voice that was unmistakably hers. It was soft but resolute, cutting through the clamor like a beacon in a starless night. She summoned all her strength to rise above the collective consciousness.

The crown's intricate design seemed to come alive, its golden vines pulsating with vibrant energy. It was as if the crown had chosen her not only to wield its powers, but also to carry the legacy of all those who had come before.

Her every step resonated with regal grace as she descended from the dais, a newfound confidence emanating from every pore of her being. The eyes of the courtiers, healers, and warriors filled with reverence and admiration. She was no longer just Babs of the Culebra line; she was now a princess, the embodiment of summer's majesty.

As she took her place at the center of the court, Babs felt an overwhelming sense of purpose wash over her. She knew that she would have to navigate the intricate politics of the fae realms, balancing diplomacy and power with grace and cunning. Her heart surged with determination as she prepared herself for the challenges that awaited.

The whispers continued to dance within her mind, their words now guiding rather than overwhelming. They shared tales of ancient rituals and forgotten spells, ancient knowledge that had been passed down from one ruler to another. Babs listened intently, absorbing every morsel.

The hall exploded in cheers, erupting into a cacophony only silenced when the queen's hand waved for quiet. Everyone settled, expectantly awaiting her words, their energy palpable as they watched what could be summer's salvation unfold before them like some ancient play. She slowly raised her hands in blessing. "With this coronation, we are at full power."

The court again erupted wildly until the queen quieted them with a wave of her arm.

The queen turned to her. "It is an honor and a burden you now carry, my child." She stepped closer and kindly placed her hands on Babs's shoulders, who was still shaking from the anticipation of what was to come. "Your responsibility as princess will be heavy and filled with sacrifice; however, I am confident that the land will reward your courage in due course. Valleys shall bloom when you need them most, rivers will run with abundance, woodlands and fields of crops will bring forth sustenance."

The weight of the queen's words settled upon her like a gentle rain, each droplet filled with promise and responsibility. She nodded, her eyes reflecting the determination and resolve that burned within her.

"I understand, Your Majesty," Babs replied, her voice steady and filled with conviction. "I am prepared to embrace this burden, and shoulder the responsibilities that come with it. I will strive to maintain the delicate balance between power and humility, to protect and nurture the natural world that sustains us all."

The queen smiled, a glimmer of pride shining in her eyes. "You possess a rare wisdom, my dear. It is clear that you have already begun to comprehend the intricate dance of nature and its need for balance. But remember, it is not just the land that relies on you — it is also the creatures that inhabit it."

Babs nodded again, her mind already envisioning the countless beings that relied on a bountiful environment. From the smallest insects to the mightiest beasts, they all played their part in the intricate tapestry of life.

"Every living creature contributes to the harmony of our realm," the queen murmured softly, as if speaking to herself. "Just as each leaf on a tree performs its own function, so must we recognize their significance. You will come to understand this sacred duty."

Babs stood there rooted in place, taken aback by all that had happened, which seemed surreal: crowned princess without expectation or preparation for such a duty! She glimpsed her aunt Habina's ashen face. Babs wondered why her aunt was looking so distressed; surely this should be a happy moment? But foreboding entered the back of her mind. Her eyes darted from face to face, searching for an answer. All she saw was joy and elation. What strange occurrence had taken place that seemed to bring such sorrow to her aunt?

The queen commanded, "Dispatch riders to the hall of letters. I want the scholars in the south consulted. Also, send word to the fiefdoms that a new age is upon us."

Verity cleared her throat. "Majesty, perhaps it's time the king —"

The queen clenched her fist, and a rumble through the ground could be felt. "Yes, I will summon the king and his party to return." She turned to her guard. "Ready their quarters."

A hush came over the crowd as the water of the portal swirled, and winter court rose up and flew high into the air. Everyone in the hall inhaled a collective gasp as Ambrosias, the winter prince, appeared. He seemed almost ethereal with his snow-white hair and icy-blue eyes glimmering like stars in the night sky. His presence commanded attention as he descended to earth and conquered it by walking gracefully upon it, feeling its pulse beneath him. His troops flew close behind, dressed in their gleaming silver armor that shimmered like satin curtains shot through with starlight. The light caught each of their beautiful wings, thus creating an aura around them that caused many to look upon them awestruck . . . not afraid but shocked at their intrusion.

The palpable tension between the queen and Ambrosias made the air feel heavy, the silence broken when the queen faced her challenger. "Ambrosias," she growled through gritted teeth. She acknowledged his status, conveying the smallest respect without a hint of fear.

All attention landed on the queen. "Be still," her voice boomed.

"Ambrosias, what brings winter court to our shores?" Verity asked as she blocked his way to the queen.

"The balancer is reborn." His eyes rested on Babs. "She holds the power to claim from the land that which is owed."

"I serve the summer court, not winter," Babs yelled out.

A woman stepped out from behind Ambrosias, somewhat smaller than the others, though her presence loomed large in the room. Her silver hair cascaded over her shoulders like a waterfall, and her eyes shimmered with such ferocity that it chilled all who gazed upon them. Babs's mouth fell open at the site of the woman. She knew her well. It was Nadine, the cunning spirit who claimed to be her sister.

Nadine looked at Babs with an intense smirk as she kneeled before Ambrosias. "Your Majesty," she said without hesitation.

Her body radiated power, yet possessed an aura of serenity even though there was a ferocious coldness about her that sent rippling chills through Babs, causing her to shy away. Her steps on the earth were confident and measured, as if she had practiced this moment in her mind repeatedly. The wind picked up around Nadine, swaying chains that bound her to a frail man dressed in rags who stood at her side. "I think you will want to hear what the prince has to say. We have a personal interest, you and I."

"Nadine," Babs whispered. Confusion clouded her mind. How could Nadine live? Full flesh and blood? And what did she have to do with the winter court?

Nadine displayed a wide grin, "Ah, you have eyes only for me? I'm flattered. Do you not recognize your own father?"

Babs could hardly believe her eyes. She would not be fooled by the seeming miracle before her. It was impossible; it couldn't be her father. The court had nothing to do with her father's disappearance, right? If they had her father, surely her family would have rescued him. A million questions filled Babs's head, making them swirl and race through like a hurricane.

"Liar!" Babs spat.

The man lifted his head. His gaze met her own, and Babs could see the man he used to be. He had chocolate-brown eyes that still held flecks of warmth and life, yet there was a sadness and loneliness in them that tugged at Babs's heartstrings. There was strength in his demeanor despite all his years kept away from home, determination and longing etched across his face. The love he clung to so hard and maintained during the long tumultuous years, clearly gave him the courage to keep on hoping day after day until he was free, and he could once more rejoin his family. Familiarity tugged at her heart.

"Father?" Babs whispered, not daring to believe it was him.

He squinted his eyes, examining Babs, taking a few steps forward, then stopped and turned to Nadine. "Nadine?" He whispered and reached out his shackled hands towards his familiar daughter. Nadine grasped them.

"Yes, Dad. I'm here. I'm always here," Nadine said softly. Tears threatened the brim of her silver eyes, which only intensified her awe-inspiring beauty. "That's Babs, my twin. I told you she looked just like me." She wiped at her face. "She's going to find and return the crown to winter so that we can go home to Mother." Nadine wrapped her arms around her father, an embrace so tender Babs felt like she and the rest of the court were intruders on something too sweet for them to see.

"My"—tears burst from his eyes—"my child?" He reached his hands out to Babs.

Ambrosias's voice broke the moment. "The winter king holds your father ransom for the stolen crown. Your mother, having given up her power for the love of a mortal, proved to be useless in retrieving the artifact." His eyes turned to Habina. "That entire generation proved useless. But you, next of the Culebra line, in your full powers, will find and retrieve the crown for the winter court so that I may have my chosen by my side and thus, by order of the king, will free your father and sister to return home."

Babs found herself speechless. Her body had gone numb. Her dad had been a hostage this whole time. Did her mom know? If so, how could it be that she hadn't moved heaven and earth to find this lost crown and get her husband back? Her insides began to shake. Gwylm stepped in between Babs and Nadine.

Babs could barely speak. "I will get you back Dad, I promise." Tears stung her eyes.

Nadine stood beside her father, glaring at Babs.

Murmurs through the hall grew to roars. A cold and formidable energy blasted throughout the room. Everyone present was readying themselves for a fight.

"Summer no longer accepts this task! I have no reason to be your errand girl," the queen announced boldly as she drew her sword and held it in front of Ambrosias, blade pointing forward with lethal intent. The summer court drew their weapons to join their queen.

Wolves began to growl, signaling their readiness to fight. Habina unsheathed her bow, controlling an arrow already prepared for defense: ready to unleash its fury upon any foe who dared go against them.

"Enough!" Ambrosias's voice bellowed. "We came to retrieve the crown, not start a war." He ran his hand through his hair, "Nadine, you stay with Babs to ensure the task is completed. Never leave her side."

Nadine frowned. Her eyes lingered upon her father.

"Queen." Ambrosias turned, his eyes full of hatred.

"That I am," she turned her back.

Rage crossed Ambrosias's face.

Verity placed her hand on Ambrosias's arm. "Your father is being summoned," she whispered.

"Then I suggest you hurry the balancer along with her task, so my business here is finished before his arrival."

"You know it's not as simple as that," Verity pleaded. "If it were so, winter would have had the lost crown long ago."

"Then I suggest you figure out how to make it simple and timely."

"Don't challenge him, Ambrosias. Your father's strength is too much for you."

Ambrosias rubbed at the back of his neck. "You know it's destined. The time of the telling has come. My chosen and I will rule both summer and winter courts, making our reign the most powerful court of all ages. My father's reign is already over, as is the queen's."

Verity looked at the ground. "At what cost?"

"My dear aunt, at any cost."

"You can't mean that."

"My mother has not one care for me. My father refuses to see me and has abandoned the realm. As if running away from his duty would change destiny. If anything, it has lit the match that formed a raging fire within my heart."

"Dear nephew, even with the telling, you have free will. You are not a puppet in a play!"

Ambrosias's eyes softened. "If only you were queen, how different things would have been."

Verity looked away.

The queen raised her voice. "No courtier of winter is granted safe haven or protection in the summer lands, and that includes Nadine. Ambrosias, return to winter with your hostage. I care not about him. You will be summoned if you are needed. Let your king know that peace with summer is at an end."

"You are not taking him from me!" Babs ran toward Ambrosias, ready to strike with all her might. The queen raised her hand, and Babs found herself floating above the ground, choking and gasping for breath that would not come.

"You *dare* question my rule!"

Babs's feet kicked wildly, as if she were dangling by an invisible noose.

"Sabella!" Verity yelled. The queen's eyes shot daggers at Verity. She flicked her wrist, and Babs crumbled to the floor. "Away with you, Ambrosias, and take your little cur."

Ambrosias shot a knowing look at Verity, grabbed the chains, and called out, "Princess, if only your family would have honored the call, you and my chosen would not be set at odds. When you feel that rage, do not make the mistake of displacement."

Babs had thought she was in a dream but now found herself submerged in a nightmare that she could not wake from. Who could she trust? What was the truth? The crown on her head felt heavy, like hot lead, and seemed to be tightening with each passing minute. Fear of the unknown gripped Babs as visions untold flooded her mind — images of war, battles long past, family feuds fueled by centuries-old grudges and betrayals . . . none of which made sense! Knowledge took shape in the corners of her mind, when amidst all this chaos came whisperings from a distance, or was it within? She felt Liande, tasted her breath. What trickery plotted its own course, lurking in shadows just beyond her grasp . . .

Babs's eyes locked on her father's as she kneeled on the floor, taking deep gulps of air into her lungs. None of that mattered. Now that she knew her father was alive, nothing and no one would stop her from bringing him back home. She knew who she had to see — Liande.

CHAPTER 16

CRICKET

The evening remained peaceful throughout the night, which was a relief for Cricket. She sat by Caroline's bed, keeping watch over her sleeping form as she snored gently. A smile formed on Cricket's face as she saw how serene and beautiful Caroline looked. At least she had gotten her much-needed rest before the big day.

When Caroline finally woke up, there was no sign of Rebecca anywhere. They spent most of the day lounging around in Caroline's apartment, scrolling through social media and laughing at memes. But soon, it was time to prepare for the wedding rehearsal at the basilica and the dinner party that would follow directly after.

With the help of her cousins, the once-ordinary bathroom transformed into a bustling makeup and hair studio. All five girls huddled together, giggling and chatting while expertly primping for the upcoming evening. Amidst the flurry of curling irons and hairspray, Cricket felt like she was a doll being pampered by Kimberly, who insisted on doing her hair and makeup. As curls were delicately pinned in place and locks were doused with liberal amounts of hairspray, Cricket couldn't help but feel like a princess getting ready for a ball.

The wedding rehearsal at the grand basilica went off without a hitch. The towering ceilings and stunning stained glass windows created a beautiful backdrop for the ceremony. The pews were adorned with lovely spring decorations, including fragrant lilacs and white tulips that brought a sense of new beginnings to the event. With everyone working together, they quickly transformed the space to match Caroline's vision perfectly.

During the rehearsal, the lively priest had a mischievous sense of humor that kept the entire wedding party entertained. He would cleverly slip in jokes and puns throughout, causing both bridesmaids and groomsmen to burst out laughing. Even Caroline's parents couldn't resist chuckling at the charming priest's wit.

Amidst the laughter and joy, Michael's and Caroline's eyes stayed locked on each other. They couldn't help but feel emotional as they recited their vows during the rehearsal.

"I promise to love you unconditionally, through thick and thin, through the good times and the bad," Michael said, his voice cracking with emotion as he looked deeply into Caroline's eyes.

"I promise to stand by you, support you, and be your rock in times of need," Caroline replied, her voice trembling with emotion.

Tears filled both of their eyes as they pretended to exchange rings and pledged their love to each other once again. All the family smiled at the emotional display.

"If you two keep that up, I'll never make it through tomorrow," Caroline's mother murmured while dabbing at the corner of her eye.

"I'll keep plenty of tissues on me to hand to you, darling," her husband replied, handing her one that he had in his pocket.

The bridesmaids were still taking pictures of the cathedral from the front of the church. Cricket listened in on the groomsmen's conversation.

"Geesh." Dylan, Michael's cousin, rolled his eyes. He stood behind Robert, the best man, who hadn't taken his eyes off Kimberly all night.

"How many weddings have you been in?" asked Robert.

"Too many to count." He laughed. "Don't mind standing on the side like this. I'll never be caught in the middle like Michael."

The other two groomsmen snickered.

Robert pursed his lips and stared off into the distance. "Well, if the right girl came along."

"Someone ready to settle down?" The guys laughed.

As they left the church, Cricket breathed a sigh of relief at how well the day was going. Both Caroline and Michael exuded a sense of calm after practicing for the real deal. They clearly were excited for their future together.

Cricket and the cousins trailed behind Michael and Caroline, giving them some space for a private moment.

"That went really well!" exclaimed Audrey.

Kimberly and Cricket exchanged glances. "Let's hope the rest of the evening goes the same way," Cricket said.

The cousins were focused on editing the photos from the rehearsal. Michael embraced Caroline, pulling her close and giving her a passionate kiss. She responded eagerly, holding on to his neck as his hands rested gently on her hips.

"I can't wait to call you Mrs. DeVere," Michael's voice carried as the couple broke apart from the kiss.

"Okay, lovebirds. Save it for tomorrow," Pricilla teased.

As the entire wedding party made their way outside, several black limos were waiting for them, each one more luxurious than the last. The smell of leather and polished wood filled the air as Michael and Caroline approached one of the limos, hand in hand.

"We could walk," Cricket said.

"Why walk when we can ride in style?" Kimberly laughed.

"Darling, I believe after all of that, we could use some alone time," Caroline stated as they settled in the back seat of the limo.

"I think we can make good use of the quick drive time. Driver, can you put up the privacy window please?" Michael called out while pulling her close to him.

Caroline nestled into his arms and closed her eyes, enjoying the luxury of the back seat and the warmth of Michael's embrace.

"I see." Pricilla smiled. "Obviously we'll take a separate car."

Cricket followed the cousins into the limo near the end of the line.

The black snake of limos pulled up in front of the Columbia Cuban restaurant, and the wedding party got out one by one, marveling at the luxuriousness of the place. The decor was authentic, with murals of Havana and antique Spanish tiles all around. As they walked in, the sound of salsa music hit them like a wave, and the scent of spices and grilled meat made their mouths water.

Caroline and Michael took a seat at the head table, surrounded by their closest family. Cricket joined the bridesmaids at a table nearby that had the perfect view for the cousins to snap photos of the happy couple. Everyone chatted, laughed, and toasted Caroline and Michael's future together.

All they had to do was make it through dinner at Columbia and get Caroline to the graveyard before the moon reached its apex to give her the elixir, freeing her from the ghost of Rebecca. They still had a few hours to get through.

The waitstaff's arms were brimming full of tantalizing dishes. The tables were laden with towers of appetizers and small plates, pitchers of sangria, queso fundido, empanadas, oh, the bread—life was good. They had barely set everything down when more waiters came flooding in behind them, weaving in and out, finding the perfect place to set down trays filled with shrimp and crab, and bowls filled with roasted pork and chicken. But for Cricket, she couldn't wait to dive into the paella. She breathed in the aroma, and a smile spread across her face.

It was good to see Caroline mingle with her family. Everyone had taken to their seats and began munching on the delicious food. Conversation flowed easily, and everyone caught up on each other's lives. Caroline's aunt Clara, began telling fanciful tales about a recent family vacation that swept them through Europe.

As the night went on, the conversation started taking some unexpected turns. Michael's uncle George, who had a bit too much sangria but was a grandiose storyteller with a booming voice, began regaling them with wild tales of chasing after an exotic dancer in Rio. Everyone was enthralled, and Cricket could see that Caroline was fully engaged.

Cricket glanced over at Michael, who was talking to his father about their shared love of golf. Their bond was clearly evident, and she couldn't help but feel a twinge of melancholy as she thought about her own predicament. If she chose a life with Bash, her path would include a night like this. She could see their families mingling. Could that work? On the other hand, there was Ambrosias. A life with him was a much less predictable path. She pushed those thoughts aside and focused on enjoying the moment with her friends and her family. This night was about Caroline, not her.

Just then, Michaels's cousin, Dylan, walked in and greeted everyone. Cricket couldn't help but notice his physical resemblance to Michael. She'd had a chance to speak to him at the basilica, and they had created a friendly rapport. As the night went on, he and the other two groomsmen, Jack and Leo, friends of Michael from way back, joined Cricket and Caroline's cousins at their table. Dylan was easy to talk to and had a great sense of humor. The other two chattered intently about stock markets and cryptocurrency. Cricket only understood about half of what they were saying.

The guys kept ordering shots of tequila for the table, and before long, everyone was stumbling over each other and slurring their words in between fits of laughter. Cricket was amused as Robert hit on Caroline's cousin, Kimberly, with clumsy flirtations and off-color comments.

"Hey there, gorgeous," Robert slurred, leaning in close to Kimberly. "What hotel are you girls staying at tonight? We have to continue the party later."

Kimberly responded, not lifting her eyes from her phone, "Oh, we're not at a hotel. We're staying at Caroline's."

Jack bragged, "We've taken over a corner of the fourth floor of the Casa Monica Resort. It has the coolest rooftop pool with a bar. You girls have to come over."

"Swimsuits optional." Dylan laughed.

Robert hit him in the arm.

"What, mate?" Dylan pretended to be injured, and flashed a mischievous schoolboy smile.

The girls laughed it off, but Cricket was tired of the conversation. "Hey, guys, want to come with me to check in with Michael and Caroline?" she asked. "They look like they need to be rescued from small talk."

Dylan looked at her with bleary eyes, but he seemed to sober up a tiny bit at her words. "Yeah! Let's go talk to Mikey! Can you believe he's marrying that hottie?" he slurred.

The table burst into laughter. Tequila sprayed out of Pricilla's mouth as she laughed.

"I would marry any of you!" Dylan waved his empty shot glass around the table. "Goddesses, each and every one of you."

"That's a left turn from earlier tonight," Robert teased.

"Obviously this one's a lover when he drinks," teased Pricilla.

"Let's keep him around. He's good for a self-esteem boost," Audrey mumbled with her eyes half-closed, slumped over the table.

Cricket was starting to form a plan on how she would get Caroline to the graveyard. It wasn't far from here, easily walkable. The party was winding down. She had counted on the cousins to be able to help, but given their tipsy state, it might be best to take her on her own to meet with Bash.

Dylan scooted his chair out. "Ladies, let's go give our best wishes to good old Mikey and his bride-to-be."

Cricket stood up from the table, keeping a watchful eye on the bridal party, as they all stumbled toward the head table. Caroline's eyes lit up at the sight of the large group.

"Dylan!" Michael exclaimed, giving him a warm embrace. "We didn't get a chance to talk before the rehearsal.

I'm so glad you could make it! That was quite a long flight for you."

"Yeah, almost twelve hours with the layover. There just aren't any fast flights from London to Florida, at least that I could find."

Michael gave him a nod of understanding, clearly happy to see his cousin in good spirits. "I appreciate the effort. Glad you could make it, mate," he said. "You're looking good!"

"Thanks, mate. Drinking man's diet." He burst into laughter.

"How's that?" Michael asked.

"You pick, either you drink or eat each day. Today" — he grabbed a cup off the table and filled it with sangria — "today is a drinking day, and the tab's on you!" He lifted the cup to Michael in salute and downed the glass.

All the guys burst out laughing.

"You're crazy, mate!"

"But you love me." Dylan smiled.

Caroline burst out laughing; manic wild laughter. Cricket felt the hair on the back of her neck rise.

It was then that Cricket saw the unmistakable glint of Rebecca staring out through Caroline's eyes.

Panic gripped Cricket's chest. The time was now. She had to get Caroline out of here and to the graveyard before Rebecca took Caroline completely over again in front of her family. She caught Kimberly's eye and whispered, "We need to get her out of here."

"Yes, yes, you are right." Kimberly shook her head. "I need to clear my head. I was wrapped up in the festivities. Water. I need lots and lots of water." She grabbed for a glass and chugged one down.

Cricket smiled. Water wasn't going to fix this in time. Cricket pulled Kimberly to the corner of the room and glanced around. All the guests were deep in conversation or drink; they weren't paying attention to them at all. She closed her eyes and held her hands up in the air, palms facing upward. She summoned the ancient power of the elements to break Kimberly's drunken stupor. A gust of wind touched her face as if confirming she had been heard. Cricket whispered an incantation and conjured a golden light that enveloped Kimberly in its warmth and clarity, restoring her reason.

Kimberly laughed. "I don't know what you just did, but, girl—you are quite a wing woman. Any chance I can get you to move to New Orleans with us?"

Cricket laughed. "That is not on my radar, but I, like your sisters, would love to visit sometime."

"Open invitation." Kimberly smiled.

With urgency in her voice, Cricket whispered to Kimberly, "We need to get Caroline out of here, now, before it's too late."

Kimberly nodded in agreement. Together, they gently nudged Caroline's arm, trying to get her attention. "Caroline, we should go take a walk outside," Kimberly whispered.

Caroline's eyes flickered to meet Cricket's, but Rebecca's presence was too strong. It was taking over. "I'm never leaving my groom," she replied, her voice flat and distant.

"That's right, you better never leave me," Michael teased.

Dylan was telling the table about the time Michael built a three-story tree house in their grandparents' backyard, unbeknownst to any of the adults, and everyone erupted into laughter, except for Caroline. Her eyes looked vacant, and her smile didn't quite reach her eyes.

Cricket and Kimberly shared a concerned glance, but they refrained from questioning the topic further.

"Let's just watch her," Kimberly proposed. "It's too early to pull her from the party. The family will notice, not to mention her groom."

"All right, but if what happened at the winery happens again—" Cricket pondered.

"Then we'll grab her and make like we're being silly. Like it's a bridal gag."

"Perfect."

As the night wore on, Caroline's behavior became increasingly erratic but not overtly so. She started talking to herself, her eyes darting around the room as if she were seeing something that wasn't there. Michael tried to calm her down. Their eyes locked. Rebecca sighed a long, satisfied breath. Here was her groom, her love. She would have the life that was denied her.

Cricket watched as Rebecca's presence continued to grow stronger within Caroline. It was like watching a car crash in slow motion—she knew what was coming but was powerless to stop it. Caroline's demeanor shifted. It was clear that Caroline and Rebecca were fighting for control, but Caroline was losing, becoming more and more like that of a woman possessed.

Suddenly, Caroline's eyes snapped shut, and she let out a lusty prolonged moan. The other guests turned to look, confusion etched on their faces. Michael reached out to his bride, and her eyes locked on to his. A seductive, simmering mood crossed Caroline's face. Rebecca's voice cooed from Caroline's lips, "I have waited so long, so long for you, my groom." She ran her fingers lightly up and down his arms.

Cricket looked on in horror as she saw Michael being drawn into Rebecca's gaze. Of course he was. This was his bride on the night before the wedding. He kissed her deeply as the family clinked their glasses with their utensils in delight from the obvious love on display.

"Oh, deary. Are you ready for the wedding tomorrow?"

Cricket turned to see Caroline's grandmother. She was a short plump woman with twinkling eyes, undoubtedly jolly, happy, and fun-loving at heart. Her wardrobe consisted mostly of large bright floral prints paired with practical sandals—which seemed slightly too small for her wide, bulging ankles—but she had more than made up for it by covering herself in gold jewelry, statement pearls, and shining rings that covered nearly every finger. She put a disco ball to shame.

"Yes, ma'am. I'm sure it will be a beautiful service, with the most beautiful bride."

"Oh, call me Nan." She threw her arms up majestically. "It seems our bride has some wedding jitters. Acting a bit strange, if you ask me. I hope you can help her keep her wits about her. Maybe some of those gummies that are everywhere these days?"

Cricket choked on her drink. "Mmmm," she muttered.

"You have a shine about you, dear. Has anyone ever told you that? A bright white light that sits like a crown about your head and shoots out behind you like radiant wings. It's quite a sight! Oh, me!" She threw her arms in the air. "Don't mind my blathering!" She patted her forehead with her napkin. "I can't wait to see the cake. I heard your mother is the best baker in all the county," she said with exuberance.

Cricket nodded eagerly, putting her drink down on the side table. She could see why Caroline and her cousins liked their Nan so much. "Oh yes! She really is an amazing baker. Do make sure to taste all of the treats she's made for tomorrow night!"

Nan waved her hand in agreement and giggled like a schoolgirl. "I know you would never guess, but I have a real weakness for sweets, deary." She winked at Cricket knowingly and said with flourish, "And why wouldn't I? Little cakes are like little slices of heaven—vanilla bean topped with raspberries, delectable pies that melt in your mouth like clouds, candy-coated memories dusted lightly in powdered sugar—life's sweetest moments captured one bite at a time! And then there is ice cream—nothing quite so luxurious as creamy swirls dancing across your tongue, hinting ever so delicately about what lies beneath its smooth surface . . . ahhh." She sighed deeply before finally concluding that there was no better way to celebrate than with sweets!

"Yes, I agree, ma'am—ah, Nan."

Nan took a sip of her champagne. "You know, Mossey and I drove the camper all the way up A1A from Key West—that's where we live now. Retired, we are. Well sort of. We do try!" She let out a long, loud laugh. "Anyway, we just pulled in. Ran a bit behind schedule. You can never account for traffic, my dear. Especially on A1A. Beautiful scenery, and so many quaint places to stop for nibbles." She burst into laughter again. "Oh, look! Mossey is starting a conga line! I just wanted to stretch my legs and mingle a bit with you young people." She cast a warm smile.

"I'm glad you did."

"Mossey, Mossey!" She waved her hand frantically in the air. "Wait for me!" Her voice rang out above the party.

Cricket watched Nan make her way through the crowd, expertly dodging and weaving past all the other guests until she finally reached her husband, Mossey. All the dancers' eyes lit up as they saw her, their excitement palpable in how quickly Nan moved from one person to the next — shaking hands with some people while giving out hugs to others. The conga line grew longer, as more and more guests joined in on this comical festive romp of a celebration! Nan's voluptuous hips swayed and strutted to the beat of the music, as she held tight to Mossey's waist.

Throughout the room, there were laughs shared between old friends who hadn't seen each other in years, families spilling into one another's arms like a huge warm hug, children making silly faces at their parents, or running off chasing after each other and playing tag in between the tables — every moment was filled with joy punctuated by the loud music. Cricket enjoyed just watching them move around so carefree. She couldn't help but notice how excited everyone seemed — especially when Nan stopped everything to give big bear hugs and special handshakes that obviously left lasting impressions on those who received them.

As the hours stretched onward, Rebecca's influence over Caroline increased. Caroline started to act wilder, her words slurring as she fought to remain in control of her actions. Cricket decided to text Bash.

> Cricket: How soon should we meet at the cemetery?

> Bash: About an hour, we'll be ready

> Cricket: Did you get your backup?

> Bash: Still working on it, see you soon

> Cricket: ♡

She looked up from her phone, and a sense of dread traveled through her as Caroline stumbled toward the door, her eyes fixed on Michael. She reached out for him, her hand trembling as she tried to grasp his arm.

Michael murmured, "Darling, I think the sangria has gone to your head. You haven't had a bite to eat. Let me get you a small plate. I know you'll like the chicken and rice. Carbs will do the trick."

"Forget the plate. Come with me," she whispered, her voice low and sultry. "I don't need food. I need you, alone."

With a wicked smile, Michael took Caroline by the hand and led her out of the restaurant.

Kimberly came running to Cricket's side. "We go after her, right?"

Cricket looked out at the moon. It was nearly at the apex of the sky. Bash had said an hour, but the sooner she got Caroline there, the better. They needed to get away from the party and to the graveyard. It was a mere five-minute walk at most.

They made their way through the crowd to Audrey and Pricilla. They both had their phones out, documenting every celebratory detail. Time, plates of food, and several glasses of water seemed to have sobered them up.

"Oh hey, Caroline is going to love the shots we've captured!" said Audrey. "I know how much I appreciated getting my guest photos after my wedding."

"Is our girl doing okay?" Pricilla asked. "No more weird stuff?"

"She just slipped out with Michael. We're going to get her and execute the plan. Caroline should be Rebecca-free in no time."

Cricket let out a heavy sigh. "Would you be able to come

with us and bring Michael back to the party while Kimberly and I extract Caroline?"

"Yeah, we've got you!" Audrey grinned.

Pricilla shrugged. "What could go wrong?"

CHAPTER 17

BASH

The squeak of Ryan's high-
top leather shoes against
the polished tiles gave away
their approach. It was an average night,
and they could hear the sounds of laughter
from all corners of the pub, along with men
talking loudly about politics, sports, and
entertainment. As soon as they sat down on
the tall, sturdy bar stools, the barman brought
them two Guinnesses.

"You two are turning into regulars," the
barman said. "Tony's sitting here." He motioned towards a
half-empty beer mug next to Bash. "He said you'd be coming in. He just ran to take a leak; he'll be right back."

"Thanks, man." Bash looked around the room. There
were a few empty tables. "Think we can get some fries and
onion rings?"

"Already have them going." He threw a towel across his
right shoulder and walked away.

Bash felt the smooth glass of the potion in his jacket
pocket. It was simple. All they had to do was get Caroline

to drink it under the full moon while standing on the grave of Rebecca. Cricket had texted that things were under control so far this evening, so hopefully that good luck would continue. They would send Rebecca to the next realm, Caroline would get her perfect wedding tomorrow, and Bash and Cricket would get to spend more time together once this wedding was done. Not that he begrudged Caroline. He just missed hanging out with Cricket.

"There you guys are!" Tony said, walking out of the bathroom. He was dressed in his regular attire: sports jersey, loosely fitting jeans, and sneakers. Several gold chains encircled his neck. "Your text didn't say much. What's goin' on?"

"Ghost business. We find ourselves in a situation. Thought it best to bring you in on it. Are you up for that?" asked Bash.

"I don't know guys. It's my night off. Plus, what could be so scary that the two of you can't handle it yourself?" Tony took a sip of his beer.

"What do you have to lose? It's just down the street. You don't have anything better to do, and you'll walk away with a firsthand account to tell your tours going forward," reasoned Ryan.

"Without telling names," added Bash.

Tony took a moment to think. He looked at the two of them, and then back down to his beer. "Fine, I'll go, but only if you buy me another beer," he said as he waved the bartender over.

Ryan and Bash agreed, and ordered another round of drinks. Tony finished his beer quickly, and followed them out of the pub.

The crowds moved like a river, parting and splitting around the trio as they made their way through the maze of humanity. The buildings and stores lining the streets gave way to smaller, winding, cobbled pathways, shadowed by the tall trees that lined each side. After a few minutes of pushing through the throngs of people, the trees began to thin, and soon enough, the old graveyard stood before them. The gravestones were ancient, the grass unkempt, and an eerie silence hung in the air.

The moody sky threatened to unleash its pent-up fury, fast-moving dark clouds swirling ominously overhead. The air was thick with anticipation, a silence so heavy that it seemed to suffocate any sound that dared to disturb its unnatural calmness.

As Bash gazed up, his breath caught in his throat at the sight of the silvery full moon peeking out nearly at the apex of the sky. Its ethereal glow bathed the graveyard in an otherworldly light, casting long, haunting shadows across the moss-covered tombstones. It was a perfect night for their mission, yet the atmosphere held a chilling quality that sent a chill through his bones.

A gust of wind rustled the leaves of the nearby trees, adding an eerie soundtrack to the already unsettling scene. Tony, Ryan, and Bash stood together, their hushed breaths mingling with the cool night air.

The trio cautiously made their way through the graveyard, each step crunching on fallen leaves and twigs beneath their feet. The earth seemed to exhale a ghostly sigh as they approached Rebecca's grave, as if it knew what was about to unfold.

Bash took the potion from his pocket, feeling its smooth glass against his fingertips. The liquid inside shimmered under the moonlight, carrying untold secrets and promises of a world beyond their own. He exchanged a knowing glance with Ryan before turning his attention toward Tony.

"You haven't told me much. What are we doing here?" Tony asked as he looked around at the gravestones.

"We're on a mission," replied Bash, his voice a mixture of anticipation and fear.

Ryan pulled out a flashlight and shined it on one of the gravestones. "We need you to help us dig up this grave."

Tony's eyes widened, and he took a step back. "Are you guys insane?" he asked, his voice rising. The air grew still around them.

"We need to find something that's hidden in the coffin that is buried right here," said Bash.

Ryan shined a light into Tony's eyes. "Everyone's lives are at stake."

Tony shook his head. "I can't do this. I won't dig up a grave," he said firmly. "It's against my religion."

Ryan threw his arm around him. "Tony, buddy, don't tell me you're scared."

Tony shrugged Ryan's arm off of him. "Fine, but if the cops come, I'm out of here," he said reluctantly.

Bash and Ryan burst out laughing.

"You're one sick dude. You would dig up a grave? Shame!" teased Ryan.

"Assholes," Tony mumbled. "You better start talkin', or I'm out of here. I've got better things to do with my time than be punked by the likes of you."

"Sorry, sorry!" Bash wheezed between laughs.

The graveyard was still as a cemetery should be, quiet and reverent. Bash could feel the air around him become thicker and more oppressive, as if an unseen force was holding its breath, waiting for something to happen. The only sound was the wind rustling through the trees and an occasional hooting of an owl in the distance. The moonlight cast a pale glow on the night, creating long shadows that seemed to whisper secrets of the dead.

As if reading Bash's mind, Tony said, "The spirits are quiet tonight." His jaw was slack. "That's unusual in a graveyard under a full moon."

Bash nodded solemnly. "We'll fill you in."

CHAPTER 18

CRICKET

C ricket and the cousins all headed out the front doors of the restaurant. There was a rush of people outside, making it hard to spot Caroline and Michael. The group navigated their way through the throngs of people, past the brightly lit restaurants and bustling shops. They could hear music playing from the clubs and loud conversations from passersby.

"Where would you go if you wanted privacy?" asked Pricilla.

Cricket scanned up and down the street.

"And that oozes romance," added Audrey.

"Can Caroline climb a fence?" asked Cricket.

"I suppose, if she kicked off her heels. She does do yoga, Pilates, and runs most days," answered Kimberly.

Cricket rolled her eyes. "There's one place, the Spanish Square." It was a beautifully manicured garden enclosed by a decorative black iron fence. It was the perfect place for Caroline to steal a private moment with Michael. Cricket, Kimberly, Audrey, and Pricilla began to make their way through the throng. They could see a winding path that weaved between the buildings and shops, passing through alleys and dark streets until it finally opened to a large expanse of grass encased by an ornate tall black iron gate. As they ventured closer, the noise of the town faded away. It was a stunning garden of paradise. Lush green grass carpeted the ground, lined by flowering shrubs and trees that offered plenty of privacy. Small pathways wound through the garden, leading to quaint benches and hidden statues. Vibrant flowers filled every corner with color. The air was sweet and light, filled with the aromas of honeysuckle, jasmine, and roses. The crisp scent of freshly cut grass added a pleasant earthiness to the mix, while the fresh running water from the fountain created an almost ethereal atmosphere. They could see the faint outline of Caroline and Michael sitting on a bench at the center of the garden, bathed in moonlight. Caroline was leaned back against him, his arms wrapped around her in a tender embrace. They were deep in conversation, and it was clear that they were in their own world for the moment.

"I feel bad interrupting them," said Audrey. "It is the night before their wedding."

"She does look to be acting like herself," Cricket said.

Kimberly looked at her watch. "I'm sure Caroline would want us to. What's the alternative, let her continue to be host to a ghost that may ruin her wedding, not to mention her life?"

"Just for the record, if, God forbid, I ever get possessed, march my ass wherever it needs to go to rid me of it. Wedding or no. No hitchhikers in this temple." Pricilla waved a hand down the length of her body.

They all snickered.

"Oh no!" Cricket exclaimed.

They all looked over to Michael and Caroline. They could just make out their silhouettes on the bench through the limbs of the trees. Caroline's clothes were no longer a barrier between them, and Michael's hands were expertly exploring her body. Caroline's moans were barely audible from where they stood, but it was enough to make them all blush.

Suddenly, Caroline let out a loud moan, and the group watched on as she ripped Michael's shirt from his body. Cricket's face flushed as she turned around and averted her gaze.

"I think we should give them some privacy," Cricket whispered, feeling embarrassed.

"I can't wait. You're driving me crazy." Michael's pleas escaped over the iron fence.

Audrey chuckled. "Yeah, it looks like Caroline doesn't need our help at this exact minute," she said, burying her face in her hand.

Kimberly and Pricilla followed Cricket's lead and turned their back to the gate. Cricket continued to examine her shoes as Caroline's moans increased in volume. Clearly the couple was finding their momentum.

Michael's voice rang out above the street noise, "Oh god, just like that!"

"Nothing to see here, move along," Pricilla said loudly through bursts of laughter at the pedestrians streaming by.

"Smack my ass, bad boy. Smack it!" Caroline ordered.

"I'm dying, just dying," Cricket lamented.

The cousins cackled, doubled over in laughter.

Caroline's moans came louder and louder in the rhythm of thumping flesh. Their heavy breathing was clearly moving to a climax.

"Oh God, yes!" Caroline yelled. "Yes!"

Cricket couldn't believe how loud they were being. Their voices carried above the cars passing by and those talking as they walked by. She couldn't remember ever being this mortified.

Audrey broke first, "Oh, for crying out loud!"

Pricilla and Kimberly rolled on the ground laughing. "Stop, stop, I'm gonna pee my pants." Kimberly cackled.

Audrey wiped at the tears streaming down her face. Her manic laughter came out in staccato snorts. "Michael needs to hurry and get his happily ever after. The whole town knows Caroline already had hers."

Caroline let out another loud moan, and Cricket's face burned even hotter. She covered her face, eager to escape the sounds of her friend's lovemaking.

"Like you've never had sex outside!" exclaimed Pricilla.

All the girls stopped and stared at her, then fell into fits of laughter.

CHAPTER 19
BABS

Babs reached for her phone, intending to send a text message to Cricket. She felt overwhelmed by all the tasks she had to complete and knew she needed to prioritize.

Babs: You have to take my truck to deliver the cake, I can't make it in the morning.

Cricket: Are you kidding me?????

Babs: Can't explain, too crazy. Can't Bash help you?

Cricket: ......

Babs: Figure it out, you know where I keep the keys

Cricket: You better be at the wedding

Babs: No promises

Cricket: Be there!

"Oh my God, your sister is still just as needy as ever. Does she want you to pick up a pizza for her too?" Nadine kicked at the grass.

"Shut up, Nadine," Babs said. "She's your sister too."

Nadine let out a groan. "I was really hoping this night would be all about us!" she exclaimed through a pouty face. "I'm finally here, flesh and blood — not a projection spell. I can't tell you how exciting it is to be walking, actually walking, these paths."

The silver-tinged moonlight cast a faint glow through the dense forest, illuminated by the occasional rustle of branches in the night breeze. Slivers of light bounced off the trees as they made their way along the path. The chirping of crickets and haunting calls of owls filled the air, adding to the eerie atmosphere.

"They're going to have to face that I'm real, now that I've been assigned to live in the mortal world as your babysitter. Let's just find this stupid lost crown, get Dad here, and all be one big happy family."

"Can you please just stop!" Babs barked.

"Look, I get you had quite a large download today: winning your challenges, having a crown shoved on your head, your queen reneging on her promise — that had to be embarrassing, seeing Dad for the first time, your sister coming back into your life after you thought you had successfully killed her. Am I forgetting anything?"

Gwylm's growl vibrated the ground.

Babs paused and put her hands on her hips. "Why didn't you ever explain things to me? At any time, you could have told me the truth. Things could have been so different. Do I mean so little to you? Was I nothing more to you than an assignment?"

"You know better than that. We're sisters—" Nadine stared her down. The temperature around them dropped.

"You definitely didn't treat me like one." Babs's insides rumbled like a volcano about to erupt. "You're verbally abusive and manipulative. Don't for one minute think things are going back to the way they were. I will not tolerate—"

"Hey, catch up with what's going on, will ya? I shouldn't have to spell it out." She pinched Babs on the arm.

Babs slapped Nadine, throwing her back against a tree. Nadine stumbled to the ground, face full of fury. She launched herself forward and grabbed Babs's arm, twisting her around until they were on the ground rolling in a cloud of dirt. Kicks and punches flew back and forth like thunderbolts between them, as both tried to gain an upper hand. Gwylm circled around them, barking and growling wildly at the scene.

Finally choking on a breathless laugh, Babs looked up through her tousled hair, still grappling with Nadine's fingers latched onto hers. "You're right . . . you win," she managed finally. "We are sisters."

Nadine let out a huff as if releasing pent-up frustration that had simmered inside her for far too long. She tumbled aside into an exhausted heap against some mossy rocks, watching leaves scatter across their garments from nearby trees shaken by all that commotion. "That's what I said *all* along . . . you idiot!" A smile started forming at the corners of her mouth but was gone before it completed itself fully. Silence settled, lifting only when Gwylm crept his way slowly in between them, cautiously placing himself snugly within their embrace so each girl could feel the calming rhythm of his breath.

"I'll take that as an apology for tearing me apart," Nadine said to Gwylm. "Let's be civil now, shall we?"

Silence enveloped the wooded grove as the sisters petted the giant wolf.

Nadine's voice took on a dreamlike cadence. "I was stolen at birth by the winter court. It could have just as easily been you, and I could've been raised all comfy with Mama and had sisters that loved me, and the queen would have put a crown upon my head. But no, I was pulled from our crib, raised without a mother, and had the privilege of witnessing your cushy happy life while none of them missed me." She continued to stroke at Gwylm's pelt. It was as if he were pulling her feelings out of her in a way that was unnatural to her. "I had Dad, sort of. It was enough." She brushed at her cheeks with the cuff of her sleeve.

It had never entered Babs's mind. Could she have endured Nadine's fate? How different of a person would she be if fortune had switched their places. Her hands began to tremble as a new wave of emotions crashed over her. "They don't know you're alive, any of them."

Nadine's shoulders drooped. "I know. The glamour was complete. That doesn't mean it didn't hurt. And you—you had this beast tear me apart. You were my only tie to home."

Gwylm sneezed at her.

"I was led to believe you were—"

"You were led to believe what your summer queen wanted you to believe. How can you stand her?" Nadine rolled her eyes.

Babs looked to her hands as she crumbled a fistful of dried leaves.

Nadine continued. "You can't defend her after that stunt she pulled in the hall. She's the reason our family is in this mess. She has lost control of herself."

Over the past year, Babs had only small interactions with the queen. Her first encounter was so awe-inspiring.

But now, with what just happened . . . She reached up and touched her fangs. It was hard to reconcile how she had always seen the queen with what she experienced today.

"She stole the winter crown to begin with. Then she lost it, or so she says. Most think she hid it away or traded it, and can't get it back."

"How do you know it was her?"

"I've heard the rumors. Many were present when she ripped the crown from Princess Liande's head."

Babs's head reeled. "That can't be."

"Oh, yeah, *that* Liande. You really know *nothing*." She smirked. "Liande bore the summer king's child. You've met him, Ambrosias."

"What?"

"After hearing of the child's birth, Sabella traveled the portal, went into a rage within the walls of the winter court, ripped the crown from Liande's head, and proclaimed a curse upon her, and all that come from her. What came next is unclear, although it became clear to me that all of summer believes Sabella is Ambrosias's mother, including Ambrosias! That's quite a spell she has going!"

"Why wouldn't Liande go after her crown, regain her power, and rule with her son?"

"After a ruler loses their crown, they can never touch it again."

Babs thought of the deal she saw Liande make with the winter king. She thought better of sharing the information with Nadine. There was too much information to sift through. Court espionage would have to wait. All that mattered to Babs was getting her father back. She needed to block out everything else and focus on finding the crown.

"Why hasn't anyone found it?"

Nadine ran her fingers along the edges of a crystal that she pulled from her pocket. "Here." She laid her hand upon the stone, and an image sprung above, of eight crowns. "Any of this look familiar?"

Babs inspected the image. She pointed at one of the crowns. "That one is mine." She reached up and touched the warm metal. "And that one graces the summer queen."

"Yes, the eight crowns belong to the royals of the two courts. When a new royal ascends the throne and is crowned, the power of all the rulers that wore that crown before, transfers to them. All the power, back to the beginning of time flows through them. They are the new conduit for them all. It's ancient magic."

Babs squinted at the translucent image of the crowns. "Are they made out of, what, antler?"

"No, they are made of the bones of the original king and queen that brought our realm into being. Each gilded in precious metal forged at the beginning of our age. There are only a few rulers, like Liande, that had their crown pulled from them. Her magic is divided between her and the crown. By the looks of her, I would say the crown took most of her power."

Babs reached up and touched her crown. "Ewww. It's bone?"

"Seriously? You doubly wield the bone magic yourself." She looked at Gwylm. "You claimed Gwylm's skull, then, using your powers, called the spirit forth, and he was reborn into this plane of existence."

"Anyone could—"

"How many familiars have you seen here?" Nadine kicked at the ground. "There are some, but I wouldn't say many, less than half the fae can call forth a familiar through bone magic." She pursed her lips. "Perhaps wielding that magic is what got you this." She touched Babs's crown. "Fancy pants."

She hadn't thought about that. She would have to ask Verity. "Do you think the crown was lost in the journey, or do you think someone has found it, and is wielding its power now?"

"I don't know who would dare wear the winter queen's crown. I would never claim it."

"Why's that?"

"The crown gives power but also drives the wearer mad. When the regent loses their mind entirely, it is up to the next in line to . . . take care of the situation."

"How is that done?"

"Kill the ruler, take the crown." Nadine waved her hand through the image and placed the crystal back in her pocket. "When the monarch is killed and the crown taken, that ruler's power is transferred into the crown and given to the one who sets it upon their head."

"So, the winter princess?"

"Winter is without one of its rulers till the crown is found."

"How does our family play into this?"

"You don't know the history of our own line?" Nadine smirked. "The Culebra house is a ruling line. Several of our ancient ones ruled in both courts."

"It can't be!"

"The madness of the Culebra rulers is legendary. Ruthless and wild. Our great-grandmother—"

"Stop talking, I will not learn my heritage from the likes of you."

Nadine rolled her eyes. "Very well, stay in the dark. It's

not important to our cause. But our family's recent history, you *must* learn."

"Fine, be quick about it. I want to get this done and over with."

"At our mother's birth, it was expected that she would be the next ruler, but our grandmother dared to fight fate by leaving the court. She feared an ancient telling that sister would go against sister. She refused to let that be the fate of her daughters. Then Mama gave up her powers when she bonded with Father. So diminished were her powers, she was unable to find or retrieve the crown when the courts demanded it. It was viewed as a betrayal to her people. Therefore, that which she loved was taken."

"Father."

"Yes, Father. Now that you are in *your* powers, the stalemate is over."

"You think I can find it?"

"No, I know *we* can find it."

Babs's phone chirped. "Ah, we can find it after the wedding."

"Oh! The wedding." A smile enveloped Nadine's face. "We get to dress up! I get first dibs at your closet!"

CHAPTER 20

BASH

The night sky was filled with the scent of fresh pine and earth, the sweet aroma of spring flowers, and the faint smell of smoke on the breeze. The warm, moist wind blew against Bash's face as he looked up at the full moon. Its pale blue light illuminated the cemetery, casting a ghostly glow on all the tombstones that seemed to stretch on for eternity.

It would have been peaceful had it not been for Tony's incessant yammering about random factoids presented on the social media pages he followed.

Bash wondered how much of human intelligence was being stunted by the introduction of social media. People once read books. Now many were barely able to read a whole tweet.

"Hey, why the sour face, man?" Ryan interrupted his thoughts. "Cricket will be here soon. Stop worrying." He took another hit of his vape.

"Ah, I'm just in a bad mood. Don't mind me. The lack of sleep is catching up with me. How are you still going strong?"

His smile widened. "You had a second beer at the bar. I switched to Red Bull."

"Smart."

"Never touch the stuff," chimed Tony, rubbing at the back of his neck. "Bad for the mojo, if ya know what I mean."

As if on cue, Bash could make out Cricket and one of the cousins each hooking an arm around Caroline, trying to pull her forward as they staggered down the sidewalk and into the cemetery. It looked like Caroline was half-asleep, maybe drunk?

Bash quickly closed the distance and came to a stop in front of the girls. "What's happened? Is she okay?"

"Calming spell. It was the easiest way to get her here. Don't you agree, Kimberly?"

"By far. I would say our girl here is just fine. Having a good old time tonight." Kimberly laughed.

Bash leaned into Cricket and whispered into her ear, "Does Kimberly know you're fae?"

"Not exactly. She's simply open to possibilities." Cricket raised her voice to include Kimberly in the conversation. "You don't need to be shy in front of her. She's no stranger to ghosts, and she finds them . . . interesting."

Bash nodded.

"Yeah, nothing freaks me out. It's cool." Kimberly shifted her arm around Caroline.

Cricket gazed up at the moon. "Did we make it in time?"

"Yes, we have plenty of time." Bash followed her gaze up to the moon, though it was barely visible through the thick grey clouds that traveled fast across the hazy bleak sky. He liked to keep track of its phases as it went from new to full and back again, like watching an old friend make a journey. He thought about what the entity had said to him about the moon being the energy source for the potion to help move Rebecca on to the next realm.

The group made their way to the corner of the graveyard where Rebecca's grave rested. Tony stood with his hands in the pockets of his loosely fitting jeans and his elbows propped against the stone wall that protected Rebecca's resting place. Three tall stone markers, arranged like standing stones in a row next to a short stump, formed an informal boundary near Rebecca's grave, separating it slightly from the rest of the tombstones. Ryan leaned against one of them, his head turned toward the others, but his attention focused on the ground at his feet.

"Possession." Tony tsked. "Nasty business."

"Have you encountered it before?" asked Cricket.

"Oh yeah, lots of times," he bragged. "Comes with the territory, you see."

"It doesn't have to," murmured Bash.

"Oh, so you were planning on your friend here to run into this trouble," Tony goaded.

"Of course not!" Ryan jumped in between Tony and Bash. "Let's just focus. No need to fuss."

Kimberly's eyes went wide. She turned to look at her cousin. Caroline's long hair flowed down her back and tumbled over her shoulders. Her head was tilted back, and her eyes were closed. "This is really going to work, right?"

Bash answered, "Let's get her to the grave and find out." Cricket and Bash exchanged glances. "I think we should lay her down, right on top of the grave." The stress had taken its toll on him, making him feel much older than his actual age. His eyes burned and felt irritated from the lack of sleep.

Kimberly's brow furrowed, and she shook her head. "Do you think your chill spell will continue to work? Caroline seemed in control for most of the night." She smiled. "Especially the second half."

They lowered her gently to the ground. Caroline's skin glowed an ethereal light blue in the moonlight, like moonbeams in water under a lake. Her lips were dark crimson in the shadow. Her calm features were impassive, like those of a sleeping child. The grass around her lay thick and green as ivy vines made a soft nest around her body. Like a burial shroud, tiny white lilies of the valleys rustled in the gentle breeze around her.

As if Rebecca's spirit was activated by the setting, Caroline's form slowly began to levitate. The group watched from below as Rebecca's spirit seemed to take hold of Caroline's body. The air turned cold.

Tony's eyes widened, and he stepped backward in shock. She hung there motionless, a few feet above Rebecca's grave. "That's not something you see every day!"

"I figured Rebecca would fight," Cricket replied. Her face was serious as she spoke, her eyes determined and her mouth set in a firm line. She stood resolutely, her back straight and her arms crossed in front of her chest.

"Yeah, Rebecca seems to like to take Caroline for a ride. At least she seems peaceful." Kimberly put both fists on her hips. "How are we getting our girl down? We don't have a carriage this time."

Cricket moved forward, her eyes glowing with knowledge and power. "I've got this." She focused her energy on the hovering form of Caroline, and chanted a magical spell in a low voice to gently bring Caroline's body back to the ground. Tiny sparks of light flickered around Caroline's prone figure as Cricket completed her chant. Slowly, like a feather caught in a gentle breeze, Caroline's body drifted down to the earth and came to rest lightly just in front of Rebecca's headstone. Cricket raised her hands to the sky, summoning the energy of the stars.

Bash moved quickly to Cricket's side and grasped her hand in his. "Use my strength if you need it," he said.

"And us!" Kimberly grabbed Tony's hand. They formed a circle of five around Caroline's figure.

Cricket nodded as she closed her eyes and held out her hands. A wave of stardust seemed to pour from the heavens and blanket Caroline's form, temporarily holding her to the earth so Bash could give Caroline the potion.

A shimmering light draped around Caroline like a protective cloak, and Bash looked up at Cricket. "Well done," he whispered.

"You're up." Cricket winked at Bash.

He smiled at her, then turned his attention to Caroline. "Rebecca, can you hear me?"

Caroline's eyes fluttered open and looked directly at Bash with a mixture of confusion and understanding. "Why did you bring me back here?" she asked. "I want to live! I don't want to die!"

Bash moved closer to her. "You are here with us, Rebecca, but you shouldn't be. We want to help you cross over."

"You must let go of Caroline. She deserves to have her own life," Kimberly urged.

Bash continued to speak, his words filled with compassion as he implored her, "I have a potion for you to take. It will help you pass to the after lands. You will be filled with peace and granted total freedom from this world into the next."

Cricket interjected. "You will have a better life beyond this one—where you can explore all that you were denied in life—love, experiences, knowledge—things everyone deserves."

"I want my husband!" Rebecca wailed.

"That's what I'm here for, doll." Tony broke from the circle. "Take my hand, cutie. I need to touch your ring. I'm going to summon your Prince Charming to help escort you to your happily ever after."

"You can summon spirits by touching things?" Cricket asked.

"Yeah." He shrugged. "My mediumship is tied to psychometry," Tony said, as if anyone could do it.

Cricket's eyebrows shot up. "Tony, let's talk later."

"As long as you're buying the beer, we can talk all you want, sweetheart."

Rebecca shuttered, and all eyes went back to her. "Take this." Bash reached into his pocket and withdrew a small vial containing the glowing liquid that promised to cross her over.

"Take the potion, Rebecca," Bash said softly. "It's your only way out. There's nothing here for you. Caroline's life is her own. You deserve a life of love in the after realm, one free of earthly disappointments and sorrow."

Rebecca looked down at the vial with fear in her eyes. "I'm scared. I've been alone in the dark for so long."

"You'll be safe," Kimberly said reassuringly as she moved toward Caroline. "Take this chance to find your peace and go where you can have freedom from all that weighs on your heart."

Caroline nodded slowly before reaching out her hand; Bash grasped it gently and guided it toward the bottle so she could grasp it for herself.

"Albert is coming?" Rebecca's voice was filled with panic.

"Workin' on it, kid," said Tony. "Bash, ya want to hurry up with that potion. If you have a cheat on tearing back the veil, now's the time. Once it's open, I can summon her Albert."

"Rebecca," Bash said softly, "this is your chance . . . Take this potion so you can have eternity with your love."

She took a deep breath before raising it to her lips and gulping down its contents in one swallow.

Moonbeams gently illuminated the graveyard, a soft white light filled the space, and the subtle sound of church bells chimed far in the distance. Caroline closed her eyes and let out an audible sigh of relief as her body relaxed.

Tony held fast to her hand, pouring all his intention into the wedding ring. His lips moved, and Bash could just make out that he was saying "Albert" over and over.

The swirling, starry blackness that marked the threshold between life and death opened right above Caroline's prone body. The grey mist seeped out from the opening and began to call to all the spirits to come and pass through. The veil between life and death opened up wider and wider. With great speed it increased, pulling at all around it.

Spirits began to rise from the graves, their forms lit up with a starry luminescence. They swirled around the graveyard in shimmering circles of all sizes and colors. Each spirit answered the portal's call as they ascended and crossed through the opening in the veil toward the other side.

Tony held fast to Caroline's ringed hand. "Bash, this doesn't feel right. It's too much energy."

Rebecca rose out of Caroline's body, her eyes twinkling with unspeakable joy as Albert flew toward her, his arms open wide and his face filled with love.

"My bride." Albert's earnest voice held an unmistakable

tenderness as he spoke. The formerly bereaved couple embraced each other before joining hands.

"You came for me." Rebecca's smile radiated happiness. She finally had peace; she was now part of everlasting love beyond mortal boundaries. Above them, silver stars filled the sky as the clouds parted. The couple passed through the portal together in eternal bliss. As soon as they were gone, Caroline's body jolted awake, and Bash exhaled a sigh of relief—they had done it.

The vortex continued to expand its form above them, and the gust of buzzing energy steadily grew louder. The ringing bells from the church were clashing together in a chaotic dance of noise. The all-encompassing sound would surely crush them all if the sound continued to grow.

Caroline was perplexed. "What's happening here?" she queried. "Why are we in the cemetery?"

Kimberly and Cricket pulled Caroline off the gravesite and back against the gate. "Kimberly, take her out of the graveyard. Get as far away from here as possible." Cricket implored.

Kimberly nodded. "I'll text you when we get back to her apartment."

"I feel like I have been in and out of dreaming for an eternity!" Caroline declared.

"I'll fill you in, cousin. Let's get out of here and let them focus on this."

Bash watched through the iron gates as the girls made their way to safety. High-pitched notes rang out from the vortex and were sustained by a singular pitch, like a chorus of angels settling on one powerful note. The scent of bog and rot poured from the swirling spiral out into the air. Bash surveyed the graveyard. Things were out of control.

Ryan and Tony stepped back, not wishing to be pulled into the vortex as its power continued to grow.

The veil between life and death had opened up wide like an ocean, its size so large they could no longer see the edges. Spirits from faraway places convened around the portal, their stories told in mysterious languages that only the dead could understand. The portal seemed to whisper its secrets to the spirits as they passed through; it was inviting and devouring.

Bash's mouth opened in horror. "It's taking everyone! All of them!" He looked up to see the beautiful spirit of a little girl in a billowing white dress, with an ethereal glow surrounding her. He knew her to be the little ghost that stayed by the candy shop. He watched as she moved forward with the grace of a river. The locks of her silver-white hair glittered like stars, and her china doll complexion shone in the light of the moon. She stopped and waved at him with a gentle smile before floating away on the breeze.

"Oh, man!" Tony exclaimed. "The priests are leaving! What was that potion?"

Bash watched as the ghostly apparitions of several shrouded priests crossed the graveyard, illuminated by a white and silvery light. Their long robes flowed in the wind like veils of smoke, and each bore an ornate crucifix in their hands that glittered beneath the pale moonlight. He looked up, mesmerized, as they ascended into the swirling portal of stars beyond.

"How do we close the vortex?" asked Tony.

A horrifying sight met his gaze. Spirits from shipwrecks of long ago poured in from the direction of the sea, their faces grim. Dark shadows trailed them like bad dreams, reaching out to them with long fingers, only to retract and disappear into nothingness once again. These lost souls moved slowly toward the gate and disappeared into its illuminated depths. The veil between life and death had opened, offering an eternity of possibilities beyond this realm.

Bash gasped as his eyes landed on the eerie scene. Floating in front of him were a group of spirits, wearing ornate military uniforms that billowed in the wind, their faces aglow with a faint light. Each ghost held a rifle in one hand slung against their shoulder. The ethereal figures slowly crossed the graveyard, passing through ancient headstones and trees before finally reaching the portal and ascending to the heavens.

Tony called out, "It's taking everyone! All the spirits from the town, the sea, everyone! We have to close it! This isn't right!"

In a majestic burst of energy, all the spirits flew at once toward the gateway of eternity, their souls intertwined with each other until their passage through this world was complete.

"I'll try to close it." Cricket's face was as stone. The enormity of the vortex was vast.

She breathed deeply as she gathered her strength, released her air magic, and channeled the energy through her fingertips with force and determination. A brilliant light suddenly exploded from her open palms, glowing so brightly that it illuminated the entire graveyard. The power of Cricket's magic unleashed a powerful wind that moved across the portal like an invisible hand.

She then took flight up toward the heavens. Her wings battered against the warring energies. She called down a storm of lightning and hail that tore through the night sky, shooting stars trailing behind it. She gathered it all, and the air around them hummed with electricity as the power of her spell continued to push back the veil between life and death. It was growing smaller, yet still was open.

Cricket gathered her remaining energy and once again channeled it toward the portal. Fire, ice, and lightning mixed as they raced in the direction of the swirling vortex, impacting it like a thunderous wave. With one final burst of energy, the rift closed with an explosion of electric sparks that flickered out into the night sky. Mist rose up from the ground mingled with a few shimmering particles that danced between them like fireflies until only darkness remained . . . The graveyard was still then, illuminated only by the faint moonlight.

The immense spell left Cricket drained, and Bash hurried to help her stand. The vortex was completely closed, and the veil between life and death had been restored. Bash put his arm around Cricket's shoulders comfortingly, as they watched the last wisps of smoke disappear into nothingness. He was thankful for their safety and marveled at what they had witnessed.

He gazed at Cricket in the moonlight. She appeared older, her face looking tight and fatigued. He vowed to himself that he would never again put her in harm's way in such a manner.

This was all his doing. He should have done more research before giving Caroline an unknown potion. Now, he had to deal with the consequences. Whatever it took, he would fix it. Cricket and her family would remain totally uninvolved. The paranormal activity ceased, and an intense feeling of emptiness settled in Bash's heart.

"What have you done?" Tony sat dumbfounded. "They're all gone. All of them." Bash thought he saw tears forming in Tony's eyes. "How could you?" Tony asked.

CHAPTER 21

CRICKET

T he basilica gleamed in the afternoon light. It was decorated for the wedding, with white calla lilies adorned with silver bows accentuating each pew. A soft warm luminosity illuminated the red wooden ceiling, and streams of sunlight filtering in through the delicate stained glass windows giving the space an otherworldly glow. The scent of incense lingered in the air, and the choir's Gregorian chant echoed throughout, settling heavy in the space.

The center aisle was lined with tall bronze candelabras that sparkled in contrast to the ornate stone flooring. High up above on a platform was an altar surrounded by a ring of burning candles, and embroidered tapestries hanging from gilded walls.

A sense of reverence and awe hung over this hallowed place, as people gathered to witness two lives being joined together as one. Everyone seemed to recognize how special this moment was. Caroline and Michael's life would be forever divided between before and after this day.

Cricket stood with Caroline and her cousins at the back of the church, waiting for the music to cue them to proceed down the aisle. They could just glimpse all the guests patiently waiting.

Cricket's heart was pounding with a combination of excitement and nervousness. She was so proud to be there with Caroline, witnessing this monumental moment in her friend's life. She was so relieved that Caroline was back to herself. She said it felt like she had been sleepwalking the last few days, but now felt completely revived.

The groomsmen came out from a side room and took their places at the altar. They stood strong like steel pillars on the right side of the platform. Finally Michael arrived. Cricket couldn't help but gasp as she saw him enter in his smart tuxedo, looking handsome and dapper. Caroline took one look at him and beamed with joy.

Cricket, along with the other bridesmaids, surrounded Caroline.

"It's time. Are you ready?" Cricket asked.

"Any last-minute advice?" Caroline asked, shaking off her jitters.

"Yes!" whispered Kimberly. "Just relax, take a deep breath. This is the first day of the rest of your life. Walk in your full power. You look amazing."

Caroline smiled and brushed her hands down the sides of her gown. It was mermaid cut, with intricate embroidered lace, and delicate rhinestones and pearls, which glimmered under the light. She chose a simple veil that didn't cover her face, but draped down the back of her gown. Cricket couldn't help but notice that she looked like an angel at that moment.

Audrey added, "She's right, you look beautiful. Try to relish every minute of the ceremony. Just focus on Michael every step of the way! Nothing matters but the two of you."

Priscilla nodded in agreement. "Above all else, have fun and savor all your significant moments on your perfect day!"

Cricket stepped forward and wiped away an emotional tear from Caroline's face. She smiled as she spoke with all her heart. "I couldn't be prouder than I am right now to call you my friend."

The music swelled up, signaling it was time for their walk down the aisle. Caroline smiled widely and relished this moment of anticipation before she stepped out into the aisle to meet Michael.

Together, the women held hands tightly during this last private moment. They lined up, then began to make their way down the aisle.

As Caroline neared the end of the aisle, she glanced back at her parents proudly beaming up at her from their seat at front row center. Cricket could see Caroline's heart swell with love. Her face radiated joy.

Cricket's eyes drifted to her mom, Gran, and sisters. She imagined a day like this for herself one day. She was so thankful for the love and support of her family throughout her life. Feeling gratitude for her own existence filled her with warmth. Her lineage was magical, something that she had found hard to accept in the past, but now embraced with wholeheartedness. Habina's return as mentor had made such a difference, while opening up to Bash had been life-changing. Cricket smiled contentedly.

Caroline finally reached Michael's side. He grasped her hand tightly, conveying his heart's true emotion without words.

The priest stepped forward, his voice melodious and comforting. His white robe was decorated with beautiful floral embroidery that shimmered in the light. He looked up at Caroline and Michael with a humorous twinkle in his eye, as if he knew this was not just any ordinary wedding ceremony — it was a mystical union of two people meant to be together for a lifetime.

"Welcome, dear friends. We are here today to witness the joining of this blessed couple in marriage. As you stand here together, I remind you that love is not a feeling, but an action. Love is about trust and loyalty — honoring your commitment even when times are tough." The priest paused for dramatic effect before continuing on with a smile.

As Michael and Caroline said their vows, Cricket couldn't keep the tears from spilling from her eyes — tears of joy for such a beautiful union of two souls destined for each other in this life and beyond.

The priest announced it was time to exchange rings. "The exchanging of rings signifies an eternal bond between two people," he said. "These sacred symbols represent infinite love, lifelong commitment, and the exchange of energy that will bind you together in harmony and mutual respect. And just as your hands will now be connected by these rings, let it be a reminder of your connection at all times — even when apart."

Cricket stepped forward, a white silk scarf draped in her hands — Michael's platinum wedding ring tied securely to its ends. She held the fabric gently. Caroline cradled one hand over the top of the scarf while gently lifting up the other corner, releasing his ring into the palm of her hand. The ring glimmered from within, like stars in the midnight sky — a symbol of hope for a future filled with love and togetherness.

Robert, the best man, stepped forward to his position next to Michael but reached into his pocket, only to find that he had no ring! Frantically he searched all the pockets of his suit—including those in his shirt—before looking up embarrassed at everyone present, declaring that he knew he had it before they left for the ceremony this morning! Murmurs from the attendees echoed off the walls of the church. Cricket's eyes landed on her gran.

Gran stood up slowly. She had been silent this entire time, just watching the ceremony with a stillness and reverence that rarely left her. Her grey hair was pulled back into a tight bun, and her eyes were bright—full of life and love.

She began to walk down the center aisle toward Robert, clutching something small in her hands. She reached the front of the church, where the wedding party was standing. Robert's head hung low in embarrassment as everyone watched with bated breath. Gran smiled at him before holding out her hand, revealing a beautiful antique gold ring with intricate scrolling along its edges framing a single solitaire diamond. She passed it to him without saying anything, her eyes glued to Caroline's. Cricket sensed an energy emanating from Gran's gaze that calmed the whole crowd.

Gran turned toward Michael and Caroline and said, "Sometimes items get lost when they are needed elsewhere, and new items come to take their place. Isn't that right, Father?"

"Indeed, the Lord giveth and the Lord taketh."

The sanctuary was silent for a moment before someone whispered "Amen" from the back of the church.

Leaning forward, Gran kissed Caroline and Michael both on their cheeks, blessing them on their journey together.

Michael took the ring thankfully and placed it on Caroline's finger with trembling hands. Tears brimmed from both sets of eyes as they shared a knowing smile.

After exchanging rings, the couple embraced in a long, heartfelt kiss amidst thunderous applause from all those gathered to witness this special occasion.

Cricket smiled, relieved that levity had been restored during what was supposed to be such a solemn moment.

The bridal party began to make their way out of the church. Caroline and Michael held hands tightly as they stepped over the threshold.

The music swelled as they stepped onto the cobblestone walkway — Cricket thought it sounded like it was from the Nutcracker Suite. The church orchestra played with grandeur and vigor as the guests followed the happy couple in joyous celebration. The air was filled with hope, love, and togetherness.

Bash and Ryan had slipped out early to ready the horse-drawn carriage.

Caroline and Michael stepped into the beautifully decorated carriage, drawn by a pair of white horses.

Bash had gone all out decorating the carriage. It was adorned with a "Just Married" sign attached to the back and trailed streamers and white lights. It glowed in the twilight like a sparkling star, ready to transport them into this new chapter of their lives. As they began to pull away, people waved their goodbyes, bubbles filling the sky, drifting away — sending them to the reception in style.

The crowd watched on as Caroline and Michael settled into the plush velvet seats.

Bash called out "Ready?" and without waiting for an answer, flicked the reins as they set off toward the Bridge of Lions. Their journey had only just begun, but already it seemed to stretch out infinitely before them.

Cricket stood in the doorway of the church, still in a state of awe from witnessing the ceremony. She felt a humbling privilege to have been a part of Caroline and Michael's special moment. She couldn't hold back the tears streaming down her face.

It was then that Cricket noticed Gran in the crowd — standing at the edge. She seemed to be waiting for everyone else to leave so she could slip away unnoticed. Not wanting her Gran to leave without saying goodbye, Cricket rushed toward her, pushing through the throng of guests.

Finally — with excitement dancing in her eyes — Cricket reached out and hugged Gran tightly and asked, "Gran — how did you know Caroline's ring would go missing? Where did you find that beautiful ring to replace it?"

Gran smiled and said, "I have seen many weddings in my years. I've come to learn that things always work out the way they should, even when it doesn't seem that way. I knew this ring was meant for Caroline and Michael, before you even told me there were issues. I held on to it till the opportune moment. Everything happens as it's supposed to — we have to be patient and trust in the process." She winked at Cricket and added one more thing before letting go of her hand.

"Remember: sometimes, what seems like an ending is actually a new beginning." With that, she turned and slipped away. Cricket was left alone with her thoughts swirling around in her head.

The crowd of guests thinned out, filed into their cars, and followed behind the wedding couple. They created a gorgeous procession that sparkled in the late afternoon sunshine as it snaked over the bridge, through Anastasia Island, and to the beach. Whispers filled the air as passersby marveled at the breathtaking beauty before the progression faded from sight.

CHAPTER 22

BABS

Babs looked on in confusion as Zadie, her sister, covered one eye with her hand while her other eye rapidly blinked. For the past few months, she had been away on an underwater archeological expedition with her boyfriend, Tom. She covered her other eye and frowned. "Something's wrong with my eyes," she pouted. "I might be having a stroke." She patted down her head, messing up her French twist, and put her hands over her bosom that pushed against her green sequin dress. "Or a heart attack. Oh my God, I'm having a heart attack. She set her glass of champagne down on the nearest tall table. The guests around them were completely oblivious to Zadie's health scare. They were all too busy enjoying the tasteful buffet and relaxed atmosphere. She kicked off her green sandals. "Get Mama!" she called out in a shrill voice, a complete juxtaposition to the calm, elegant reception. Jazz music emanating from a mini stage nearby carried throughout the area. Crisp white linen draped each table along with flickering candles adding subtle lighting scattered across various nooks within different sections of ground they rented out for this event—mixing modern contemporary decorations while maintaining its natural elements in between palm trees and driftwood logs. Babs appreciated the unique aesthetic. All the details crafted together meshed seamlessly. Time momentarily stopped as evening overtook the day and the sunset-filled sky transformed to indigo, bringing forth endless stars to illuminate the celebration.

"I'm dying!" Zadie screeched.

Babs rolled her eyes. "What are you going on about?" She brushed her sweaty palms down her sides. The gold chiffon dress she was wearing had a deep V-neckline that showed off her slender neck and accentuated her curves as it cascaded softly against her skin like waves of liquid metal. The intricate beading around the waist spotlighted Babs's frame, while still allowing enough room to move with ease. Her strappy sandals were an ode to comfort, but spoke of luxury—all tied together by gold statement hoop earrings which glowed in the candlelight. Wearing a fancy dress felt foreign to her; the wedding reception was a stark contrast to the life she had been living. It was unsettling to see everyone acting like things were still normal, while her own life had taken an unexpected and bizarre turn.

"I'm not sure. My eyes aren't working right. You are fuzzy! When I see you out of the corner of my eye, I see something different. Then I look right at you and"—she frowned—"and a blurry blur! I keep seeing a blurry spot out of the corner of my eye! I don't know, something's off. Maybe I have the bends. But Mer don't get the bends!"

"You're fine. Nothing's wrong with you." If anyone would see through her glamour, it would be Zadie. It wasn't like she could show up to the wedding as herself. Her fangs were hidden away while a translucent glow enveloped her head to conceal the ancient crown that had been bestowed upon her. Apparently, once crowned, the relic wasn't to leave your head.

Despite the warning that the crown would drive her to insanity, she couldn't help but think that she was already teetering on the brink of madness. The sight of her dad as a prisoner had her head reeling.

Attending this wedding was the last thing she wanted to do. However, it could be the last normal human event she took part in. She reached up and touched the crown on her head. With a wave of concentration, she focused her energy and pushed at the glamour, willing it to become stronger.

"You'll get better at it as you go." Nadine's voice entered her mind. *"Look how good I am at it. No one here can even see me."* Babs's stomach rolled. That was something else she was going to have to deal with, introducing Nadine to the family.

She sent her thoughts back to Nadine. *"Zadie is sensing you, so work on that. You insisted on coming. At least stay silent."*

"Oh, I'll stay silent, sis. Only you can hear my thoughts. But I'm not leaving your side till we succeed, Princess."

Babs felt her cheeks flush.

"Zadie, look at me now. Has your sight improved?"

She cocked her head to one side and shut one eye. Then she looked away quickly and back.

"Maybe?"

"It's been a long day. Wanna do shots? There's a bottle of tequila on that table over there; I can nab it for us. We can stroll along the shore and split the bottle. It'll give everyone else time to get the party going."

"Who are you and what did you do with my sister?" Zadie laughed.

Babs grabbed the unopened bottle, and they walked to the edge of the crashing waves.

"It's a big day. I passed my challenges, Cricket's friend got married, you're back — it's a day worthy of pause and remembrance."

She took a swig and handed the bottle to Zadie. "Truth or dare?"

Zadie jumped up and down, a large grin dominating her face. "Truth! Truth!" She took a big swig.

Babs looked out over the ocean. The waves rhythmically and ceaselessly came in. She felt a twinge of melancholy as she realized life was about to change for her and her sisters, that the odds were stacked against them. Most likely they would be torn apart from each other. But then she had a glimmer of a vision of them all together on this beach somewhere down the line or maybe even on another beach at some far-off place, knowing their bond would remain unbroken forever no matter what obstacles lay ahead. Smiling sadly, Babs embraced Zadie tightly. She thought about Zadie and her life, living on the ship with *Yara* and *Dulcinea*, and the fact that she had been with Tom for a few years now. That took guts to hand someone your heart when you knew that it would end.

"Tom?"

Zadie laughed and brushed a strand of hair out of her face. "Is that a full question?"

"Yes, tell me about Tom. We're at a wedding, walking on the beach under the stars, splitting a bottle of tequila. Tell me your truth about Tom."

"You want to know my heart?" Zadie stood still, letting the sand pull at her feet. All merriment left her face, a rare occurrence. She placed a hand on her chest, opened her mouth, and began to sing. Her Mer song wailed across the crashing waves, lyrical and sorrowful as she sang of loves long gone, and pains so deep that they changed one forever, of loves that lingered. As Zadie sang her mournful song, Babs's eyes filled with tears — encompassing every emotion felt within each word sung until at last her grief turned into hope for what may still come.

A gust whipped up around them, softly blowing both their hair against their cheeks, as if nature itself were attempting to wipe away those tears while enveloping both sisters' hearts with its soft embrace. Zadie stopped, looking out toward the sea, her body leaning in as if being pulled. Then she looked back at her sister, face tear streaked, smiling.

Babs squeezed her hand. "Oh, so that's how it is, is it?"

CHAPTER 23
BASH

Bash leaned against a palm tree that was bedecked with twinkling white lights. He viewed the many circular tables with white linen draped over them that were adorned with tall silver vases filled with ornate flower arrangements. Breezy white linen tents sat clustered in groups all up and down the beach, providing resting areas for guests. Lounge chairs, candlelit lanterns, and table upon table filled with gourmet finger foods were scattered about. The upbeat band played tunes everyone recognized as people danced with their shoes kicked off, enjoying the sand on their bare feet.

Bash felt a sudden wave of sadness wash over him as he looked around at all the people enjoying Caroline's wedding reception. He thought of Cricket—her infectious smile, her wit, her intelligence—all the little things that made his heart ache, knowing what he needed to do. He glanced over and watched her laughing and dancing with the other bridesmaids.

He felt a pang of melancholy as he observed how radiant she looked with the glow of the twilight reflecting in her eyes. His heart ached within him as he thought over the past year how happy he had been with her. They laughed and joked together. She was so easy to be with. She understood how it felt to be different, and she embraced that side of him. He didn't have to pretend. Until Cricket, Ryan was the only other person that he could be that open with.

He watched on as Michael and Caroline took the center of the makeshift dance floor and began performing a wonderfully choreographed waltz. Everyone clapped at the end, watching them twirl about expertly under the night sky.

"Hey there, buddy. What are you doin' hanging back? Not a dancer?" Robert strode up to Bash and handed him a craft beer. "If not a dancer, at least be a drinker!"

Bash smiled. They clinked beer bottles together. "I wish I could dance, but it just wasn't in the cards."

"Same with me. I just stick to drinking and watching," he joked. He glanced back at Caroline and Michael. "It should be criminal for a couple to be that happy."

"Is that your professional opinion, counselor?" Bash smiled as he watched Michael and Caroline twirling around each other. Even though the sadness was still there, something inside Bash shifted slightly, and he felt a little more hopeful. "Your buddy Michael really won the lottery with Caroline. She'll keep him on his toes."

"Oh, I don't doubt that for a minute." Robert chuckled. "I hope they enjoy New Orleans. Lots of change all at once, ya know."

For the first time since he'd arrived at the reception, Bash allowed himself to relax just a little bit. "Caroline seems really excited about it. And I heard that her cousin Kimberly is thinking about moving out there."

"Really? Which one is she?"

"I would say the one in the pink, but they all are in pink." Bash grinned.

"Blush," Robert corrected. "These things matter."

Bash pointed. "That's her right there."

"Good for her!" He tipped his beer back and finished what was left. "I think I'll ask her to dance before I have another." He shook his empty bottle at Bash.

"I thought you didn't dance."

"Hey, for the right girl, I'm willing to make an ass of myself."

"Good talking to you, man. I'll catch up with you later."

"I'm sure. It's gonna be a long night."

Bash watched Robert weave through the crowd, making his way slowly toward Kimberly. They talked for a little while before he took Kimberly in his arms for a slow dance. As they moved closer together, Bash couldn't help but notice the way she looked up at him with joy and merriment. It was clear that they both were having a great time. The twilight seemed to give the evening an ethereal glow, and Bash admired the beauty of it all.

It was inevitable that Cricket would find someone else who could make her happy like that too. That would be for the best. His heart ached for just a moment as he watched Robert spin Kimberly around the dance floor gracefully.

He finally walked over toward Cricket, who had stopped dancing and made her way over to one of the tent areas filled with pillows and blankets. She curled up into a seat in the corner, and Bash sat beside her just listening to the waves crash against the shoreline, while everyone else continued to celebrate around them.

"There you are." She smiled at him. "Are you not feeling well? You haven't come out to dance at all tonight."

He reached for her hand, savoring the feeling. Their hands fit perfectly together. He ran his thumb across the top of her delicate, soft hand.

She adjusted her posture, sitting up straight. Her skin was still warm and flushed from dancing. She leaned in closer to him, and he caught a whiff of her sweet perfume blending with the salty ocean breeze.

"What is it?" she asked, her eyebrows knit together.

"Nothing, we can talk later. It's not a topic for tonight." He leaned back away from her. "Let's enjoy the reception."

"Oh no you don't, mister. Tell me what's going on."

"I don't want to ruin the evening. Tonight should only be about Caroline."

"Caroline has you to thank for this night. If you hadn't given her the potion and freed her from Rebecca, tonight wouldn't have been possible. The wedding couldn't have gone on."

He stood up and ran his fingers through his hair. "At what cost?" he said louder than he had meant to. "Sorry, I just— I screwed up. I didn't know who, or what, gave me the potion. I was so focused on Caroline, my vision was so narrowed, I didn't see the bigger picture."

"What are you talking about? What are you saying?" Cricket's eyes were wide, filled with worry.

"All, *all* of the spirits are gone. That portal sucked up every last one of them." Bash looked up and down the beach. "They're all gone, and it's my fault!"

"Okay, I see." Cricket fidgeted with her necklace. "I was so relieved that Caroline was okay, I went right into maid of honor mode and just checked the Rebecca thing off my checklist. I didn't think about what happened or what it could mean. I'm sorry."

"Cricket, you have nothing to be sorry about. This isn't on you; it's on me. As of yet, I'm unsure of the extent of the damage I have caused."

"What do you mean? The event is over. What else could be wrong?"

"Well, for one, I have no idea what was in that potion. Caroline seems fine. But what if it has lingering or long-term side effects? What if it slowly kills her? All I was told about it was that it wasn't made from things that are in our realm."

"Bash, I think you are overreacting—"

His speech was staccato and reached a high pitch. "And why did this Liande give me a potion in the first place? She said she had seen me, watched me. What is that supposed to mean?"

"I'm not sure, but I know that we can figure it out"—she reached her arms out to him—"together."

"No, that's not going to happen." He stepped back away from Cricket, hitting his head on the tent. "We need to go our separate ways." He felt his jaws clench as he folded his arms across his chest. He was resolved. His heart was like iron.

"Are you—" Cricket stammered. "Are you breaking up with me?"

"It's the only way. I need time to figure things out. I need to work on myself."

"Bash, be reasonable."

"There's so much I don't know. I need to get away and take some time."

"You're breaking up with me, at a wedding?" Her mouth went slack.

"I can't continue to blunder my way through this. Someone is going to get hurt, and it will be utterly my fault."

"One of our best friends' wedding?"

"I think I'll see if Ryan can get away. Maybe get a cabin in Georgia and take the bikes."

"Are you serious right now?"

Zadie popped her head in the tent, her slender arm propped on her waist. "Hey, we heard raised voices. What seems to be the problem?" Babs dipped in right behind her.

"Oh, you want to know what's going on? Bash, my sisters want to know what's going on. Are you going to tell them, or should I?" Cricket had both of her hands on her hips, her legs planted firmly apart, her stance combative.

Zadie and Babs looked at Cricket, then glanced quickly at Bash.

Babs grabbed Zadie's arm. "Looks like this is a private conversation that doesn't require four people."

"Oh, I want to stay!" Zadie slurred.

"Nope, not gonna happen," Babs declared with a fierce glare. "Sis, we will wait for you by the champagne table." She gave Bash a leveling stare. "It's within earshot." She dragged Zadie out of the tent.

Bash shook his head. "Look, I'm sorry this is happening at a wedding, Caroline's wedding. But the truth is, as incredible as this past year has been, and as much as I love being with you—really love being with you. The fact is, I'm not ready. I'm sorry." He shrugged.

She started pacing in a tight circle.

"Say something," he pleaded. "Say you understand."

She scowled at him and walked out of the tent to join her sisters at the champagne table. He watched as Babs handed her a flute filled with bubbly liquid. Zadie embraced her, and the two swayed together. As he stepped out of the tent, Babs locked eyes with him. With a grimace dominating her face, she paused and softened, lowered her head and gave him a slow nod as she wrapped her arms around her sisters.

CHAPTER 24

BABS

Babs and Zadie flanked Cricket on Mama's backyard swing. Tikaboo covered every inch of Cricket's lap and part of Zadie's. They were all wearing snuggly pajamas, their hair thrown up in messy ponytails, and cuddled under their own favorite fluffy blankets. The most wonderful aroma filled the backyard from several lit candles which cast a warm, gentle light around them. Soft jazz music played from Cricket's phone, creating a soothing atmosphere. They each had their own pint of ice cream and unceremoniously wolfed it down as they chatted.

"What exactly did Bash expect to find in Georgia? Does he think all the ghosts flew away to the mountains?" Cricket asked in between rabid bites of ice cream. She expressed her opinion that he was being irrational. She thought that he just needed a few days to think. "And how could he possibly think breaking up with me at the reception was acceptable?"

Babs listened intently without saying much, her mind reeling from other pressing matters.

Zadie just finished off her ice cream and burped contentedly before interjecting, "Well I'm just glad you two are able to express your feelings honestly — even if it's not going how you planned," she said sagely, glancing between both Cricket and Babs, who rolled their eyes at this statement.

Babs gazed at the familiar open backyard surrounded by towering trees. Beyond the dense thicket lay their garden, a peaceful sanctuary. Fireflies illuminated the area, their bright lights resembling precious gems. Overhead, bats flitted in and out of the shed's rooftop, emitting high-pitched squeaks as they darted through the night air. It was such an idyllic atmosphere that for a few moments they all simply sat in silence until Cricket broke it with, "Well, I'm gonna go talk to Bash tomorrow."

Babs released a heavy sigh — the timing of Bash ending things with Cricket couldn't have been worse. As she indulged in her own tub of ice cream, she realized there was nothing she could say to comfort her sister.

Tikaboo jumped off the swing to chase a moth.

Cricket smiled lightly, obviously turning over what Zadie said in her mind. "It seemed so out of the blue."

"Oh, come on!" Babs exploded. "The dude is struggling with his mediumship. This isn't about you, Cricket, it's about him and where he is in life. I would think he could expect a little understanding from you. Give him some room to breathe. You were friends before. If that's what he needs from you right now, be a good person and give him that. Or, if you aren't capable of reeling it back, at least give him the space that he needs."

Zadie's eyebrows shot up. "I suppose Babs has a point." She put her pint and spoon down. "He did get rid of all the spirits in St. Augustine by accident. That is worth taking a beat, don't you think? I mean, no one blames him. It's not his fault."

Cricket's face turned green. "Why didn't I see it? Ryan has always been there for Bash. I guess it makes sense that he would feel like getting away with him. But he could have just said that. He didn't need to break up with me."

Babs shifted in the swing causing it to sway gently. "Well, you said it yourself, earlier. He's worried about Caroline's safety. He's second-guessing his judgment. Just give him time to work it out. With all that rattling around in his head, he doesn't need to be worrying about you too."

"That's a good point," Zadie chimed.

Cricket sighed. "It's hard for me to think clearly right now." She nodded. "I know that what you said makes sense, but I still feel heartbroken."

"Of course you do." Zadie patted her knee.

"Maybe," Cricket finally spoke up after an intense silence from all of them, "the breakup was for the best."

Her sisters exchanged a silent glance before giving their approval; it was enough to reassure Cricket that everything would work out.

Zadie sighed. "Besides, life is ever-changing and nothing is permanent."

They lazily swung in the swing, sleep threatening to end the evening.

"Now that that is settled, why don't you tell us about Ambrosias?" Babs asked. "Your path was destined a year ago. Now that you have cleared space, you can get on with the direction your life is really meant to go."

"What?" Zadie asked.

Cricket felt her face go flush. "Um, there's a lot to tell I suppose, but I don't know where to begin."

"What are you two talking about?" Zadie was at a total loss.

"We are talking about the winter prince, Ambrosias, who held claim on our sister in front of both courts while you and I were busy busting the Drake curse last year."

"Ohhhh, well, you broke the curse, I just held the waterfall in place." Zadie's face scrunched into a pout. "Why are we just hearing about this now? You kept a secret from us for a whole year?"

Cricket's face went white. "He—he is . . . difficult to explain . . ."

"Wait, did Bash know?" Zadie asked.

"Yeah, he was with me when it happened." Cricket stumbled through her words and began to tell the story of how, when she had tripped and fallen in the queen's chamber, her hand had gone into the body of water. That small act seemed to have called Ambrosias to her, who declared her his chosen before both courts. "From that day, we have been connected, at least in the dream world."

"And what is the nature of this relationship?" Babs's eyes drilled into Cricket's.

"If I had to really examine it, I have to admit we have a unique connection which has stirred up something inside me like nothing else I have experienced—but it's a feeling that I don't necessarily trust."

"What do you mean?" Zadie asked.

"When we're together, there's an energy. Time stands still. It's dreamlike. The nature of the relationship? Complicated."

"Yes," Babs answered, sliding off the swing. "It sounds complicated." She began to pace like a caged animal. "It's about to get more complicated."

"Babs?" Cricket asked.

Babs weighed her words in her mind. She remembered Liande's words and whispered them aloud, "and the Culebra line will be divided, sister against sister." She felt the blood drain from her face.

"What did you say, Babs?" Zadie asked.

Babs stopped and crossed her arms across her chest. "Ambrosias has put the two of us on opposite sides!" Babs slammed her fist against her leg. Cricket and Zadie startled. "The winter court has been holding Dad prisoner since the day of my birth. Mama, Gran, and Habana shielded us from that truth. I'm trying to put the pieces together, but I don't have all the information."

Zadie spoke up—her voice shaking, betraying the anger that was brewing. "They knew where Dad was? How could they keep that from us!"

Babs watched Cricket's face as she tried to make sense of all this new information. Cricket said in a small voice, "I want to be mad at Mama for not telling us the truth, but in a way I understand. I can see how it seemed like the right thing do back then . . . but at some point, couldn't the truth have been revealed?"

Babs abruptly interrupted with a hard glare directed toward Cricket. "You and I can get Dad back from winter. Unlike the generation before us, we won't let things spiral out of control . . ."

Zadie piped up. "I don't get it. Why would they take Dad? What is one mortal to them?"

Babs continued to pace. "Taking Dad was a punishment for Mama."

"A punishment for what?"

"The crown of the winter princess was stolen, and many suspect it is hidden in the human realm. It was expected that Mama, who had a connection to earth, would be able to locate and retrieve it, but she relinquished her powers to be with Dad, rendering her unable to fulfill this task. As punishment, Dad was taken as an incentive."

"Incentive?"

"For our family to find and give back the crown. They refused or have been unable to find it all this time."

"We must ask Mama! If all three of us confront her, she'll have to give us an answer." Cricket interjected.

Babs rolled her shoulders back. "After Dad was taken, there was an attack on our family. That was when Maj left for the sea, Habina was thought dead, and Mama and Gran decided the sub was to be sealed off, for our protection."

"Babs, how do we get Dad back?" Zadie asked.

"Dad will be given back to Mama once we deliver the crown to winter." Babs cringed. "At which time it will be placed upon your head, Cricket. As the next Princess of Winter, you will rule alongside Ambrosias."

Cricket looked away from her sisters.

"Is anyone worried about failure?" Zadie questioned. "If Mama, Maj, and Habina with Gran couldn't do it—"

The reality of the situation crashed in on Babs with a sharp clarity.

"We can do this. Our family needs us to step up," Cricket reasoned.

It was up to them to release their dad from this twenty-five-year separation. Uncertainty rolled like a tidal wave in Babs's stomach—but one thing was certain; she couldn't allow further suffering because of a duty her family needed to fulfill that should have been handled long ago.

A feeling of resolve fell over Babs. No matter how difficult or dangerous things may become, she would do whatever it took to get her dad back from winter court, and ensure the Culebra family stayed united—telling be damned.

The sound of slow clapping came from behind Babs. "Well done, sis."

Babs saw horror cross both Zadie's and Cricket's faces. She turned to see Nadine, an amused smile lighting up her eyes as she stepped out of the shadows. "Nadine—"

"Not going to"—she reached up and touched Babs's head and slid her fingers down the side of her throat—"reveal all? That's okay, we can keep some things between just the two of us. We always have." She sauntered to Cricket the moonlight outlining the long waves of her hair. "What, no hug?"

Cricket stood frozen, her eyes wide with disbelief as she stared at Nadine, her long-lost sister. "You're dead," Cricket managed to whisper, her voice trembling with a mix of fear and anger. "You died at birth."

Nadine chuckled softly, a sinister gleam in her silver eyes. "Death is overrated, my dear sister," she taunted, her voice dripping with venom. "No love for your long-lost sister after all these years?"

Cricket's confusion left her jaw slack. Babs stepped forward, her expression hardened.

"Enough games, Nadine," she said through gritted teeth. "Tell them the truth."

Nadine tilted her head slightly, a sly smile playing at the corners of her lips. "Oh, which truth? I played this little family reunion over and over in my mind, and I have to say, it's living up to my imagination. Any ice cream left for me? No?" she asked smoothly. "Cricket." She shifted her gaze. "Want to hear all about how winter court stole me out of my crib and made everyone think I passed? Or do you want to whine some more about Bash?"

Zadie's eyes squinted together. "What? How do you know about—"

"Zadie, are you going to run away to Tom? Right when everyone needs you?"

"Nadine, reel it in!" Babs said through gritted teeth.

"Babs wasn't crazy. I was always with her," Nadine cooed. "Always."

"How is that possible?" Cricket asked.

"The only thing you need to focus on is finding that damn crown. Cricket, quit your whining about Bash. Zadie, quit pining over Tom."

"Who do you think you are?" Zadie huffed.

Nadine threw her hands to the air, and suddenly the atmosphere around them shifted. Babs felt a surge of power coursing around them, an energy so potent it made her head spin. The night sky above them seemed to respond, as if it were a canvas waiting for Nadine's brushstroke.

With an eerie calmness, Nadine raised her hands toward the heavens, her eyes blazing with determination. The moon, once a serene orb of silver light, transformed before their very eyes. Its surface rippled and twisted, turning a deep shade of crimson. As the moon changed, shooting stars streaked across the sky in brilliant arcs of fiery red and gold.

Nadine's voice boomed. "I am the most powerful of the four of us, and you will help me free our father."

The bats that had been circling above them became disoriented by the sudden chaos, their high-pitched screeches filling the air. They scattered in every direction, wings flapping wildly as they sought refuge from the unnatural spectacle unfolding beneath them.

But it was Nadine's face that turned Babs's stomach. As she channeled her magic, her features contorted, shifting and morphing until her flesh turned as pale as bone. Her eyes glowed with an otherworldly light, piercing through the darkness like twin stars.

A cacophony of wailing sounds filled the space around them, as if the very fabric of reality were unraveling, a chorus of voices, both human and animal, crying out in anguish and terror. It threatened to shatter their eardrums and drive them mad.

Cricket's voice shook as she found her words amidst the chaos. "Nadine . . . what have you become?"

Zadie stumbled backward in fear, while Nadine revealed in the chaos she had unleashed. Her laughter pierced through the tumultuous symphony, blending with the howling wind and the screeching bats. "You see, dear sisters," she shouted over the pandemonium, "what it is to be fae!"

Her skeletal form waved its bony hands, and with a twist of its fingers, the shooting stars multiplied, creating a mesmerizing display that streaked the sky in an array of violent hues. The moon's crimson glow intensified, casting an ominous aura over everything below. The sheer force of her magic caused tremors to ripple through the ground, shaking trees and unsettling stones.

Nadine stumbled back, a smirk crossing her face. "Do we understand each other now?"

Babs dropped her glamour and stepped forward, her own magic swirling around her like a protective shield. The voices of those that ruled before her murmured in her ears, feeding her the spells to unleash. Her crown, now visible upon her head, glimmered with a brilliance that rivaled the moon itself, adorned with intricate patterns of silver and gold. The air crackled with energy as she released her true power, the power of the crown. She closed her eyes, feeling the ancient energies of the forest surge through her veins.

As she opened her eyes, a blinding light radiated from within her. It danced and flickered in hues of emerald and gold, weaving a spellbinding tapestry in the air. The wood-land creatures, drawn by the raw power emanating from her, emerged from the depths of the woods to bear witness to this extraordinary display.

Foxes with fiery-red fur, and eyes filled with wisdom stood side by side with rabbits adorned in coats as white as snow. Majestic deer with antlers crowned like a king's scepter gracefully stepped forward, while squirrels chattered excitedly atop branches that seemed to sway in time with Babs's magic.

Gwylm, Babs's loyal wolf companion, stood faithfully at her side. His fur shimmered with an ethereal light, reflecting the magic that flowed through their bond. His eyes locked onto Nadine's skeletal form, a deep growl rumbling from within his chest.

Babs lifted her delicate hands, fingers outstretched. As she did, the trees surrounding them appeared to come alive. The ancient oaks and towering pines swayed and rustled their leaves in harmony to an invisible melody carried by the wind. Their branches reached out toward Babs, as if longing to touch the source of their awakening.

The air crackled with energy as Babs channeled her magic, intertwining it with Nadine's chaotic display. She closed her eyes and focused on harnessing the raw power within her. The chaos began to subside gradually, and all returned to proper balance.

A whisper escaped Babs's lips, barely audible. "You have misjudged my abilities, dear sister," she declared, unwavering. "You're not in control anymore." She tipped her head back and flashed her fangs.

Nadine turned her gaze towards Cricket and Zadie, but quickly focused back on Babs. "We'll see, Princess. We shall see."

ACKNOWLEDGMENTS

I extend my thanks to Rebeca Sams Willis for her invaluable insight and steady support. Her contributions came to be crucial in my writing journey.

CHRISSY CHICORY

invites you into her mesmerizing urban fantasy world with *Seriously Challenged,* the second tale in the Culebra Chronicles. A graduate of Bradley University with a bachelor's in science, and an associate's in library science from Illinois Central College, Chrissy weaves her artistic vision and literary passion into her storytelling. Having been an esteemed member of the Florida Star Fiction Writers for three years, she deeply values the kinship and inspiration shared among her fellow writers. In her leisure, Chrissy enjoys exploring the mysteries of beachside towns with her Cavalier King Charles spaniel and engaging in spirited discussions with her author friends over lunch.

WWW.CHRISSYCHICORY.COM

www.ingramcontent.com/pod-product-compliance
Lightning Source LLC
Chambersburg PA
CBHW030802020726
47499CB00006B/1741